This Here and Now

Stories by
Robyn Parnell

Scrivenery
Press

Published in the United States of America by:

Scrivenery Press
P.O. Box 740969-1003
Houston, TX 77274-0969
http://www.scrivenery.com/

First Edition

This is a work of fiction. Names, characters, places, and incidents, unless otherwise specifically noted, either are the product of the author's imagination or are used fictitiously.

The author and publisher wish to acknowledge the periodicals in which the following stories first appeared: "So Much Not Neither," "The Burghers of Troutdale," and "People Like You," *Lynx Eye*, 2000, 1999, and 1997 respectively; "One and One" and "A Tie in the Road," *ProCreation*, 1999 and 1998 respectively; "Kiss Me I'm Irish," *Bellowing Ark*, 1989; "The Anti-Cancer Diet," *Ellipsis*, 1988; "We'll Talk Later," *Oasis*, 1993; "A Middle Piece," *Innisfree*, 1993; "How Heavy is Blood," *Timberline*, 1994; "Where Things Are," *Burning Light*, 1994; "Rescheduled," *Strictly Fiction II* (an anthology), 1995; "Landscape," *Pangolin Papers*, 1996; "Sister Dentia and the Reading List," *pica*, 1996; "Leave It Up," *Uno Mas*, 1996; "Clinic," *Happy*, 1996; "Hope," *Roswell Literary Review*, 1998; "Sound No Trumpet," *Windhover*, 2000. "This Here and Now," "The Book of Joel," "Modus Operandi," "Benediction," and "Googie" are published for the first time in this collection.

Cover design by Françoise Merot, based upon a photograph by Kaz Chiba. Editing by Leila Joiner. The book block is digitally typeset in Minion *and* Minion Expert, *by Adobe Systems Incorporated (www.adobe.com). The headline typeface is* ICG Papyrus *(www.eyewire.com).*

01   02   03   04   SP   10   9   8   7   6   5   4   3   2   1

LIBRARY OF CONGRESS CATALOG CARD NUMBER **00-112027**

ISBN **1-893818-09-8**

This Here and Now

For Eli and Sadie, whose inquiries ("Where do grownups come from?") keep me curious, whose observations ("Mom is really complicated") keep me humble, and whose snuggles keep me...and for the one who told me that "Just because you can't always doesn't mean you won't ever." Thanks, Mark.

Acknowledgements

I thank every person I've ever met who has suffered fools gladly. As for the rest of you...

I thank Leila Joiner, Ed Williams and the gentle folk at Scrivenery Press for their enthusiasm, respect and support. Leila and Ed's combination of grace, competence, warmth and wit is rare amongst mere mortals, not to mention literati. (Which I just did. Sorry.)

Von Binuia, Pam McCully, Pete Shedor, Neal Storrs, Jon Ther, Donna Walker-Nixon and Stephen West are just a few of the editors in whose journals my stories first appeared (and I trust they've been able to settle the majority of those pesky lawsuits). Their insightful critiques and even rueful rejections were encouraging and instructive. The slavish compliments were also greatly appreciated.

Family, friends, teachers and colleagues have always been a source of inspiration, and I continue to rely upon their bemused forbearance. Thank you, Chet and Marion Parnell; Davis and Patricia Baldwin; "Teddy" Clucas and Santa Ana High School's '73–'75 *Generator* staff; Lynn Hawley; Ernie Kyger; Frances Patterson; Mrs. Solomon, my third grade teacher; Bob and Shirley Waggoner; Lisa Worthington. Additional muses include the FCC-UCC Tuesday morning book group; 3rd floor Bixby Hall, UC Davis; the Baha'is of Washington County; Balmer Yummers; Oregon Pinot Noir, French champagne and English breakfast tea; the air at Manzanita and the elephant seal at Pescadero.

No animals were harmed during the making of these stories, despite what crossed my mind whenever I sat down at my desk on a chair that was covered with cat hair.

I appreciate death and taxes, the Law of Gravity, and all forces natural and artificial that keep me grounded, and I am grateful to be unable to acknowledge the generous support of MFA Creative Writing Programs, Fiction Workshops or Art Council grants. What follows is all my fault.

"We are here on earth to do good to others.
What the others are here for, I don't know."
—W.H. Auden

"Tell the truth and run."
—Yugoslavian proverb

Contents

Benediction

Arla zipped up her windbreaker and briefly considered the propriety of breaking a sweat on the morning of her husband's funeral. Standing on the front porch of her house, she bent sideways at the waist and began her warm-up stretches.

"Going for a walk?"

Arla jerked upright at the sound of her mother's voice. "Don't *do* that to me!" she gasped.

"Didn't mean to startle you, hon." Marion Dayne sat on a rotting leather armchair in the corner of the porch. "I thought, maybe, this morning you'd try to sleep in. I suppose…I'm sorry."

"For what?"

"For thinking that you could sleep in."

"I've been up since four-thirty." Arla yawned. "Lynne said she'd get the baby if she wakes, but Anna usually sleeps 'til eight. I need to get out, do something, before they all get here."

"I know what you mean."

"I bet you do." Arla eyed the coffee cup her mother held. "Apparently, the mere thought of being around Miguel's family has driven you to drink. I thought your doctor said no…"

"It's decaffeinated," Marion sniffed defiantly, "so don't go telling on me to your father." She winked at Arla and raised the cup to her lips. "Yes…this is it." She swallowed slowly, savoring the steamy brew, and looked out past the porch railing. "Maybe I'll start walking in the morning. It's peaceful, this time of the day, before everyone gets going."

"Peaceful. Uh huh."

"Honey, your father and I haven't seen any of the Toros family since the wedding. And I don't hold much stock in first impressions."

"They usually turn out to be the most accurate." Arla plopped down on the porch beside the armchair and unzipped her windbreaker.

"I try to give people the benefit of the doubt. Sometimes, especially in tragic situations, they really pull through." Marion reached out and lightly stroked her daughter's hair. "They might surprise you."

"Like by not showing up? That would be a pleasant surprise."

Marion sipped her coffee and gazed at the horizon. Arla tapped the toes of her shoes together several times. She untied her shoelaces, retied them, and cleared her throat.

"At least they're bringing Rosie," Arla said.

"Rosie?"

"Miguel's niece. She was at the wedding. Remember Carl and Lena, Miguel's older brother and sister-in-law? They were the ones who wanted to watch TV during the reception."

"Oh, now I remember Rosie. The little retarded girl?"

"Mentally chall– yeah." Arla nodded. "The little retarded girl. She's their daughter. I've only seen her five or six times, since. They trot her out for weddings and baptisms and such. It's too bad; she's a real sweet kid. I want her to sit by me at the church. She's the only one of his family I can stand."

"Isn't that a bit harsh?"

"They've never liked me. I'm sure they're blaming me for the accident; they probably think *I* ran him over."

"*Arla!*"

"Keep an eye on my car when they get here. I bet Mr. Toros checks the front bumper for dents."

"You've always been a bit hard on his family." Marion spoke tentatively, looking into her coffee cup. "I know you've tried not to influence us; you've never said anything directly but there were clues in your letters and phone calls. Maybe they were, at first, a little disappointed that you kept your name. You know how some people are about such things. But surely all that means nothing now. It's not as though they dislike you."

"No, Mom, you don't get it. It's not that I think *they* hate *me*. That's the hard part." Arla stood up and inhaled deeply. "I'd better go before everyone gets up and tries to be useful. Whose idea was it to have people over both before and after the funeral?"

"Mr. Toros," Marion said. "It seemed odd to me, too, but he mentioned something about a family tradition."

"Other than their family tradition of eating every two hours, it's nothing I've heard of before."

"Your father and brother will be up soon." Marion Dayne stood up, raised her coffee cup and toasted the rising sun. "I'd better go make some of the real stuff."

"It's the Millennium, Mom." Arla squinted into the low glow from the east. "Let the boys get it themselves."

Mrs. Dayne looked at her daughter and forced a smile. "I don't mind. The Toroses are bringing the food. I need something to do."

"I know," Arla said.

"Maybe your sister could use a hand with Anna. I haven't changed my granddaughter's diapers since I've been here. I suppose in a few months she won't need them."

"I hope so."

"I can tell she's like you…and Lynne, and Stephen, too, come to think of it. All my kids were early learners. Maybe I could iron your dress for you?"

"Sure, Mom." Arla rested her hand on her mother's shoulder. "You could iron my dress."

Steam rose from the roofs of the neighboring row houses, making them resemble a chain of double-decker teapots, Arla thought, when she returned from her walk. Ascending the porch stairs, she detected *sotto* voices from her living room. She tiptoed up the remaining stairs, sidled along the porch and crouched under the living room windowsill.

"Thank you, Mrs. Dayne. Yes. I spoke with your husband last night."

I know that voice.

"We appreciate you coming over," Arla heard her father say. "She seemed agitated, and we couldn't get her to take anything."

"I'd like to help, if I can." The deep bass tones of Dr. Turner, Arla's general practitioner, reverberated through the living room despite his obvious attempts to speak softly.

"When I got the call last night," the doctor continued, "I thought it best to notify a family member. I hate to betray a confidence, but obviously…"

"Obviously, she's a bit nut-*ty*, even for someone who's just lost her husband." Stephen Dayne emphasized the *T*s in 'nutty.'

Don't mince words, brother dearest. Say what you really think.

"I mean, wanting to set him on fire out on the…"

"Stephen!"

"Hey, Mom, I'm just worried about my sister."

"We're all concerned."

Oh, oh, trouble: Mom's using her "everybody-calm-down" voice.

"Did she take anything?" the doctor asked.

"No," Marion Dayne answered. "Neither the sleeping pills nor the tranquilizers. 'I don't take drugs,' she said. I think she's upset that we went behind her back, to you."

I'm more upset with that busybody receptionist at the city hall. I was trying to be a responsible citizen…this is what I get for living in a tittle-tattle small town.

"And it's not nutty, Stephen," Marion continued. "I don't think that's at all appropriate. It was what Miguel wanted; it was his idea, when they made their wills, last year. It's perfectly understandable that she would want to honor his last request."

"We don't even know if that's true," Stephen said. "Sure, some folks get cremated, or that thing where you're put in a drawer…"

"Interment."

Thanks, Dad.

"...whatever, instead of a regular burial, but how many people do you know who, seriously, want to be burned up in a boat?"

It's so unfair. It's the only semi-original thing Miguel ever thought of in his life...besides marrying me.

"Now, wait a minute, Stephen." A slight, reedy voice gently yet firmly entered the conversation. "Dr. Turner, what exactly did you hear yesterday?"

Nice to hear from you, Lynne.

"I had a phone call from Amy Jenkins, at city hall," Dr. Turner said. "She told me that Arla had called her, wanting to know if a license or permit was needed to conduct a 'Viking funeral'—those were Arla's exact words, according to Amy—for Miguel."

"I've heard of those," Lynne said. "Arla didn't make it up."

Dr. Turner cleared his throat. "Apparently, a Viking funeral is when the deceased is cremated, in his battleship..."

"I think they were called 'longboats,'" Lynne offered.

"...cremated in his boat, at sea," Dr. Turner continued. "And since the closest thing we have to an ocean is Nellie Pond, Arla wanted to check with the proper authorities to see if she needed a city permit, to, uh, take Miguel's canoe out. Ms. Jenkins..."

"Should mind her own business," Lynne huffed.

Atta girl, sis.

"Ms. Jenkins was concerned, and contacted me." Dr. Turner ignored Lynne's remark. "I think she did the right thing; and I'm also thinking that perhaps we shouldn't worry too much about Arla."

"Well, I do," Stephen said. "A *Viking* funeral? After the Toroses made all the arrangements—coffin and cemetery and all?"

"They shouldn't have done that. Not without consulting her, first," Lynne said.

"Honey, they were just trying to help," Mrs. Dayne said. "I think it was considerate of them. Arla's had so much to deal with;

she's had no time to even think about a funeral service. The sheriff's department was here, going through Miguel's things, trying to get Arla to remember if he had any enemies or if she had ever heard anyone threaten him."

"Do they think it was intentional?" Dr. Turner asked.

"One of the deputies said that with a hit-and-run, you never know," Mr. Dayne said. "They're assuming it was an accident, but there were no witnesses. They don't want to rule anything out. There were no skidmarks. He was doing his usual run; it was foggy…I don't know. *They* don't know. Probably a drunk driver."

"Arla's out walking. I think it's the route they used to do together, before he took up running." Marion's voice broke.

Please, don't, Mom. Not now.

"It's been a shock, we all know," Stephen said, "but she's not acting like someone who just lost her husband."

"You'd feel better if she got hysterical in front of everyone?" Lynne raised her voice. "That's not her way."

"She never *has* been easy with her feelings. She didn't even cry at her own wedding," Marion said.

"I think this Viking-bonfire thing is a warning sign," Stephen said. "She's gotten almost no sleep since we've been here. That does weird things to people."

"It's not weird," Lynn insisted. "It's what Miguel wanted."

I love you, baby sister. Stephen, go suck an egg.

"Why would *he* want a *Viking* funeral?" Stephen sputtered. "He's Spanish, for God's sake! *We're* the Norwegians!"

"Lower your voice," Mr. Dayne said. "The baby's still asleep, and the Toroses could get here anytime. They don't know anything about this and I don't want them to. Does everyone understand? Arla has enough to deal with."

Arla crept down the porch stairway; then slowly and loudly tromped back up the stairs and opened the front door. Dr. Turner was nowhere in sight. She declined her mother's offer of a cup of tea, saying she wanted to go upstairs to see Anna before the guests arrived.

I'm sorry, Miguel. Lo Siento. I tried.

"Come on in." Arla responded to the knock at her bedroom door.

Lynne opened the door and motioned for her brother to enter. Arla stood in front of the full-length mirror, next to the armoire.

"Everybody's here," Stephen said. "They're waiting for you."

"It's a funeral brunch," Arla snapped, "not a debutante ball."

"You're not the only one who loved him," Stephen said.

Arla sighed. "Sorry I've been jumping on you, but if I hear one more time about how I'm not making it easy on the others…"

"I didn't say that," Stephen said. "I just want you to remember, to maybe think about, the fact that you're not the only person who loved him. I took him fishing last summer."

"Get him out of here," Arla hissed to Lynne.

"Stephen, would you please go get Anna and take her next door, to Mrs. Allen's?" Lynne shooed him out of the room. "We'll be down in a minute." Lynne closed the door and turned to her sister. She removed a loose thread from Arla's sleeve, took three steps back and gave her sister an admiring once-over. "Probably not the best time for compliments, but you look nice."

"Thanks. Purple was Miguel's favorite color, for me. Do I look ready for battle?"

"For battle?"

"That's what I feel like." Arla sat down on the bed and tugged at the neckline of her dress. "I should give them a few minutes to get warmed up. When they see Stephen take Anna next door they can talk about what a bad mother I am, giving Miguel's child to a stranger. That's what they call her: 'Miguel's child.'"

"Mrs. Allen is not a stranger," Lynne said. "They know that. Anna's too young; I've never seen a toddler at a funeral. I'm sure everyone understands and respects your decision."

"Maybe I'll have one of those pills after all," Arla sighed.

Arla leaned against the refrigerator. Stephen, balancing a tray of pastries in each hand, kicked open the swinging door that separated the dining room from the kitchen.

"I'll have one of those," Arla said. "I'm on a break."

"A break?" Stephen set the trays on the counter next to the sink and handed her a doughnut. "You've been downstairs for a whole ten minutes."

"True, but you must admit I've been behaving myself."

"Now that you mention it, I didn't see you bat an eye when that lady…what's her name—Lena? Miguel's cousin?"

"Sister-in-law," Arla said. "The one who slapped Rosie's hand when the poor kid reached for a doughnut. She's Rosie's mother."

"Yeah, her. She told me to take the trays away or Rosie would eat everything. You didn't blink when she started in." He raised his voice in imitation of Lena's. "'How *will* you and poor little Anna make out?'"

"Yufuh huh." Arla crammed a raspberry cruller into her mouth.

"What happened?" Stephen poked her in the ribs. "Did you take your Valium like a good girl?"

"What's with this *my* Valium thing?" Arla frowned. "'Arla, did you take *your* medication?' Since when is it *my* Valium? I didn't invent it; I didn't even request the prescription. I took *one*, okay? Right before I came downstairs. I don't feel it, though."

"The doctor said it takes twenty minutes to get into the bloodstream," Stephen said. "You took it on an empty stomach?"

Arla nodded her head and licked her fingers. "Are there any more of the fruit ones? I haven't had a thing all morning."

"Then you better have another." Stephen looked at his watch. "We're leaving in five minutes. You're riding with Lynne and me."

Arla removed a carton of orange juice from the refrigerator. "I told Rosie she could ride with us, too. Why don't you sneak a chocolate croissant for her?"

Stephen took a step toward the dining room. "You coming?"

Arla poured herself a glass of juice. "Go *habla* with your brothers-in-law. I'll be out in a minute."

Lynne walked up the center aisle of the church and sat down in the second pew from the front. She slid down the length of the pew, toward her brother, who was sitting at the end by the side aisle. Stephen leaned forward, his forehead resting on the back of the first pew.

"There were five of these this morning," Lynne whispered, shaking a small medicine bottle. "There's only one left now."

"What?"

"I just now took this from her purse. I was with her upstairs. I saw her take one, and we were both with her in the car. What happened when you two were in the kitchen? Did you upset her?"

Thumpa-thumpa-thumpa.

Lynne looked toward the center aisle, where Rosie sat in the first pew, quietly humming to herself and scribbling in the coloring book Lynne had given her. At the end of the pew, next to Rosie, Arla sat sideways, with one leg stretched out into the aisle. She drummed the side of the pew with both hands, bongo drum-style, and watched the mourners enter the church.

Thumpa-thumpa-thumpa.

"She had a doughnut and some orange juice," Stephen said.

"And, apparently, three more of these." Lynne shook the bottle and glared at Stephen. She slid down the pew, toward Arla and Rosie.

"Hi," Arla beamed.

"Hi." Lynne leaned forward and put her fingers to her lips.

"Why are we whispering?" Arla whispered. She turned around and wiggled her fingers in Stephen's direction. "Why's he sitting way down there? Oh, that's right; he needs his space. Lots of space. Biiiiiiig space. One of his ex-girlfriends told me."

Rosie hunched over her book and concentrated on her coloring. Lynne reached behind Rosie and patted Arla's hand. "It's stuffy in here. Let's go get some fresh air."

"Where's Mom and Dad?" Arla pointed at the pew behind her, to a spot beside Lynne. "This is reserved for them, right?"

"Shhhhh." Lynne strained to reach around Rosie. She cupped her hand and feigned caressing Arla's hair while she tried to turn Arla's head to face the front of the church. "They're talking with the minister. They'll be here in a minute."

"I can't see anything this way." Arla pushed her sister's hand away and turned back around. "Would you look at that? This isn't a *Catholic* church!"

Arla gestured toward a group of Miguel's relatives, who one by one knelt and genuflected before taking their seats in one of the back pews. "Oh, great." Arla's voice rose well above a whisper. "Here comes the Spanish Inquisition."

Lynne turned to Stephen. "Can I get some help, please?"

"Too late now." Stephen slid closer to Lynne. "You can't bounce the widow from the funeral. Besides, if people hear anything, they'll think it's Rosie."

"Hail Mary, full of grace; four balls, take your base!" Arla elbowed Rosie. "That's what Miguel used to say in Sunday school."

Rosie pointed a yellow crayon toward the picture she was coloring. "Big Bird," she said.

Stephen leaned in front of Lynne and waved his hand in front of Arla's face. "Hey, Arles, you can chill out for a while. We'll talk to everyone after the service."

"What, I got it wrong?" Arla asked. "Hail Mary, blessed art thou although a woman and blessed be the fruit of your loom, Jesus."

"Jesus fruit of the loom." Rosie hummed and colored. "Jesus fruit of the loom."

Arla giggled. "Size thirty-four, I'd wager."

Marion Dayne walked up the center aisle and sat down next to Lynne and Stephen. "What is going on?" she whispered through clenched teeth.

Stephen made a "v" sign with his fingers. "Arla got religion."

Ten minutes into the post-funeral reception at Arla's house, Marion glanced around the living room and then motioned to her husband. Frank Dayne nodded acknowledgement and followed his wife into the dining room.

"What should we do?" Marion whispered. She pointed toward the kitchen, where Arla was talking with Lynne. "I don't think it's worn off. We shouldn't have let people come over."

"We couldn't *un*-invite them," Frank said. "Lynne's keeping an eye on her." He glanced over his shoulder at the living room. "People are paying their respects to Miguel's parents. Everyone probably thinks Arla is off…grieving, somewhere."

"Maybe. But they'll want to say a few words to her, eventually."

"I know." Mr. Dayne sighed. "It'll work out. I'm going to get a glass of wine. One for you?"

Marion shook her head. "We should watch, make sure she stays away from the liquor."

"Arla doesn't drink," Frank Dayne said.

"She doesn't take drugs, either," Marion Dayne replied.

"I wish someone would take the sign off the door." Arla sat at the kitchen table, grimacing at the cup of coffee in front of her. "This stuff is awful."

"I followed the directions on the can." Lynne sat across from her sister. "What sign are you talking about?"

"There must be a sign on the front door: 'All ye who enter here cast aside your conversational fluency.'" Arla walked to the sink and dumped her coffee. "Haven't you heard the clichés? Everyone memorized *Reader's Digest*'s 'Homilies for the Bereaved' before they got here. Or maybe Stephen's at the door, passing out copies. And how come everyone but me gets offered a glass of wine?"

"This isn't very good, is it?" Lynne pushed her cup aside and looked up at Arla, who stood, arms folded across her chest, in front of the sink. "They mean well. No one knows what to say."

"Then why haven't they shut up since they arrived?" Arla gestured toward the door to the dining room. "Two rooms away, behind closed doors. Those are the muted voices of mourners? Sounds more like a Cecil B. DeMille cast of thousands, rehearsing Pharoah's climactic death scene."

"Good Lord, Arla!" Lynne valiantly suppressed her laughter and feigned indignation. "Why'd you take all those pills?"

"I thought everyone wanted me to." Arla opened the door to the dining room, looked around briefly, closed the door and removed a bottle from the refrigerator. "Don't tell Stephen." She poured wine into two punch glasses. "The pills wore off long ago."

"Oh, really?" Lynne raised a disapproving eyebrow but took the glass Arla offered her. "Shouldn't you, maybe, go out and spend some time with Miguel's parents? Oops...sorry."

Arla sat down at the table and sipped her wine. "Did you see how they practically dragged Rosie away from me after the service?"

"Maybe they thought she was bothering you."

"They think I'm a bad influence."

"You two *were* a little loud..."

Arla waved her hand dismissively. "Her own parents want to send her away, but I'm a bad influence 'cause I actually talk *with* the girl instead of at her."

"Send her away?"

Arla nodded. "It's no surprise. They've always treated Rosie like a pet, and now that she's becoming more of a bother to care for...She's approaching puberty. Miguel told me, after the last time he visited Carl and Lena."

"Will she go through that?"

"Sure. Her brain topped out at age four but the body keeps going on. I don't know what they're afraid of: that maybe, one day, right in the middle of 'Hawaii Five-Oh' reruns, she'll pull out a tampon and pretend it's a hand grenade."

"What?"

"Rosie likes to play army."

Lynne poured herself another glass of wine.

"I think they're more comfortable with me in here. This way they don't have to lower their voices when they talk about poor me and my 'situation.'" Arla ran her finger around the edge of the punch glass. "It's amazing how smoothly they made the transition from, 'How can she leave Miguel's child in daycare and go off to work' to 'Thank God she'll have something to keep her busy.'

"And that *provider* thing! I've heard it twice today. How will Anna and I make out, now that our provider is gone? I've always been a provider, too. Only now it's with a capital *P*, I guess."

"Oh," Lynne said, "so *that's* what you were doing while you were neglecting your child, leaving her to be raised by strangers. You were being a provider! Thank you for clearing that up."

"Any time. Now, clear something up for me. How come Miguel, when he was off providing, was never accused of abandoning Anna?"

"I'm supposed to answer that?"

"There is no answer for that," Arla snickered. "I must be having a delayed, feminist-allergic reaction to Mrs. Toros's tuna-tamale casserole."

"Yum." Lynne wrinkled her nose. "I had some."

"You could have washed it down with that coffee," Arla smirked.

"No more truth serum for you." Lynne took both her and Arla's glasses to the sink.

"I am so tired." Arla leaned forward and rested her head on the table. "This day must end, and soon. I need a nap."

The dining room door opened part way, and Miguel's father peeked into the kitchen. He looked pensively at Arla. "I hope I'm not disturbing you," he said, "but Rosie's asking for you."

Arla slowly lifted her head, as if she were overwhelmed by the effort. "That's okay." She smiled wanly. "Please, send her in."

Mr. Toros nodded and shut the door.

"I think he meant for *you* to go out *there*," Lynne said.

"Sniveling weasels," Arla muttered. "Sending their developmentally-dissed grandchild in to flush me out."

"Looks like they'll have to settle for me." Lynne headed for the living room.

"Don't let the doorknob hit you in the butt on your way out," Arla called after her.

Rosie tottered into the kitchen. She held a carrot stick in her hand. "For you, Aunt Arlie."

"Thanks, Rosie. Arumpf!" Arla loudly bit into the carrot. "How did you know I was hungry?"

"I just knowed. I watch you."

"Well, thank you, sweetie."

"Uh-huh." Rosie crinkled the hem of her dress with her fingers. "Mommy says Uncle Miggy died."

"Yeah, sweetie." Arla put the carrot down. "Yes, he did."

"I had a hamster. It died."

"A hamster?" Arla grinned. "They're nice pets. I had one when I was a little girl."

"Daddy said he's a girl, but I named him Miggy," Rosie said, "'cause he had brown hair. Not black. Brown, like you and me and Uncle Miggy."

"Were you sad, Rosie, when your hamster died?"

"Yes. Oh my yessy yes yes." Rosie raised her voice to a soft squeal. "He was so pretty and soft." She laid her head on Arla's lap, wrapped one chubby arm around Arla's waist and stroked Arla's leg with the other. "I loved to petted him, like this."

"Oh, Rosie," Arla whispered. "Don't be so nice, sweetie. Not right now."

Rosie continued to pet Arla's leg, and began humming a familiar tune. Arla recognized the melody: a hymn from the funeral service.

"Damn." Arla's chin trembled. She caressed Rosie's head, and ran her fingers through her niece's scrambled, nut-brown curls.

"Pretty boy Miggy," Rosie crooned. "Pretty boy; soft boy."
She looked up at Arla and smiled. "It's raining on my hair."

The Book of Joel

It had become obvious to Joel that God—anyone's and everyone's god—was a woman.

Joel took no pride in his realization, nor did he find even the slightest comfort therein. Still, he accepted it as a man should, even if his acceptance meant that he therefore could no longer handle that realization—or any other insight—as a man would. Like the Divine Man would. Even if it meant that, from this point onward, it wouldn't matter if he handled anything like the man he now knew he would never be.

Scriptures of all faiths, tongues and centuries are mangled through and by translation. Caretakers and scribes attempt to cloak, soften, and mitigate; their manipulation of pronouns, however faithful the intent, makes their complicity all the more callous. The dismal certainty—sooner or later, even and yet, intimately and ultimately—always will out.

They slip up, and it slips out. It oozes out, through the translucent, ancient and ongoing narratives. Creaking, seeping, and finally cracking; dribbling its dusky marrow from primordial papyrus through megabyte modem. Holiness is thus revealed.

Jealous, petty, and whining. Expecting total devotion and exacting impossible demands. Vengeful and bitter; proud and resentful. Haughty. Exclusive. Female.

Which is why, on that justifiably raw November morning, when Joel buttoned his long-sleeved, plaid Pendleton over the seven-round mags jammed into his shoulder holster; when he zipped up his Nordstrom outlet gang-banger denim baggies, donned an oversized, mud-spattered, knee-length khaki raincoat and rolled his gray woolen soccer socks up and over the seven-inch, double-edge, spear-point Peace Keepers sheathed to each ankle, he knew the visit he must pay would be to a gathering of the most openly clueless of Her blasphemers.

Joel grabbed a stapler and a pair of tarnished haircutting shears from the kitchen utility drawer. He removed a frayed yellow notepad from underneath the telephone answering machine. Scrawled throughout the notepad's pages were the names, addresses and descriptions of the churches he'd been evaluating since May.

Joel flipped through the notepad with his left hand; with his right hand he dangled the shears, point down, over the notepad. He closed his eyes and counted aloud.

–A one and a two and a three-four-five...

When he reached eleven he dropped the shears, stifling a gasp when the shears' point nicked the end of his thumb. Swiftly, silently, he drew a cleansing breath, opened his eyes and beheld the name on the first of the four pages the rusty point had pierced.

–Of course. The goddess worshipper-denouncers of the Reformed Independent Baptist Church of Vernonia.

Joel thrust his thumb deep into the pocket of his raincoat, using a wad of tissue he found there as a pressure bandage. He leaned forward and hawked a gob of spittle onto the notepad, aiming for the drops of blood that had obscured the church's Sunday service start times. He smeared the fluids around with his finger, careful not to tear the paper, until the red had been diluted and he could make out the blurry black ink. Wielding the open shears like a razor, he sliced out the notepad pages that the shears' point had pierced. He stapled the pages together, crammed them into his shirt breast pocket, and removed two .32 semiautomatic Beretta pistols from a plastic bag in the cupboard above the telephone answering machine.

The crisp click of boot heels ricocheted off the walls and floor of the church's mottled-tile hallway. The notepad pages crackled in his shirt pocket, rubbing against his clavicle with each step. Joel had no concern to soften his step. No snapping twig would divulge his approach; he knew the Independent Reformed minions were long enfolded in the 9:30 a.m. service. He strode down the hallway, toward his intended position: the main sanctuary doors that led to the Fellowship Hall.

"Hello."

Joel whirled about and dropped to one knee, fumbling with both hands in his front coat pockets. Though ensconced in a pale-cheeked, watery pink-lipped, ashy gold-tressed face, the eyes that bored into his were as fixed and dark as a barracuda's.

"My name is Vashti."

A she-cub, perhaps all of four years old. Joel slowly rose to his feet, all the while attempting to seize and return the shock of her impaling gaze. It was as if a Kewpie doll had switched assembly lines at the toy factory and had received the Ninja warrior eyes by mistake.

"You passed it." She pointed behind him, down the hallway. "It's that way."

"What's that way?" It was out before he could stop himself. Joel looked up and down the hallway, fingering the pistol butts in his pockets. She seemed too young to be unaccompanied.

"The bathrooms," she said. "A boys' one and a girls'. Grownups can go in both when they take kids. You can choose."

"I don't need…"

"When you're big, you can go alone. It's okay." Vashti looked him over. "You can go by yourself. I'll wait for you."

And his countenance fell.

—*Just as it is written.* Joel wordlessly rebuked and then forgave himself when he could not help but recall the verse. When a four-year-old declared, Thou art the Man. Even if She is not.

And because God is what God is, Joel resigned himself to one last realization. Vengeance would have to wait, even as, throughout the resounding void that would comprise his eternity, so would She.

"Right here." Vashti wriggled her right foot, tapping the toe of her Vaseline-polished, black vinyl ballet shoe on the floor. "I'll be here."

Which is why, on an ice-bright Sunday morning, before he entered the Gentlemen's restroom of the Reformed Independent Baptist Church of Vernonia; before he threw the latch and jammed a stack of paper towels in the crack between the floor and the bottom of the restroom's door; before the ringing, staccato pop-pop was followed by a muffled thud sliding down the door; before the brown paper towels turned crimson and crackled as they expanded with absorption, Joel tore off a piece of paper from the stapled-together bundle he'd stuffed in his shirt pocket.

"Yes," he said to the girl-child. "You can wait."

Joel tore the paper in half, spit on each half and rubbed the pieces together between his palms, shaping them into small, moist, plug-shaped wads. "Here." He gently placed a wad into each of Vashti's ears. "Now, go like this." Joel took each of her hands in his own and cupped them over her ears. "It's going to be loud."

A Middle Piece

"Midnight dreams are deceptively veiled harbingers; even good fortune is swathed in somber attire at this hour. In the early morning one dreams of one's most private desires, and reveries that hold fast before waking are of promises never to be kept.'"

This is what I got when I asked her what her most memorable dream was. I expected either a scene-by-scene recounting of a particular favorite or "How could I possibly choose!" Instead, I got a reading from a dream analysis book. I got pseudo-mystic categories; I got dreamy divisions.

I got you, babe.

Nap dreams are to be savored for their droll illogic, then promptly dismissed. One must not look to them for deep revelations or hidden meanings; they are hallucinatory, fleeting fantasies—the "dandruff of the superego," she calls them. *Never* tell a nap dream to an analyst.

"How about to a financial analyst?" I asked her. "Or is it only the psychos who need to be protected from the—get ready, Bren, I made this up myself—from the naked fantasies of the unconscious?"

"Never try to teach a pig to sing," she said. "It wastes your time, and annoys the pig."

Because I don't dream, Brenna worries for me.

Everyone dreams, she insists. For some reason, you can't remember yours.

If a tree fell in the forest and there was no one to hear it…I don't remember my dreams. Isn't that, consequentially, the same as not having them?

"*Full-time* English teachers don't make up words like 'consequentially,'" she said. "Everyone, every *thing*, dreams. The cat dreams."

"It's not a made-up word," I said. "And how do you know the cat dreams?"

"His nose twitches." She traced my profile, from brow to jawbone, with her finger. "You snore sometimes. But your nose never twitches."

I watch her again, as she sleeps. The breeze through the open window flutters the hair on her arm. Brenna never complains of the cold, never wakes up to pull the covers tight. She insists on keeping the window open, even in winter.

The gentle night current ruffles the note she left on my dresser. She leaves pieces of paper with phone numbers and suggestions. We discuss and consider; ideas hover over the cereal bowls, floating in and out of conversation. A name is mentioned over breakfast.

"I'll think about it," I say. Later that evening, a notepad appears on my nightstand. Names and phone numbers.

"It's done on an outpatient basis," she told me at breakfast. She passed me the marionberry jam and wiped up the oatmeal that was spilled on Ben's highchair tray. "Local anesthetic, minimal discomfort—mostly the doctor/surgery fear men have. The hardest part is shaving, and you can do that at home. They give you instructions."

Where does she find the time to investigate all this? There are several medical office complexes on her route. I asked her if she got her information from the employees there.

"Don't be silly. No one talks to mail carriers anymore. I do my research." She wiped Ben's mouth with his bib, kissed us both and went into the bedroom to change into her uniform.

The doctor's name and number are here tonight, gesturing to me in the breeze while she lies dreaming.

She comes home briefly for lunch, taking some fruit and leaving a travel brochure.

"I forgot to mention that it takes two to three months to be effective. Two negative sperm counts in a row, then they give you the go-ahead. You could schedule it for the week after we're back from vacation—before your tan fades," she teases. "Then by the time everything's back to where we'd have to start using something again, we won't."

"That's assuming we'll be getting enough sleep to have the energy to even *want* to." She winks at me and backs out the door, apple in one hand, letter sack slung over her shoulder. "They say the second ones are nocturnal, like hamsters."

She wants to walk along shimmering, white sand Caribbean beaches. She wants to go to a nude beach, "Before I show," she says, pushing her palms against my stomach when I laugh. "Damned tree sperm." She blows her nose. "I've got to get away from this. There's no pollen in Bermuda, you know."

Where does pollen go after dark? She doesn't sniffle at night, even though she sleeps with her face turned toward the open window.

Some nights when I can't sleep, and watching her isn't enough, I write in my journal.

"Why not 'diary'?" she asked. "Why 'my journal' instead of 'my diary'?"

"What's the difference?"

"The difference is that you'd never call it a diary. Men write in journals; women keep diaries. No, girls who dot their *i*'s with circles keep diaries. Other than that there's no difference, though most men assume or hope there'd be one, content-wise."

"Why don't you keep a dream journal?" I suggested.

"I don't need to; I remember them. Why don't *you* keep one?"

"I don't remember them, remember?"

"Maybe it would help." She ran her toes up and down the length of my shinbone. "The excuse of writing in the journal might legitimize your need to remember them."

I grabbed her foot. "You mean *your* need for me to remember *my* dreams. Thanks for the tip, Ms. Freud."

"Anything to get you started. I'm onto your little secret. This journal is practice, isn't it? All English teachers have it: 'But what I really want to do is write.' So why don't you?"

"And give up my pedagogy? Shun my gift of imparting knowledge to eager young minds?"

"Really, Cal. You'd make a good writer precisely because you're a lousy teacher."

"I'll think about calling that doctor. In the morning, maybe."

She stroked my neck with the back of her fingernails and whispered, "I love it when you're responsible." Arms stretched over her head, she lay back on the bed, grasped the windowsill, and convinced me from under half-closed eyelids.

Sometimes when she's sleeping I think I can see her eyes through her closed lids. I try to see the light blue dots, so pale they often seem almost white.

Her dreams are vivid, larger than life and, she swears, always in color, except once: in the middle of a dream when Godzilla "made a guest appearance" and the scenario switched to black and white. She was so excited when that happened that she woke up in the middle of the dream and then woke me up to tell me.

"Consistent with its own reality—the only Godzilla movies I've seen were black and white! Isn't that amazing?"

"Consistency is the refuge of the unimaginative," was my not-quite-fully-awake response.

One who ceases to have any recognizable form of brain activity between the hours of 11:30 p.m. and 7 a.m. should not even imply a lack of imagination in someone else. My penance for such blasphemy was to listen to her read from the dream interpretation book she got at the library.

"'If you dream you are falling, you may feel out of control in an emotional situation...some Slavic peoples believe dreaming of defecating inside a house (not in the bathroom) foreshadows a loved one's death.' That's from the chapter on symbols."

"What about the whistle dream? Remember, you dreamt about a man in a blue trench coat who sat whistling in an aisle at Nordstrom's. It was a sad tune, and it made you..."

"Not everything has an explanation," she said.

"You mean interpretation," I said.

"Whatever. Go back to sleep."

She says she works on the names in her sleep. I see the book on the nightstand on her side of the bed.

"Didn't you once say you thought a boy's name should have personal or historical significance?" she asked.

"I don't think so. I'm not against those criteria, just as long as it's nothing too common, like John or Mark, or Mohammed."

"Tell me, Cal, why do Hispanics consider it an honor—I mean, I can think of no other reason—to name a boy child 'Jesus'?"

I can't always tell when she's teasing.

"Must be a cultural thing," she continued. "Can you imagine, in an English-speaking country, Jesus O'Malley? Jesus Ole Hansen? Jesus Armstrong Hale III? Jesus Davis, Junior?"

"I get it. You want something respectable, maybe even Biblical. How about Adam?"

"Adamantly not." She grimaced. "Too intimidating."

"David?"

"Too common. He'd be one of five in his class."

"All right then, what about Habbukuk?"

"Too Middle-Easty. Sounds like a stuttering hijacker. You're on the right track, though. Something unusual or unique."

"Like Barrabas?"

"And you wonder why *I* insist on picking the names?"

Our son is Ben, not Benjamin. She was adamant about that. "Your parents didn't insist on Calhoun or Calvin, right? Cal was enough for them," she says, "and you."

Ben, or Benjamin, means "son," in Hebrew or Aramaic, I can't remember which. Meanings are important to her.

Girls need strong names, she said. "Like Abra. It means 'earth mother.' Or Alma, or Astrid."

"Too matronly," I said.

She touched her (still) flat stomach. "Matrons are strong." Slowly her fingers traced an ever-widening circle, starting at her navel. She reached for my hand, and placed it on her chest. "And sensual, too, wouldn't you agree?"

She once told me that her name means "firebrand." That's wishful thinking; that's *Brenda*. I looked it up. Brenna means "raven-haired."

"If it's a girl, it gets my last name." She says this at least once a week.

I can live with that. What if it's another boy?

Every time I ask that question she pauses as though hearing it for the first time, looks at me blankly and says, "I'll let you know, then."

I laugh more, now, than when we were dating, when I was trying to be a good audience.

Brenna says she's forgotten what she really wants to be when she grows up. Maybe later, she says, when both kids are in school.

I always assumed she loved her job.

The pink ring on the kit's dipstick matched her eyes, swollen with tears, the morning she did the test. She called to me from the bathroom. She sat on the toilet seat, holding the stick next to her face, and forced a smile. "Red on the outside, white on the inside."

Brenna cried in her sleep that night. I pretended to let her wake me, although I had been up for hours, watching her.

"I know it's late," she said, "but you have to promise something, now."

"Anything. You know that."

"No, not for me." She sat up and hugged her knees to her chest. "Try to be aware of the little things, and how they fit into the big picture. Like cornbread, when you make it in the square pan? Make sure Ben gets the middle piece, sometimes. The one in the center that doesn't have any hard, crusty edges on it. I know *I'll* remember. I want you to make an effort when it's your turn."

She remembers having to give the prime cuts and pieces of everything to her younger brothers and sisters. She was the oldest and had to "set an example." She said Ben shouldn't have to be an example for anyone but himself.

"Bren, he's only eighteen months old."

She arched her eyebrows. "Boys mature slower. We'll have to start now if anything's going to sink in."

I check on Ben, who, like his mother, usually sleeps the whole night through. They'll be a little over two years apart, I think. I return to our bedroom and take the piece of paper with the phone numbers on it out of my wallet.

What if something happens? What if she changes her mind?

She says she's never changed her mind about anything, except for her first impression of me.

I slip my feet under the covers. Brenna sighs and stretches an arm toward the window. I inch sideways, my face close to hers, and strain to see behind the closed lids.

She admits to sometimes dreaming of lovers, but says they have no faces. And, *yes*, they are anatomically correct, except for the afore-mentioned detail. That's all she'll say. "Go have some fantasies of your own," she says, when I press for details.

Sometimes, when she's sleeping on her side, I spoon myself around her from behind, close but not touching. I place my hand on the curve above her hip and slide, fingers gently tapping, down toward her stomach, touching softly, just enough to enter and change her dream.

Give that lover a face.

Brenna keeps a Bible on her side of the bed, next to the baby names book. I've seen her reading it when she thinks she's alone.

I remember an Old Testament story from Sunday School. God took Abram outside one night, showed him the stars and said, "So shall your descendants be." That meant, I was taught, that there would be a lot of them. The countless multitudes.

So shall my descendants be. I look at the heavens, and see Brenna's blue-white eyes in every flickering star.

"The choices we make, whether thrust upon us by circumstance or initiated by our action or lack thereof, are all that matter. We close our eyes, spin the bottle, point in the dark and say, 'I'll take that one.' We say we had no rational choice to do anything other than what we did."

That was the first paragraph in my journal. I tore out that page and started over.

I dreamt I was dreaming. I climbed a rope ladder that stretched from the bedroom window to the moon. The moon was in a quarter phase and resembled a silvery sliver, like one of the illustrations in Ben's favorite poetry book. The ladder rungs felt like strands of cotton, barely supporting my weight as I climbed. I was drawn toward the moon's face: a fiery yet friendly crescent-shaped eye above a smiling, pale pink mouth. I reached the top rung and lost my grip. I tried to break my fall by grabbing at the rungs, which metamorphosed into strands of a spider's web when I touched them.

I awaken facing the foot of the bed, clutching Brenna's ankle. I turn around and lie back with my head against the windowsill. Brenna mumbles, and I place my hand on her shoulder. Still asleep, she whispers, "Soon, sometime soon."

Tomorrow I'll make the travel reservations, and a doctor's appointment.

There are few stars visible tonight, and no moon. Not nearly enough light to write by.

This morning I'll start again, a new entry. I dreamt that I dreamt I was dreaming.

The Anti-Cancer Diet

I know what you're thinking: broccoli. Oh, and maybe some *cauliflower* now and then for a real treat. Plus lots of bran muffins and fish oil. But it doesn't have to be like that; I'm here to tell you.

You see, there are a lot of well-known facts that just aren't widely accepted by those in the general population who have all the influence and all the power. Now, I am not contradicting myself—a fact can be, and in fact often is, both well-known and yet obscure at the same time, because we are talking about common sense, something that has been forsaken by man in the late twentieth century. And women; excuse me, you know, I, too, am sensitive to generalities.

No, thank you; I drink nothing but mineral water. It's easier to obtain than you might think for someone like me, for a person of my means. I prefer to describe myself in terms of what I have rather than what I have not, so I say, "my means."

And what I have—are you getting all this down?—is worth a lot to this world, by that I mean this immediate society. So you see, I come to you with something to offer. I have collateral, you'd say, for this loan of your resources.

A man of my position has a lot of time to think and to ponder. It is absolutely *amazing*, the things people will throw away. I get the newspapers that way and I see the magazines and I know that people read and report with no thought of correlation or collaboration, and so it's easy for me, you see, because obviously a man of my means has no ego struggle; I'm not afraid to seek and to ask. And to take, to accept, which is even harder, don't you agree? That's what a friend of mine confirmed: you could not even give away all you had at your Christmas food bank or shelter or whatever he called it, as it is hard even for some of the people you'd say are in his—which is also my—"situation" to be that humble for that long.

You know what they say: "You can't have everything, where would you put it?"

I'm sorry to take so long, but I've always been stifled by applications or forms of any kind. It must be the categorization.

I know the state disapproves, but to be correct you must list my address as the bench in front of the All-Mart drugstore. And I don't mean "The State" as in the anonymous, all-encompassing, impersonal bureaucracy. I don't mean to sound so cliché, as I for one do not believe in clichés, but I can see that you do, because your experience shines through you. You are a beacon of light, illuminating through the opaque, but still very red, tape. You went through it, you learned at the hand or desk of the very best, and now you do it for the charity, for the love of it.

Yes, there is no daytime phone.

Your forehead crinkles give you away. I don't mean to ramble, but I see you are surprised that I am so articulate. Streetwise, but with the documentary-perfect tongue of the uneducated, the left-behind, that's what you expected—it's okay, I know—and I'm sure that most of the time you're not disappointed.

And I am not ungrateful; I know of your character, of the reputation of Grace temple or whatever, and that you offer freely without proselytizing and so perhaps you will bear with me while I proselytize to you?

My collateral, as I said earlier: the ultimate gift of an idea, as opposed to a material, corporeal substance.

To call it a diet is actually a misnomer, but it is a most purposeful attention-getter, because I know that today you must package everything as a "diet" to get noticed. It is more a way of life, a change in lifestyle, that is as life-affirming as it is rearranging. It will shake you up, it may even annoy you, for as what I would assume to be your blueprint, the Bible, says: "The first shall be last, and the last shall be first."

Thank you; I know that's not verbatim.

The answer is right in front of our eyes. Demographics, statistics...can it be that we are blind to the obvious?

You can eat as much broccoli as you like, as long as you wash it down with a generous portion of a diet soft drink. Now, right there, I know what you're thinking, but I do not subscribe to the theory of artificial sweeteners despite the mice studies. Copious amounts of diet colas, yes! The more the better. Have you ever actually heard of anyone dying from bladder cancer? That was just some research doctor—I have it on good authority that they can't cut it as regular, patient-seeing doctors so they retreat to publish—who was going for a Nobel prize. Whatever happened to those studies, do you even remember? Of course you don't, because it doesn't matter.

But I go beyond myself again. I'll lay it right out for you and then we'll finish up, I promise. Your patience is as great as— and even competes with—your generous and beautiful spirit.

Turn the page over and there's room. You can get this all down, as it's not very long. The truth is, as I have found, rarely as complex as the documentarians would have us believe...and I have nothing to give you under "other significant background information," anyway.

Besides the diet soft drinks, there's donuts. Basically, it comes down to the fact that women who live in trailer parks or low-cost housing developments or those retirement villages, and who subsist on a physical and intellectual diet of low-cal sodas, donuts, and tabloids, and who wear synthetic stretch garments— particularly the vibrantly-colored slacks—simply do not get cancer. This is not wholly my original idea or even observation, but one I have made and substantiated over the years, although not by conventionally documentable means. So, as I cannot claim sole authorship for this idea, I do not reserve sole proprietorship for its presentation or marketing.

Yes, of course there's more to it than that. Weight is also a factor. Being overweight helps; not obese, but enough zaftigness to strainfully caress the seams of one's garments. I do not know why being of the female persuasion helps, but apparently it is of some protection. Career aspirations and outside interests other than the tabloids and plentiful daytime television viewing have yet to be fully analyzed, though I believe it may actually be the rays—yes, from the TV set itself—that afford some protection. We, of course, don't fully understand it yet, but at one time we—meaning *They*, of course—thought that prolonged exposure could make one sterile, remember?

Two days for processing? Now, this is an example of the progress of the private industry over governmental floundering, despite the best of intentions.

Oh, far from it, my good woman! Having the experience I have had in this kind of situation, two days is truly a miracle. And that's my point, that's why I offer you—not personally, but as a representative of the practical, organizational, get-it-done-and-then-sing-the-hymns side of your beliefs—the opportunity to use your facilities to eventually provide more than a mere temporary relief to those in need. I am of course grateful for the chance, but I in return offer the Giver the chance to be grateful and thus complete the circle.

I know about licensing…you're nonprofit, but I assume you had to get separate licenses or permits for this shelter, which involved more applications and City, maybe even County, forms.

You did? You see, I am not really surprised. I could tell you had experience in this matter. And now I will do something I do not often do. I will ask you, as you the person, to help both me personally and collectively, as the collective "we": that is, us. A collaborator for my collateral. A colleague! I like the sound of that better, and I do sincerely need your help to put this together in a more…*coherent* form. Yes, I am not afraid of that word, which I know is oxymoronish when used or applied to a man of my means.

Such a wistful smile, but it's true. They're only words, and as we used to say, "Sticks and stones..." You know the rest.

How many times have you laughed today? It's nice to hear...no, we haven't missed anything. There is no home phone number—what do they think!—nor one for messages. I will come back in two days to claim my just desserts. One more thing I forgot to mention, I think I'm allergic to petroleum-based fabrics, especially polyester. I scratch and sneeze when around them; not to be picky but I'd prefer natural fibers.

No, no, now I am not teasing, or are *you* teasing *me*? But please, you must answer now for me: will you help me? Can you use your network of what must be some influential contacts to find a grant proposal writer of some experience? Shelters like this, no matter how storefront in appearance, do not just spontaneously generate. Philanthropists—I can almost smell them! There must be one amongst your supporters who would find it in his or her heart—or even ultimate best interest, as cancer strikes with such pugnacious whimsy—to fund this theory of mine to its respectable documented fruition? Besides, we could make big bucks.

One more laugh from you and the third time will truly be the charm! You see, I'm not all-serious. Not every one of us anti-cancer mentors are terminally earnest and grave.

And once again I must thank you for your immediate help, and in advance for your discretion in revealing these secrets to a select few, until the proper time. For I can tell that you are a person of honor, and although I do not share nor profess your particular religion, I can attest to the motivation it gives you, and I know that you will not let this fall into the wrong hands.

Just kidding about the wrong hands part. You expected, at the very least, a dab of paranoia, didn't you?

Of course I'm teasing. *Again.* I'll see you, then, on Thursday afternoon, Miss...Ms...?

I like that. Did you know that your name means "woman warrior" in Gaelic?

"May the road rise up to greet you..." Or meet you. I forget. It's an Irish prayer or blessing. Also, "May you be in heaven an hour before the devil finds out you're dead."

I can see they're waiting; I must apologize for holding up the line. The others are not like me; they're so without hope. But in the long run I'm sure we all fit into the same boat, or ark, two by two. Although I do not drink in the alcoholic sense, I look forward to Thursday, to toast what I hope will be the good news— the gospel, if I may, as that means "good news" in Greek, doesn't it?—you will have for me.

We'll Talk Later

Rex hadn't always had difficulty swallowing stringy vegetables. The problem had developed gradually, as had his awareness that his first name was more commonly given to pit bulls and high-strung terriers than human beings.

"Rex, eat your string beans," his father implored. "Remember the clean plate club agreement?" Mr. Duncan considered every scrap of food remaining on his children's dinner plates to be an affront to his meager, yet honest, dog-walker's salary.

"Don't call me that," Rex answered. "That's not my name." Rex had decided to find a name more suitable to his liking, and until he came up with something new, he had halfheartedly vowed not to answer when addressed by his current moniker.

"Young man, I'd rather not get into that nonsense at the dinner table, if you don't mind. Your given name, the name you were baptized with, the name your great-uncle was proud to claim on his veteran's disability forms, is *Rex*. I suppose you'd rather be another one of several million Johns, Jims, Daves, Bills or Bobs?" Mr. Duncan scraped his knife along the edge of his plate, wiping bits of butter and mashed potato on the rim.

"I'll be twelve in less than ten months, and I suppose that makes me titled…"

"You mean, '*en*titled'," his mother whispered from across the dining room table.

"…entitled to make some decisions about my, uh, destiny." Rex paused and drew a deep, loud breath. "Besides, I looked it up in the family genes Mom was workin' on…"

"*Genealogy.*" Mrs. Duncan spoke even more softly than before.

"...and we never had no Uncle Rex. You named me after Mrs. Harkey's German Shepherd!" Rex tried to sound indignant.

"Well, you *do* have those big brown eyes," purred his sister, Nina, "not to mention the similar gait and coloring."

One week ago such a remark from Nina would have brought her a glob of potatoes smashed into her ears, but Rex decided to play it cool. He also didn't know what "gait" meant. He suspected it was one of her vocabulary words and probably had some cruel, biological (he couldn't bring himself to even think "sexual") connotation.

"You kids!" Mrs. Duncan stood up and started clearing the dishes from the table. "If only your book reports were as clever as your verbal sparring at dinner; well, I don't know, we'd just have to write a book about it!"

Nina rolled her eyes at Rex, twirled a strand of her shoulder-length hair around her index finger, and mumbled to herself.

"What did you say?" Rex whispered, leaning toward Nina. Mr. Duncan took his plate into the kitchen and helped his wife load the dishwasher. "Did you call Mom obscene?"

"Obsequious." Nina gave Rex a rare smile. "I may be using it wrong. There's got to be a specific word for how bizarre our parental units are. I mean, how can I be related to *that woman*?"

Rex, unsure of how he should respond, shrugged his shoulders and nodded his head.

Nina's eyes widened. "Non sequitur." She smiled at Rex, who frowned and scratched his head. "I bet that's it. Not to worry, bro—I'll look it up and let you know."

Rex laughed. She probably made a joke, he thought, and, if so, he'd best pretend he got it. He stayed at the table while Nina helped her parents in the kitchen. Twirling his fork between his thumb and forefinger, he remembered overhearing a conversation between his parents, many months ago, in which his father referred to Nina as "...thirteen going on thirty-three." Rex supposed that had something to do with Nina's vocabulary books, and the fact that she seemed to be taking her teachers' evaluations seriously.

"'Destined for superior intellectual achievement. Without a doubt, the brightest junior high school student I have ever had the privilege to teach.'"

One evening, four months ago, at the dinner table, Mr. Duncan had read Nina's first semester eighth grade evaluation to the family. Rex had listened politely, feigning interest in his sister's report card while he ate his spaghetti. He asked to be excused from the table, and then ran next door to Megan's house.

Megan Winger was Rex's classmate, next door neighbor, and best friend. Megan was also eleven, and also had an older sibling whose academic achievements were held up by her parents as the educational pinnacle to which children should aspire. Rex and Megan had howled with laughter when Rex recounted Nina's teachers' remarks, and then when he told Megan that Nina had bought, with her own allowance and babysitting money, a textbook.

"It was a book of words," he sneered, "one of those vocabulary books. She did it on her own; she admitted it. She seemed almost *proud* of it." He pinched his nostrils together with his fingers and spoke in a nasal, high-pitched tone. "It's advantageous to learn a new word every day and use it in conversation."

"She really said that?" Megan giggled and punched his arm.

"Yeah, swear-ta-God," Rex said. "Then she used one of those words on me. Actually, she got me to use one and then turned it around to make fun of me, like I *really* care."

"I know, she's so good at that," said Megan. "Like Vince. Sometimes it bothers me that I'll never be as smart as him, even though he's older so it's not fair."

"Anyways," Rex said, "what she did was this: she said it wasn't my fault that I'm not good in school. She said she heard there was a name for it, so I told her maybe I was—oh, man, I can't remember it now. Remember that thing, something about your brain being sideways, that Alan Fernow has and so he gets those different math workbooks? Mis- or dis- something."

"Dyslexic?" Megan offered.

"That's it," Rex said. "So, I said, maybe I'm dyslexic, and then she said," Rex raised his voice again, "'No, nothing so technical. You're probably just slow-witted.'"

"Whatever *did* ever happen to Mrs. Harkey's dog?" Mrs. Duncan interrupted Rex's reminiscing. She walked into in the dining room, wiping her hands on a dishtowel. "Didn't the poor thing die under mysterious circumstances?"

Mr. Duncan spoke loudly from the kitchen while he loaded the dishwasher.

"Mysterious-schmerious. It jumped the fence and got into the Winger's garbage, remember? Ate a whole batch of Ken Winger's chili that Anne had thrown out when Ken left on a business trip."

"Dad, that's just a rumor," Nina said.

"No, it's the honest truth," he said. "I heard it from the horse's mouth, from one of my clients who goes to the same veterinarian. Poor pup died of third degree intestinal burns."

"Yeah, burned his spleen off!" Rex said. "I love that story!"

Nina flipped her hair off of her shoulders, and directed her comment to the ceiling as she sashayed out of the dining room.

"Dogs don't have spleens."

Megan came over to Rex's house early the next morning. As per their previous day's agreement, Rex telephoned her the moment his parents left the house to go grocery shopping.

"We're going on an adventure," Megan had told him, "and we'll need supplies." She made him write them down: he was to bring a small paper lunch bag, four plastic baggies, four rubber bands, and two large, yard-size plastic garbage bags. She would bring the same.

Rex and Megan walked to the end of their street, turned left at the corner and headed for the overgrown, weedy fields of what had been, many years ago, a junior college athletic field. First stop, Megan told him, would be the Henlor house. The Henlor's was the last house on the short, dead-end street onto which they'd turned. The cul-de-sac ended at a narrow dirt road, which led to what had once been the junior college parking lot.

"If we're going to the dump, why can't we ride our bikes?" Rex shifted his large bag, which held the rest of his supplies, from shoulder to shoulder.

"It's not that far," Megan said. "Besides, we may find a lotta stuff that we want to bring back, and it'll be easier to carry it than ride with our bags full."

"I don't get it," said Rex. "Your brother really crawls around in garbage for a college class?"

"Yeah. 'Garbage Anthropology' is what he calls it, but it's really got some other name. I don't know that much about it. He says that by looking at what people throw away you can find out how they live or what they do. Leftovers and scraps tell a story."

"Oh, I get it," Rex said. "You find some Kleenex and maybe, if you're *real* smart, you figure out that they blow their noses."

"I don't care about all the what-people-do stuff, I just can't believe we didn't think of this before." The breeze shifted, and Megan sniffed the air. "All these years of living by the dump; you just *know* people have been throwing away great stuff and we've missed it. Remember the perfectly good refrigerator box your parents threw out last summer?"

"What if we both see something we like, at the same time? Who gets it?" Rex asked.

"We'll negotiate," Megan said. "Okay, stop. Here's the Henlor's car. Get out your brown bag."

Rex looked at the tan Buick Skylark that was parked in the Henlor's driveway. The car was covered with dust and had cobwebs in the wheel wells. It looked as though it hadn't been moved in years. Grayish-white streaks dripped down the side of each of the front doors, starting from under the side-view mirrors.

"Now what?" Rex asked.

"We're gonna stop this mess, that's what. I thought, since it was on the way, why not?" Megan took her small paper bag and put it over the mirror on the driver's side. She instructed Rex to use his bag to cover the mirror on the passenger door.

"Gross—this is *bird shit* all down the door!" Rex gingerly covered the mirror with his paper bag.

"Really, Einstein," said Megan. "I saw it the other day when I went to check out the dump. There's this bird, probably with a nest in one of the Henlor's trees, and he flies down and lands right on the mirrors. Both doors have got it so he must change sides. He sits on the mirror and pecks at his own reflection!"

"I saw a mockingbird do that once, in our backyard," Rex said. "He flew into our sliding glass door and knocked himself out. I thought he got brain damage, 'cause he got up and kept flying into the door, over and over. Mom said he saw his reflection and thought he was chasing his enemy or defending his territory. But he didn't *crap* all over our door."

"How could he?" Megan asked. "Anyway, I watched this bird for about ten minutes; he kept pecking at the mirror. I figure, when he's got nothing else to do he comes and sits on the mirrors and fights with himself. That's why those poop streaks are down the sides of the doors. So, if we cover the mirrors, there won't be a reason for him sit there anymore."

"Did you figure this out by yourself, or did Vince help you?"

"It's my idea, but he helped, in a way," Megan said.

Rex put his index finger in his mouth and made gagging sounds. "Who cares if the Henlor's car gets *covered* with bird poop? They're never gonna wash it. I don't think it even works."

"That's not the point," said Megan. "I used the scientific method; I problem-solved, just like Vince says. He talks a lot about that when he's home during his breaks and he pretends to help me with my homework. What you do is, first, figure out what the problem is, then figure out what to do. You form a hypothesis—that's when you find out what the problem is—and then you come up with ways to fix it."

"You thought of this so you could form a hypotenuse?"

"*Hypothesis*, dummy."

"I'm dyslexic," Rex sighed. "I can't be a scientist."

"You could go into show business," Megan said. She grabbed his arm and pulled him away from the Henlor's driveway. "I read somewhere that lots of movie stars are dyslexic. C'mon, let's go."

"I don't know about that. You'd have to be able to talk good in front of lots of people…"

"I suppose you're gonna walk dogs, like your dad?" Megan made barking noises and ran ahead of Rex. She squeezed through a hole in the chain link fence that separated the city dumping grounds from the abandoned junior college parking lot.

"He doesn't *just* walk dogs," Rex panted. He caught up with Megan, and together they ran toward the dump. "He does something else, but I don't know what it is. Nina says there's times when he's 'unaccounted for.' I hate it when she talks like that…she *always* talks like that. But she doesn't know what he does, either."

"Why don't you ask him?" Megan asked.

"He doesn't like to talk about work when he's home." Rex stopped abruptly, and stared at a "No Hazardous Materials" sign in front of the dump. "He's always trying to get us to talk about family stuff, especially at dinner. We're all supposed to take turns and say how our day was or what we did. Nina told me she thinks he's a spy or sells drugs or something like that, and one day we're going to wake up and his picture will be on the front page of the newspaper."

"Yeah, right." Megan sat down and dumped the contents of her large bag on the ground. Rex plopped down next to her. He removed the small bags and rubber bands from his large bag.

"I can never tell when she's joking," Rex said. "So *I* told *her* if that happens, she'd have to quit school and help Mom knit those Christmas ornaments and toilet paper and soap dish covers—the ones my mom gives your mom, to sell at your church raffle for the old folk's home…what's it called, 'Golden Acres?' I told her she'd have to sell them or we wouldn't have enough money to eat!"

"You'd all starve. Those things are so ugly, the only reason people buy them is because they feel sorry for the people in that home. They feel guilty 'cause they put their relatives there," Megan said. "That was pretty good, though. What did Nina say?"

Rex snorted. "She said, 'You shouldn't sell true art; art comes from in here.'" He thumped his palm on his chest.

"I am *so* sure," Megan said.

"Where does all this stuff go?" Rex asked.

"Watch me." Megan tore two holes in the bottom of one of the large bags, put her legs through them and then pulled the bag up to her neck. Around each hand and foot she put a smaller plastic baggie, using the rubber bands to secure the bags around her ankles and wrists. Rex did the same.

"All right," said Megan, holding the remaining bag in her hand, "use this as your stuff bag. Remember, be picky, 'cause whatever you take, you carry. And we gotta be back by noon."

Rex held his body-bag up around his neck with one hand, grabbed his loot bag with the other, and ran toward the dump. "Betcha I'll find the best stuff!"

That night at dinner Rex couldn't wait until the all the food was brought to the table. He had to tell them about his and Megan's adventure.

"Crawling around in *garbage*?" His mother sounded more mystified than angry. She brought the salad bowl into the dining room, set it on the table and began tossing the salad. With her arms bent at the elbows she snapped her wrists upward, using brisk, flipping motions that brought the salad tongs a good eight inches above the top of the bowl with each flip. She ignored the pieces of lettuce that dropped onto the tablecloth as she tossed and tossed.

"I suppose I can see the attraction to a child, but...what do you think, honey? It doesn't sound like legitimate *science* to me."

"Your mother's right. I think Vince may have been pulling his sister's leg on this one, Rex." Mr. Duncan cleared his throat, picked up the lettuce bits his wife had dropped from the salad bowl, and placed them in a neat pile on his plate. "May I keep calling you Rex until you decide on another name?"

"I bet Megan is telling the same story at her dinner table, and Vince is having a laugh on both of you," Nina said. "I'm sure *his* parents are impressed with him, for getting the both of you to pick through other people's trash."

Nina looked impassively at Rex, and continued. "How come you're not grabbing for the food like usual? Lost your appetite, or maybe you found some homemade chili in the dump?"

Ignore her, Rex thought; she *hates* it when you ignore her.

"You weren't there, so you don't really know, do you?" Rex tried to keep even the slightest hint of irritation out of his voice. "We had fun, even if we didn't find a whole lotta stuff that would tell us anything about the town, or whatever the anth-pology would say. And I got three really neat things." Rex pulled a small bag out from under his chair.

Mr. Duncan raised his eyebrows. "Now, wait a minute. You're not bringing garbage to the table?"

"Just three things I found worth keeping, and I washed two of them. I couldn't wash this one." Rex pulled a crumpled piece of lined notebook paper out of the bag. He laid it on the table, smoothing the wrinkles as best he could.

"This is *so* great. I don't know how we found it, it was like it just jumped up and we saw it." Rex lowered his voice and read from the paper: "'…he gave me a fichus, which I later used to beat his head in after he…' That's all there is." Rex looked around the table at his family. "Isn't that *mysterious*?"

Nina rolled her eyes toward the ceiling, pushed a bit of chicken casserole around her plate with her fork, and moaned. "Is there a *point* to this?"

"Megan says it's probably part of a poem someone wrote," Rex said, "and then they threw it away later when they reread it and saw how stupid it was. I think it could be, maybe, a spy code or a murder confession."

"In your wildest dreams," Nina snickered.

Rex's parents looked at each other and smiled. Rex put the note back into the bag. He looked across the table at his mother.

"Shut your eyes and hold out your hands." Rex took a Swiss Army knife from the bag and placed it in her outstretched palms.

"Rex! You found this at the dump? It's in perfect condition!" His mother caressed the pocketknife as if it were a hamster. "I never got one when I was a child. My brothers did, but never me. You remembered me saying that, didn't you?" She smiled at Rex, her eyes bright and shiny with unshed tears.

Nina sighed loudly. "Big day for you, huh, Mom?"

"Thank you for thinking of me, Rex." Mrs. Duncan put the knife into her apron pocket, and glared at Nina. "I'm going to keep this with me, always, like a good scout."

She's in a good mood, Rex thought. I'll try one more time.

"I got some more information about the water ski camp."

"Not this again." Mr. Duncan tapped his fork on the table.

Rex pretended not to have heard his father. He spoke rapidly, figuring to say as much as possible before he was interrupted.

"It's two weeks, like Forestry camp last year, and it doesn't cost any more than that one did, and they have safety instructors to teach us first aid, which would be great to know anywhere, not only at a lake, and so far there's four other kids from our block going: Megan and Joshua Sun Tree and…"

"You complain about *your* name?" his father guffawed. "You want to make up a name like 'Sun Tree?'"

"I read about families like that," Nina said. "The parents were these Sixties nerds who secretly wanted to be revolutionaries, but they were too chicken to take drugs, so they gave their kids weird names in the Seventies and Eighties."

"That's his real name," said Rex. "*As I was saying*, Megan and Joshua and the Than twins…"

"I didn't know Chinese people water-skied," said his mother.

"*Vietnamese*, and they don't, not now. None of us do. That's the point, it's a camp to *learn how*." Rex clenched his fists under the table. "We'll all learn; then we can all water ski. Ask the other parents. They think it's okay."

"But honey." His mother used her 'there-there' voice. "We've been over this before. We don't know anyone who owns a boat. It's not as if you will be able to go out and ski once you learn how. You won't have the opportunity."

"We *have* been over this before, and we're going to settle this now before I get sick of hearing about it," Mr. Duncan said. "It's not that we don't want you to go to a camp this summer. We said you could go again this year. It's just that your mother and I would like you to pick something more useful."

Rex looked down at his plate. "I'd probably make friends with people at the camp, and their families might own boats. It could be my birthday present, early, and then you don't have to get me anything else, later."

"I've always thought water skiing was a low-class sport," Mr. Duncan said. "People with fast cars and big boats…Have you ever been in a neighborhoods where you see the vans, or trucks with trailer hitches, and boats parked to the side of the garage? The kind of people who do moto-crossing and those kinds of things. Remember how you hate the snowmobiles when we go up to the snow? It's those same kind of people: loud and fast. It's a tacky and wasteful kind of recreation, Rex, when you think about it."

"And it isn't good for the environment," his mother added. "Remember when in Forestry camp you learned about pollution and natural resources and tried to get us to stop using plastic wrap?"

"Drop it, bro," Nina muttered to Rex. "This is a lost cause."

"What else did you find at the dump? Maybe a musketeer's sword for your old dad?" Mr. Duncan elbowed his wife and grinned.

"Another mystery." Rex looked around the table, wide-eyed and sincere. "Megan thinks it's a woman-thing; we don't know for sure." He reached into the bag, pulled out a light tan, dome-shaped piece of rubber and set it on the table next to his glass of milk.

Nina stared at the diaphragm, and then at Rex. She covered her eyes with her hands and mumbled, "I don't believe this."

Rex ignored her and spoke to his parents. "Megan says it's one of the things women put in their bras so their chests look bigger."

"Well...not exactly." His mother blushed and looked to her husband, who shook his head and whispered, "Not on your life."

"So what, *exactly*, then?"

Rex glanced around the table. His parents looked uncomfortable, as if they were sitting on their silverware. Nina, who obviously knew something by the expression on her face, stifled a giggle.

"That's okay." Rex tried to sound nonchalant. "It's something embarrassing, I can tell. I'm on the right track."

"No, not embarrassing. We don't want you to...to get the wrong idea," Rex's father stammered. "This just isn't the right time. Let's get that off the table and we'll talk about it later, okay?"

"No problem." Rex returned the diaphragm to his bag. "You don't have to tell me anything, if it bothers you. Megan and I will figure it out. We'll use the scientific method."

Rex looked around the table. His mother passed the casserole to his father. Nina was actually eating her salad. They're trying to change the subject, he thought.

"We'll use the scientific method to figure it out." Rex spoke loudly. "We'll form a hypotenuse."

"Isn't that 'hypothesis'?" his mother asked. She passed Rex the casserole dish. "Have some chicken."

Later that evening, when he knew they would be watching their favorite sitcom, Rex approached his parents' bedroom door.

They're going to feel guilty about brushing me off at the dinner table, he thought. I'll wait until the time is right, and then hit them up for ski camp.

He listened before knocking on their door. Instead of the usual drone of the television, he heard voices and laughter. He decided against knocking and put his ear to the door.

"I suppose we should take advantage of this, and use it as an opportunity to discuss the facts of life…now, stop that! I'm trying to be a responsible parent." His father's baritone whisper rose in a spasm of unsuccessfully suppressed laughter.

"We didn't handle that well, did we?" Mrs. Duncan giggled.

"I was trying not to laugh," Mr. Duncan said in his usual tone of voice, not bothering to whisper. "I couldn't help but think of the irony…"

"I know, I know," Mrs. Duncan said. "Our 'diaphragm baby' finds a diaphragm."

The voices faded into muffled laughter. Rex heard a noise and turned to look behind him. Arms folded across her chest, Nina leaned against her bedroom doorway.

"C'mere," she said.

Rex followed Nina into her room and sat on her bed. She shut the door and sat down next to him.

"It's okay, you know."

Rex stole sideways glances at Nina as she spoke. It had been a long time since she had just looked at him, like a normal person, he thought. There was no sneer, no smirk, no insult behind her eyes, waiting to leap out and rub his face in a mess of big words.

"I've overheard them, too. Remember that, when you have kids of your own. The walls have ears." Nina tried to make eye contact, but Rex averted his eyes and picked at his shoelaces. "They wanted to have two kids. Just maybe a bit farther apart. What the hey, we'll both be out of the house earlier this way."

Rex looked at her blankly.

"You don't know what I'm talking about, do you?" she said.

Rex scratched the bottom of his shoe.

"That was a rhetorical question; it means you don't really have to answer."

"I *know* what a diaphragm is." Rex hesitated. "I mean, I think I know, but I'd never seen one before. I'm so stupid."

"Not stupid," Nina said, softly. "Maybe a little ignorant." She poked him in the ribs. "Don't you ever watch any TV shows besides 'Star Trek' reruns?"

Rex untied and retied one of his shoelaces.

"You don't, do you?" She smiled at him. "Oh well, I don't suppose there's contraception in outer space, is there?"

"It's not funny," Rex said.

"Sure it is," Nina said, "if you keep it in the proper perspective. You don't like your name, right?"

"What does that have to do with it?"

"Well, things could be worse. They could have named you 'All-Flex' or 'Ortho.'" Nina leaned back on her elbows and, Rex thought, seemed enormously pleased with herself.

"Those are types of diaphragms," she said, "like Cheerios or Wheaties are types of cereals."

"I knew that."

"Of course you did." Nina sat up and wrapped her arms around her knees. "That's what you get for eavesdropping." She looked toward their parents' bedroom. "It's funny, how you can hear Mom so clearly from behind the door... I can usually barely hear her when she's standing right next to me. She always talks so quietly, like she's in church or at the library."

Rex stood up. "I almost forgot, I was supposed to go over to Megan's after dinner. She wanted to know what you all said the rubber thing was."

He started toward the door and then turned around. "Promise..."

"I won't tell anybody," she said. "Cheer up, bro. Play your cards right and you may be able to go to ski camp after all."

"Huh?"

"Just think about it, okay?" Nina clicked her tongue against her front teeth. "Can you believe it? *He* walks dogs, *she* makes those butt-ugly soap covers for senile citizens, but people who water ski are 'low-class.'"

"I know we had poultry last night, but I was feeling nostalgic for the Sunday dinners we had when I was a child." Mrs. Duncan aimed her comments toward the dining room, where Rex and Nina were setting the table. She took three different flavors of bottled salad dressing from the refrigerator and brought them to the table.

"We had a big roast chicken, every Sunday, but I thought this might be more fun." She returned to the kitchen and removed a platter of Cornish game hens from the oven.

The family sat down at the table, and Nina glanced at Rex. Rex cleared his throat. "I've found a couple of names I like," he announced. "I'll let you hear the choices so you can tell me which one you like best."

"That's awfully considerate of you," his father said.

"Pray tell, don't keep us in suspense," Nina said.

"I'd like my name changed to either Ortho or All-Flex."

Nina slapped her hands to her face. "I had nothing to do with this," she hissed through her fingers.

Mr. and Mrs. Duncan's faces slowly turned various shades of purple and pink, respectively.

Rex casually reached for the rice bowl. "All-Flex is my favorite. It sort of rhymes with Rex. Maybe it was that -ex sound you were going for in the first place."

Rex's mother grabbed the salad bowl and began aimlessly tossing the salad. She looked at her husband.

"Well, this is the right time, obviously. Anne Winger asked me today if we'd like to send Rex to their church's 'Family Life' camp. It's for fifth and sixth graders; they have it every year at a mountain retreat. Megan will be going this year. Anne left some sample course materials for us to review, and I think it looks like a really good thing. They take a responsible and wholesome approach, and they have volleyball and swimming and crafts and…"

"Honey, your skirt." Mr. Duncan picked lettuce leaves and radish slices from his wife's lap. "It sounds like a great idea."

"I hate it when they talk to each other like we're not here," Rex whispered to Nina.

"Rex, would you like to go?" his father asked.

"What's 'Family Life' camp?" Rex asked.

"Sex education," said Nina. "You know: 'The Facts of Life.'"

"I know some of that already. I mean, everyone knows where babies come from," Rex said, chewing a mouthful of rice. "How come you never sent Nina to that camp?"

"I didn't need to go," said Nina. "I went to the library and looked up everything I wanted to know."

"It's not that we think you don't know about…about babies," his mother said. "There are a lot of details that are difficult, sometimes, for parents to teach…" Her voice trailed off and she looked at her husband.

"And it's important to know things correctly, rather than hear rumors from your peers," his father said. "If you have the right information you can make, uh, responsible decisions and…"

"What's the big deal?" Nina interrupted. "Ask me, I'll tell you. What do you need to know? Sex is for losers. *I'm* going to go to Caltech."

Mrs. Duncan blushed, and whispered to her husband. "Al! Say something!"

"I don't want to go to that camp, and I won't learn anything if you make me," Rex said. "It sounds boring. I bet Megan's parents are forcing her to go. At least they're letting her go to water ski camp."

"Maybe we can work something out," said Mr. Duncan. He looked at his wife and patted her hand. "Now, I'm not promising anything, but maybe you could go to both camps, too."

Rex said nothing. His toes tapped wildly on the floor underneath the table.

"I'll look over those course materials," Mr. Duncan said, winking at his wife, "and then we'll talk, later, okay, Rex?"

"More rice, anyone?" Mrs. Duncan picked up the serving bowl. "Somebody eat the rest so I won't have this little dab left over."

Nina took a pen out of her pants pocket, scribbled on her napkin when her parents weren't looking, and passed the napkin under the table, to Rex.

"Touché," read the note.

Rex looked up at Nina and smiled. She smiled back and mouthed, "It's French. It means 'right on!'"

"I know," he whispered.

One and One

In *through the nose,* out *through the mouth; in through the nose, out through the nose* and *mouth...*

What was it her high school gym teacher had said, those many years ago? Could she ever have imagined that, someday, she'd regret not having listened? Gail concentrated on her breathing and tried to ignore the sharp, grasping stitch beneath her ribs.

In *one-two-three,* out *one-two-three. Establish a rhythm,* that *was it.*

Gail closed her eyes, and saw once again a cavalcade of swirly-browns spinning in front of her. The vision momentarily, literally, took her breath away, and along with it the stitch in her side.

One *and one and* one *and one...*

Gina counted the revolutions, her feet pumping up and down on gleaming pedals, her mind reverberating with the sing-song cadence by which she paced herself. She smiled into the rising sun, flush with the early morning exertion as well as with the satisfaction she always felt after overhauling her bicycle's bottom bracket.

One *and one and* one *and one.*

Gina cycled north, on roads outside the county's urban growth boundary, past the few individual family farms that had withstood the pressures of corporate land buyouts. The farms, ten- to twenty-acre blocks of filbert, cherry and pear orchards, were crazy-quilted by country roads named for various Oregon Trail pioneers.

I never can remember…who was it and where is it? The one whose grave I keep meaning to check out. Third graders make an annual field trip—part of their state history curricula. Just as annual is the follow-up to the kids' visit, the petulant Letters to the Editor from indignant Cemetery Preservation geezers who claim that the kids leave Twinkie wrappers and other undignifiables on the headstones of lesser notables. Joseph Meek, in the Old Scotch Church cemetery—that's it!

Meek's body's original resting-place was three miles north of the cemetery; his grave had been relocated years ago to make room for the highway. Gina had managed to absorb that much of the local lore, even though she was in the fifth grade when her family moved north and so had missed the field trip. Know the history, and the history is yours, her father had insisted.

One *and one and* one *and one and…*

Gina's legs made a smooth, seamless rotation, which pleased her. She concentrated on that pleasure and tried to stifle the growing, guilty impression that her early morning time could have been better spent. Perhaps, rather than fiddling with her bicycle's crankset, she should have been reviewing lab notes in preparation for her Intro to Biology midterm exam.

Heading east toward the road that paralleled and then crossed the highway, Gina exulted in the comparison with the same ride of just yesterday afternoon. No more annoying clickaty-clicka. Amazing, how *one* pitted bearing can throw off everything. Shiny round bearings, silver-smooth in the palm of her hand; the musky scent of the lubricant. She marveled to think that most people leave the sensual pleasures of routine maintenance to the sullenly-acned, adolescent males at the local bike shop…

And then she was upon the windshield.

In *one-two-three,* out *one-two-three.*

Gail desperately looked right and left, searching for the nearby pay phone that she knew did not exist. She ran south, back down the road she'd come, focusing on the Fisher farmhouse which was a mile past the "You're less than two miles from Laurel's Country Gardens" sign.

Remember, you passed it twice—on the way out and then on the way back and by the way, just where were you going? Gail was grateful that, later on when she recounted the accident to her husband, he did not ask her that question. Clay knew she drove a lot these days.

Move the legs; one-two-one-two; can a person actually forget how to run?

Gail ran. At first it was more of an unbridled, frenzied canter, then she willed herself to control: breathe deeply; reach out and back, arms and legs; obtain and maintain a rhythmic pace. She quelled the rising panic in her gut by repeating to herself how the bicyclist looked (*a bit shook up, but young and strong*).

Gail ran, thinking about how she would finally agree to Clay's request to purchase cellular phones for the cars. She thought about the windshield, the dirty windshield she should have rinsed off—in the morning's dusty-gold glare she had no idea the bicycle was even there! And then the rainbow of brown, suddenly somersaulting across the hood of her car, interrupting her reverie of...of whatever she'd been thinking about before the accident. A flash of cinnamon hair, bronze skin, chocolate eyes and copper bicycle frame; a slow motion ballet, tumbling across her windshield.

Somewhere between that thought and the Fisher farmhouse she stopped thinking and kept running.

Gina removed her helmet and performed a quick body parts check on herself. Everything still attached, although violently shaking with what she assumed was an adrenaline overdose. She fingered the shredded, synthetic blend of what had once been her cycling shorts, and saw something resembling raw hamburger beneath the tatters. That's one incredible road rash, she thought.

Her bicycle straddled a ditch a few feet beside her, its front forks bent at a grotesque angle, the front wheel nowhere in sight. She shielded her eyes against the sun and tried to concentrate on what the woman was saying to her—a woman who had sprung from the car and run to her side; a woman in her thirties or forties to whom she heard someone—herself, presumably—say, "I'm okay, just shaken up." The woman whose faded, flowery house dress was too big for her or she was too big for the dress; but it couldn't be both, could it? Gina tried to focus on what the woman was saying: something about possible internal injuries, need a blood pressure reading, stay there, don't move, I'll get help. The woman turned and ran down the road, her voice fading, and the sound returned, echoing through Gina's skull—dull, metallic thud of frame meeting frame and then the shriek of brakes as she and her bicycle parted company.

One *and one and* one *and one...*

Gina hunched forward, head between her knees, and concentrated on her breathing. She slowly raised her head and watched the fading form of the woman who ran down the road. There was something comically divine about that flapping, ridiculous housedress, she thought.

Gail cursed her sensible shoes and kicked off the low-heeled, beige slings. A tingling sensation ascended each leg as her stockings snagged on the gravel road; she envisioned matching sets of racing stripes from toe to knee and on up. She felt her arms pumping and tasted the salty drops that dribbled into her mouth from her forehead and upper lip. She felt her body parts moving together in seamless rapidity, and wondered what a sight she must present. Turning up the dirt driveway, yelling for Jan Fisher to call 911, she felt exhilarated beyond belief.

Gail knew she must have looked ludicrous, as ludicrous as the very idea of even thinking that anyone would have cared about how she looked. There had been a time, long ago, when she would have had no such thoughts; a time, Gail remembered, when she *was* her own body, instead of a stranger shrouded in someone else's fleshy shell. Somewhere on that road, somewhere between thinking about the windshield she should have cleaned, the windshield suddenly both obscured and illuminated by the thumpa-thumpa-thud from nowhere... How long had it been since she'd had a desire to move, a desire to do something other than sit, drive, or crawl?

She was certain she ran faster that morning than Clay drove that night, the night when Danny wheezed and turned red and finally stopped breathing. It seemed at the time that they fairly flew to the hospital; now she wonders how they could have gone so slow. She remembers cautioning Clay: It won't do Danny any good if we crash before we get to the hospital.

And then it was as if someone had pushed a button on Clay's VCR remote control. Her life advanced one frame at a time, one slow step up from freeze frame, when the doctor came out of the Emergency Room with an I'm-so-sorry look on his face, and asked to see the cookie Danny had been eating when he collapsed—the chocolate chip cookies the Fisher kids had brought by, and who would have thought a twenty-month-old boy would be allergic to walnuts? No, Clay told the doctor, come to think of it, Danny had never eaten nuts because Gail didn't like them. Nuts of any kind left a funny taste in Gail's mouth; she never had any in the house, which was fine with Clay 'cause he could take 'em or leave 'em and so there they were, every other farm a filbert orchard, in the filbert-growing capital of the whole damn world, but they grew grass seed and talked about raising llamas because Gail didn't like nuts.

At Clay's request, Gail had taken down Danny's pictures from the hallway and the dressers and the side of the refrigerator. Someday, Clay said, they'll go back up, but not now. "Not now" means not ever, Gail soon realized. She could accept that. Gail's body carried its own photographs. The throbbing veins behind her knees; the loose, fleshy abdomen; the dark, vertical line which bisected her torso from the navel down (the line the doctor said would fade); the empty, sagging breasts. These remained, but as the months and then the years went by she realized she was forgetting what Danny looked like. When Clay was outside she'd get the photo album and remind herself.

Gail remembered standing over Danny's crib, inhaling the sweet and pungent toddler earthiness. She remembered the physical grace and foolishness, all pudgy arms and legs scampering and stumbling through bright red clover in the north pasture, and she beseeched Nameless Spirits to illuminate the sparse miracles and ample tragedies that framed one's life.

When Gail arose the morning after the accident, and the mornings after that, she no longer went driving. She walked behind her house, to the pasture. She ran to the pasture; in the pasture; up, down and around the pasture. She ran for soccer teams never joined, games of tag never played and puppies never chased.

"You're crazy", Gina's brother said, when he learned of her intentions. "Don't give her anything she can use; nothing that could be interpreted as an admission of responsibility. Why you admitted running the stop sign in the first place is beyond belief for someone who supposedly sustained no brain damage."

Gabriel paced back and forth in the apartment he shared with his younger sister. "Typical, naive student. Get out in the real world and you'll see. You don't know a thing about this woman, Gina. You don't know what she'll do."

No. I do know a thing, this one thing. I know where I was—right through the stop sign—and the poor lady probably thinks…

Gina fingered the stiff, macramé crucifix that hung on a chain around her neck, and reread a copy of the accident report. No doubt she'd given this totally innocent woman nightmares about the cyclist she had almost killed. In all the confusion, after the sheriff and paramedics arrived, she'd never spoken to the driver.

"Infliction of emotional distress, negligence…*she'll* probably sue *you*." Gabe refused to let it lie. "Her lawyer will find some
reason; *she'll* find a reason. White people sue at the drop of a hat."

Gina hated it when he talked like that. She hated his pre-
dictable, pathetic follow up—some cutting remark in Level II
Spanish, as though it were natural for him. Yet another
discomfiting reminder of their native monolingualism, a reminder
that their familial affinity with what Gabriel calls "their own" culture is about as genuine as the Taco Palace on Division Street.

Gina leaned her bicycle against the graying, split rail fence.
She looked past a mailbox labeled "Country Clover Acres, The
Madsen Family," and squinted into the late afternoon sun.

One *and one and* one…

Gina took a deep breath and walked toward a cloud of dust
that rose from a field north of the farmhouse. A woman wearing
a pastel yellow, mumu-ish dress ran around the field in her stock-
ing feet, kicking a neon orange foursquare ball through the red
clover.

"Hello there!" Gail wiped a reddened, freckled forearm
across her sweaty brow. Her smile was demurely effusive, as if she
were welcoming a beloved though seldom-seen cousin to Sunday
supper.

"Hello; good afternoon. My name…" Gina hesitated. She
extended her right hand, and sneezed three times as the dust from
the woman's disporting enveloped her. "Excuse me! I'm Gina
Casares."

"I know." Gail giggled shyly. "Sorry about the dirt." She
waved her hand, shooing the airborne particles that, backlit by
the setting sun, resembled a ring of golden confetti encircling her
head. "I'm glad you stopped by, Gina. I'd like to thank you for
saving my life."

This Here and Now

"Choose your sunglasses as carefully as you do your jewelry. Sunglasses are a fashion accessory and say much about your style."

It's probably true.

Kelly hunched over her second cup of coffee and read the "Weekend at Macys" ad in the morning paper.

"Are you ambitious?" asked the Question Man, page three. One man answered, "I work ten hour days four days a week to have time for skiing and gardening and I do not accumulate as much tension."

As much as what?

Kelly accumulated much tension. She not only tolerated but cultivated tension—life-affirming tension, which was not to be confused with the kind of tension that arose from her bi-monthly Sunday dinners with her sister, Melinda, and brother-in-law, Barry. Barry's postprandial ritual—unzipping his fly, untucking his shirt and rubbing his woolly belly while belching, "My compliments to the chef…oops! Chef*ette*, hey hey!"—made her want to throw up, join the Navy and get a tattoo, in that order.

Life-affirming tension was also not the kind that arose from Kelly's weekly visits to her chiropractor.

"You are a head-tosser, I can tell. And I will tell you right now that you are going to have neck problems for the rest of your life unless we can correct this nasty habit of yours." Dr. Charney, Kelly's chiropractor, had a habit of referring to Kelly's movement patterns as nasty habits.

"Postural atrocities abound; look around you, Kelly! People walk, sit, stand, run and simply *move* incorrectly. And *we*, Kelly," Dr. Charney intoned with her sincere, doe-eyed gaze, "*we* must correct these habits. We replace old, nasty movements with clean, fluid, spine-affirming motions. You will still express yourself; you will still feel the rhythms of your environment, which cause you to react thusly. But you will *not* toss your head."

The whiplash injury had responded to treatment, despite Kelly's often giving in to the urge to fling her head back and forth after one of Dr. Charney's adjustments.

How can I do this?

Kelly turned to the horoscopes. "Friends share good news with you. Recognition is finally yours for a project begun long ago. A romantic gesture keeps your spirits soaring for the rest of the day."

Kelly chuckled, her spirits rising, if not quite soaring. She recalled the wino who tried to look up her skirt when she gingerly stepped over his seemingly lifeless form on her way into the coffee shop. *You've got to take those romantic gestures when and where you can find them.* She had learned not to be picky.

"An old dog *can* learn new tricks," her father had said, over and over again, when at age fifty-seven he had taught himself to speak Portuguese. "Brazil! That's where the future is for bright young ladies like yourself. Mark my words."

Two years since he'd read that *National Geographic* article about the slums of Rio de Janeiro and he still wouldn't let up.

"It was your mother's last wish, that you should go to Rio after you graduate and help those people who live in paper shacks."

Kelly thought that if she gave any consideration to her father's obsession she would either go mad or somehow make sense of it. No one on either side of her family was Brazilian or Latin American or had even a rudimentary understanding of either Portuguese or Spanish. And her mother's last wish, as much as could be determined from the nearly illegible note, was that she not be buried in her linen suit. A simple housedress would do.

Kelly's toast arrived, along with coffee refill number three.

"Excuse me, ma'am; I've changed my mind. Could you get me the English muffin after all? And make the next round decaf, thanks."

Kelly set the newspaper aside and reached into her book bag for her sketchpad. "A is for Architect," she wrote above a pencil sketch of a prison cell.

How am I going to explain, after all these years? I can't get into the beginning design class at the junior college…can't even complete my general ed courses.

Over the years, Kelly had honed her story: she'd finish her prerequisites at the community college, then transfer to the university to get her architectural degree. She'd repeated the story so often she'd started to believe it herself.

She flipped through her sketchpad. Each page was filled with variations of the same drawing: a small, box-like room, completely enclosed except for one wall of evenly spaced, vertical bars. A man's head, with spiral pinwheels for eyes, hovered behind the bars.

A lot of explaining to do.

Kelly returned the drawing pad to her book bag. She sipped her decaf and glanced at her watch.

Melinda…where are you, Melly? Dr. Charney will want to know if I laid off the caffeine, like she advised. She'll also want to know if I remembered the source of the whiplash injury.

Dr. Charney had frowned, tapping her pen to a nervous, three-quarter waltz beat, when she looked at Kelly's x-ray.

"We usually, we almost always, see this kind of injury as the result of a sudden or violent jerking motion. Your movement patterns, while hardly exemplary, should not account for this degree of vertebral displacement. You are certain you cannot recall an incident?" *Tap tap tap.*

"Stress and poor posture have cumulative effects and would, over time, exacerbate the problem, but there must have been a precipitating event. A parking lot fender bender, however insignificant it may have seemed at the time…Try to remember. It may be helpful."

Believe me, it would not be helpful. Maybe I should "remember" a minor auto accident.

Kelly flipped through the newspaper, looking for the comics.

Barry had been his usual charming self during that last family dinner. After dessert, Kelly had excused herself to get a glass of water. She heard her parents and Melly, laughing and chatting, in the living room of Melly and Barry's apartment. Barry entered the kitchen; she turned away from the sink to face him. The words were out of her mouth before she could stop them.

She had no idea she could sound so in-control.

"Nice CD player, Barry, though it'd look better if you'd remove the price sticker. Six hundred, say six-fifty, total, for that and the CDs. What did you do with the other three-fifty?"

Barry grabbed her shoulders with his massive, simian hands, jerking her toward him and then shoving her back against the sink.

"What are you talking about," Barry hissed. He released his grip on Kelly, raked his fingers through his slick, thinning brown hair, pursed his bony lips and forcefully exhaled, as if clearing a snorkeling tube. Barry forced a smile, attempting to mask the anger of discovery in his eyes even as he saw the flare of recognition in hers.

"You've spilled water all over your blouse," he softly sneered. He turned toward the living room and raised his voice. "Anyone else out there want refills?"

Kelly scanned the business section headlines about the Savings and Loan recovery. Bail out or hold out? What is the prudent investor's wisest choice?

She hadn't actually seen Barry take the money, but she and Melly were the only ones who knew their mother had been hoarding the bills, sticking them inside the restaurant-sized onion powder jar in her pantry.

"There's nothing in the checking account," Melly had explained earlier that week, when she borrowed forty dollars from Kelly. "Barry's next paycheck goes for the rent, every penny of it."

At the next Sunday dinner, Melly bragged to her family about how Barry had got an almost-new CD player from a friend.

"We got it for a great price. 'A steal,' as Barry put it." Melly giggled, and beamed at her parents and her sister, who were seated around her at the living room table. "Barry's so patient and thoughtful and clever to wait for a deal like that when he's wanted a CD player for months."

No hope. She tells him everything and believes what he says. One thousand dollars.

"That cruise to Hawaii I've always dreamed about." Their mother had proudly waved the onion powder jar in front of her daughters, one afternoon when Kelly and Melinda had stopped in for a visit. "Your father has no idea I've been saving this, but I know he'll be proud of me for being so thrifty."

Then, one week later, a frantic phone call. "Do you remember me saying anything about moving the money?" Quietly weeping, her voice barely audible, Kelly's mother said that what she had dreaded was finally coming to pass. This was the proof she couldn't ignore. "Misplacing *one thousand dollars*! For God's sake, Kelly, it's not as if I've lost my keys." She had Alzheimer's disease, she sobbed, just like her brother, and would die a shameful, lonely death, as he had.

Kelly's mother had been so fearful of developing Alzheimer's disease she'd removed all traces of aluminum—from foil Christmas decorations to cooking pots—in her house. She'd read about a doctor who had proposed a link between aluminum exposure and Alzheimer's.

"What doctor, Mom?"

She couldn't remember.

"It starts with your memory; dear Lord, the little things go first. Before you know it—well, *you* don't actually know it—you're wandering away from home, half-naked, muttering gibberish. It's the family that suffers."

Kelly's mother chose her words carefully, despite her panic. "It's the family that suffers" was also the first sentence of the neatly folded note she left on the front seat of her car, next to her purse.

Six days after spilling water on her blouse in her sister's kitchen, Kelly was making funeral arrangements for her mother and anticipating the same for her brother-in-law.

What am I going to say?

Kelly picked up the classified ads section and wondered which editor was responsible for putting the obituary section immediately preceding the Pets Lost & Found notices.

"Lost 8/30, 'Eva,' tan Doberman bitch. Call Paul after 6 p.m."

Good name for a female Nazi dog. C'mere, you tan Doberman bitch! Has an S&M eroticism to it. Paul probably meant this ad for the Personals column. The "Lost 8/30…" must be some kind of code denoting certain bedroom preferences.

8/30…eight-thirty? Kelly looked at her watch and slapped her forehead.

Idiot! We agreed to meet at eight-*thirty, not seven-thirty.*

Kelly asked for more coffee ("Nix the unleaded, gimme the real stuff this time"). She cut her English muffin into tiny pieces, spreading the pieces alternately with butter and orange marmalade. She lined up all the buttered pieces on the left side of the plate and the marmalade pieces on the right side, popped a buttered piece into her mouth and returned her gaze to the paper.

It's been a slow week for the dead, she thought, skimming the lone obituary, and one helluva month for the living.

"Believe it or not, I seem to thrive on stress. And my sister and I are very close. We get together often, just to talk."

Kelly had rehearsed her tone and mannerisms in anticipation of sympathy calls, and had perfected a combination of muted grief and the-show-must-go-on grit. She was thus able to reassure her chiropractor during her last office visit, when Dr. Charney had offered condolences and expressed concern as to how Kelly was going to handle, "spinally speaking," the effects of two family tragedies within such a short period of time.

Kelly had been supportive of her father's decision to move to Arizona. Two days after their mother's memorial service, Melinda met with Kelly at the coffee shop. Melly had spoken tentatively, gradually strengthening her tone, as if she were in the process of talking herself into agreeing with what she was saying.

"Dad says the change of scenery will do him good. He's always liked the dry climates, and he can continue to study his languages by correspondence course."

Kelly shook her head. "Poor old fool. I bet he thinks there are more Portuguese speakers in the Southwest."

Melly exchanged a bemused, knowing glance with her sister. "I hadn't the heart to tell him it's *Spanish* they speak there. He says that he has to get on with his life, and he thinks he'll be in the way of *our* lives." Melly's voice faded out, then in again, as she tried to imitate her father's gruff laughter. "Besides, your mother never liked the desert, so here's my big chance!

"And I think *he* thinks you'd finish your prerequisites or whatever if you didn't have…so many family concerns. He never said so directly but that's a definite impression I got.

"But, Barry has a way—well, *we* may have a way—to bring him back." Melly blushed. She looked down at her cup, her voice sounding, Kelly thought, like what a honeycomb would sound like if it were a musical instrument.

"I didn't take that job because Barry thinks, *we* think, when I get pregnant I'll have to quit, anyway. There's no time like the present, so we're going to start 'trying,' as they say."

At that moment, in the same coffee shop where she now sat, Kelly had looked at her sister with what she hoped would pass for an adoring, expectant aunt's face, and she knew what she had to do.

People spend their entire lives searching for a moment of clarity, of utmost certainty—a moment that usually goes unrecognized if it even comes at all. Kelly recognized the voice. It was a voice inside her head like the crazies claim to hear, although unlike the crazies she would never try to pass it off as anything other than her own. It was not the voice of Jesus or Satan or the neighbor's black Labrador. It was not the voice of God commanding her to be the instrument of Righteous Vengeance.

It was also not the voice of God telling her *not* to do it.

I believe you're out there, somewhere, God. So speak now or forever hold your peace.

"*Beloved husband of; loving brother of; survived by. Memorial services will be conducted…*" *Barry will sound so much better on paper than he does in real life.*

"*Survived by.*" *Be a survivor, Melly. You could learn.*

While Melinda spoke of children, Kelly thought of accidents.

I'm going to have your sad eyes one day, Melly. Have you seen yourself, warming your hands around a coffee cup? Shy, yet engaging, almost lover-like, you ask about my plans. I could get full-time at the library, but how to explain? That I went to school mainly to impress, to inspire, you? Ah, Melinda—I can't even rearrange my bedroom. I won't save the Third World with practical, low-cost housing. I don't even know if I can save you.

Kelly reread the front section of the newspaper while she finished the last piece of buttered muffin.

What do I say?

Once the possibilities had been narrowed down the actual planning was surprisingly simple. Accidents are the number one cause of death among young adults; Kelly recalled seeing several headlines to that effect in the medical journals she filed at her job in the community college library's publications department.

Well, then, it's simple. We need an accident.

The radiant stars of heaven most likely will pale in comparison with the hospital's Emergency Room lights, Kelly had thought. Approaching the Admitting Office from the side, she strained to hear the muffled voices that emanated from behind the reception window's translucent glass panels.

"Different clientele, I'd say. Not like downtown. Two bathroom falls for every GSW, except on weekends. Three DOAs last summer, within a week of each other. Old geezers up on their roofs with a six pack and a hammer, fixing leaf gutters or…"

Kelly cleared her throat. "Excuse me, I'm Kelly Hewson. Is there any word about my brother-in-law, Barry Knarles?"

Kelly was directed to a hallway, where Melly sat on a couch opposite doors marked "Emergency OR—Authorized Personnel Only." A woman dressed head to toe in green surgical scrubs sat next to Kelly's sister. Ageless except for the blue-gray circles under her eyes, the doctor held a clipboard in one hand, touched Melly's shoulder with the other hand as she spoke, in a voice as soft as flannel, Kelly would remember, about organ donations.

"Oh, Melinda." Kelly took her sister's hand and knelt down in front of her. The doctor excused herself and stood up.

"No, that's all right." Melly's voice, an octave higher than usual, wavered. "Time…is of the essence, you said."

Yes, doctor. Stay. Please. Sign it, Melly. Let them take it all. Everything but his heart.

"It's so soon after Mom's funeral, but what with that and Dad in Arizona, it's more important than ever to keep up certain traditions, don't you agree? It's you and me now," Kelly had told her sister. "And Barry. Just us three, but that's more than some people have. Our 'Bye-bye Summer' barbecue, my place this time. I'll dig out the hibachi. It's in the garage, somewhere."

It had almost been too easy, getting Barry blasted before they'd even finished the chips and salsa. Kelly set out two six packs on the table, turned on the television and switched channels until she found a ball game. Her sister was in the kitchen, carving melon balls for a fruit salad and, as always, seemingly oblivious to her husband's drinking. Kelly chatted with Melly and walked into the living room every few minutes to make sure another open beer can was by Barry's side. When he started on can number five Kelly asked Melinda if she'd mind getting the potatoes ready.

"I need to borrow your husband to help me get the hibachi."

Kelly now rejoiced at the sight of the garage ceiling cabinet, the one she'd cursed for its height and inconvenience. She'd had to use a ladder—the gloriously wobbly old ladder—to reach the cabinet's lowest shelf. The previous afternoon she'd anchored the ladder's front and back legs between the workbench and her car's bumper. Once the ladder was tethered and steadied she'd moved her hibachi to the cabinet's top shelf. Her gigantic gray toolbox was heavy, even when empty...timing was important and the angle must be just so. She'd pushed the hibachi to the back of the shelf, put the toolbox in front of it and then filled the box with every tool and weighty, tool-like object she could find. It took all of her strength and concentration, standing on the top ladder rung, to position and then tip the toolbox forward so that it would lean against the cabinet door when the door was shut. Two wood chips wedged in the door made a tight fit and kept the door shut against the weight of the leaning toolbox.

Barry had taken his beer with him, down to the garage. God, what luck! Kelly thought, following him down the stairs. Her adrenaline-fueled gait unconsciously mimicked his sloshed swagger.

Barry set the ladder in front of the cabinet. He put his beer can on top of the ladder and slowly climbed the steps.

"Thanks, Barry. The door's old and gets stuck and, well…" Kelly affected a helpless, Southern belle tone, "I know how you love doing *man's* work."

Barry puffed up his chest, gave Kelly a lecherous wink and jerked the cabinet door open.

Slow down. Trip; again. Stall…every second may count.

First walking, then crawling up the stairs to the apartment, the sight of all that blood… Kelly discovered she needn't have rehearsed her reaction.

The toolbox had grazed Barry's left temple before striking him on the shoulder. With a yelp of surprise he'd pitched backwards, headfirst, to the garage floor.

Kelly closed her eyes. She took a deep breath, counted to ten and opened her eyes. Barry lay face up and spread-eagle on the cold concrete, amidst scattered tools in a small puddle of beer and a widening pool of blood.

Say something. Someone may have heard him fall.

"Barry? Barry—BARRY! HELP!"

Again. Louder. Are the neighbors here—damn! Forgot to check that out. They don't speak much English, anyway.

Kelly stumbled up the stairs, into her apartment, and yelled for her sister. Melinda ran into the living room. Kelly grabbed the phone, dropped it when she tried to dial, and screamed for Melinda to call the paramedics, 911, a doctor, an ambulance.

"Barry fell off the ladder. Oh God, Melly, it looks bad."

"Solar Flare's Eruption Expected To Jangle Earth."

Who writes these headlines?

According to the Washington Post, the largest solar flare in ten years erupted on the sun yesterday. Possible effects include disruption of communications and scrambled electronic signals. Intense showers of charged particles are expected this afternoon.

"If your friend doesn't get here soon…honey, you've had enough coffee to float my dead daddy's boat, if you catch my drift." The waitress, one hand on her hip, poured Kelly's sixth refill. "The little girls' room is up by the kitchen."

Kelly switched sides in the booth. She wanted to see her sister's face when she walked into the coffee shop. She hadn't seen Melly since Barry's funeral, three weeks ago, although they spoke every night on the telephone.

I can't take it if she… This is the right thing to do. It was the right thing to do. Survived by his wife. Beloved husband of Melinda Hewson Knarles. She survived him. And now, perhaps, me.

When Kelly returned from the bathroom Melinda was sitting in the booth.

"I always know where you're sitting. It's the place nearest the door, with the newspaper scattered around and a circle of toast crumbs where your plate was." Melinda wrapped her hands around her coffee cup. "Funny, isn't it, how even in the summer my hands are so cold?"

Kelly smiled at her sister. "You look great."

"Oh, yes." Melinda blushed, shaking her head. "Aren't your chiro appointments on Wednesday? I hope you didn't reschedule on my account because we can always…"

"No no no; don't worry 'bout that." Kelly flapped her hand in front of her face. "My symptoms disappeared so I canceled. Thanks for coming. I know you're busy—arrangements and all— but the phone's not the same."

Melinda nodded. "I can't believe how much there's been to do. Things to take care of."

"Whatever it is, you must be doing it fine. Melly, this sounds so cliché, but you really do look great."

She really and truly does. And not just in comparison.

"Actually, you'd be surprised." Melinda gazed out the window. "I know *I* was. I don't want to steal the spotlight from your news, but I've got to something to tell you, too."

"Sure, go ahead." Kelly's right leg shook under the table.

"I'm okay. I'm really okay." Melinda's voice rose with the "okays." She cleared her throat. "Sometimes I feel so bad, almost guilty, when I get these bouts, these spells, of missing Barry. Of missing him so much that I forget to miss Mom."

Melinda laughed, lightly. Kelly paused, noted the laugh was genuine and added a few moderate chuckles of her own.

"But I know that's a normal reaction. He'll always be with me. No one can ever take that away. And I'll be better tomorrow than I am today...and today is the beginning of the rest of my life. Like all those corny, stitchery-sampler sayings."

"I feel so...unqualified." Kelly reached across the table and grasped her sister's hand. "Unqualified to give advice, or say that it'll get better with time, even if I'm sure it will."

"I know." Melly squeezed her sister's hand, then reached into her purse for a tissue. "I promise not to start again," she sniffled. "It just came to me the other day. I had the TV on while I paid some bills. There was a PBS show, something about older women, women and aging. A lady in her sixties, recently widowed, had been married for years: children, grandchildren and all, always a housewife. I thought about what the narrator had asked her: what will she do? Everyone, her friends and family, told her that now she would 'live for her grandchildren'...I'm not doing a good job of explaining this, am I?"

Whatever it is, you're doing a wonderful job. What do I say when it's my turn?

"The widow said something like this: 'The way I see it, a door has been opened for me. I can walk through it, to God knows what, or I can do nothing and continue as I have been.'"

When I remember my sister, it will be with her eyes of this here and now.

"This probably sounds weird, but *I* feel like that woman. In a moment everything seemed clear to me. Not all better, but clear. I feel—I think—I should walk through that door." Melinda pushed her cup aside and took Kelly's hands in her own. "What do *you* think?"

Kelly looked at her sister, and thought.

A Tie in the Road

Now they've even got me thinking like them.

Left to my own devices, I never would have noticed it. I would not have given any significance to the fact that I saw it, other than to note its existence.

Dissociation is increasing my powers of observation.

I had been running a few errands before the church board meeting. In my car, at the stop sign, I scribbled a reminder on my notepad to schedule a tune-up for the muffler-rattling, carbon monoxide-belching, associate-pastor's-salary-excuse-for-transportation. I waited to turn out of the library parking lot. I waited for the elderly Vietnamese gentleman in the mellow-yellow Mercedes to turn, stop, keep going, signal...you've got the right of way, mister, do *something*.

"What is it about old men in new cars?" I wrote on the notepad.

I drove out of the parking lot and ran over a necktie that lay in the road to the right of the center divider line.

I pulled over to the side of the road, shifted into neutral, engaged the parking brake and left the motor running. I walked over to where the tie lay, took a good look at it, then ran back to my car and "peeled out," like a teenager, leaving real skidmarks.

By the time I returned to the church office my notepad had three messages on it:

–Schedule tune-up ASAP
–What is it about old men in new cars?
–Remember the tie in the road story

Of course, there was no "tie in the road" story. Yet.

Daniel and Ahlene's counseling session, their second that week, was scheduled for after the church board meeting. Scheduled at my request. It's unusual, so many sessions for such a well-adjusted couple. How did I get them to agree to that schedule? I can't remember my excuse. They have lives outside of my office; they are busy, active people. "We need to work on/we're really making progress with…" Those would be the usual reasons.

It's unprofessional, Elizabeth, I say to myself. No matter that you're not charging them.

Then I think of Daniel, slouching and smiling in the overstuffed chair, across from my desk. And of Ahlene, of how she inhabits more than sits in the wooden rocker, next to her husband. I see Daniel lean conspiratorially toward me, one hand placed to the side of his mouth as if to whisper, though he speaks loudly.

"To baby or not to baby, that is the question. Pastor Libby, together we may be able to open this pitifully shut mind," he gestures toward the rocker, "to consider the fine art of reproduction."

"You're confusing an open mind with open legs," Ahlene drip-drawls in reply. "And I've heard no complaints about the latter."

I reach for my tape recorder as soon as they leave; I remember the content but can't get the accent right. It's quite an affectation, Ahlene's combination of Hispanic and southern belle inflections.

I heard her, before I saw them, the evening they arrived for their first session. The church janitor dropped a wastebasket on his toe and swore loudly, and Ahlene and Daniel walked through the church office's open door.

"'*Dammit*' isn't God's last name." Ahlene's acid tones corrected the janitor. She and Daniel walked past him, down the hall toward my office.

"I've always wondered, what *is* his last name?" Daniel mused.

"'Schwartz,'" Ahlene said. "Old Testament, I think. First Abominations, chapter three."

Verbal voyeurism is unbecoming—especially to a woman of the cloth, Elizabeth. If you want to be a part of their repartee, why not invite yourself over for coffee?

Once again, I digress.

The tie in the road was not a wondrous sight to behold. It was rather plain looking: dirty and twisted, navy blue, with vertical stripes that once may have been yellow.

It never would have occurred to me, before meeting them, to think about thinking about noticing something…and now look what I've started. 'Round and around and around. I'm no good at this sort of thing. I almost flunked my introductory philosophy course in college; no one wanted me on their debate team in seminary; I threw up on the "Teacups" ride at Disneyland.

"You can't find something unless you look for it, and then if you do, you must prepare for the possibility of finding it."

One of my counseling participants offered his version of that rusty philosophical gem last Thursday evening. I'd had the usual presuppositions about how introspective a blue-collar man would be; I'd steeled myself for yet another routine recounting of marital discord, and then the husband waxes pseudo-philosophical. His white-necked, blue-veined, pink-collar wife sat next to him and glared at me. It's always one or the other's idea to come for counseling, never both.

But…that tie. How long had it been there, and why hadn't someone picked it up? Road kills don't last long around here. One never sees an old, dried-up squirrel on the street—it's either freshly squashed or there's only tufts of fur remaining to mark the spot. Whatever government department handles such things gets right to it. I suppose lower priority is given to removing a flattened cravat, unless it's a cheap one that starts to unravel within an hour of impact (this 'burb is very image conscious).

There are always explanations.

A young corporate up-and-comer, on his way to work, is suddenly overwhelmed by a gut feeling. He loosens his collar and rips off his necktie, right there, in the middle of the road. "Free at last! Free at last! Thank God Almighty, I'm free at last!"

Or maybe the lone tie is all that remains from a tragic, freak accident. Young Up-Comer had no grandiose visions of liberty, no intention other than to cross the street. Preoccupied with his mental review of meetings to attend, memos to compose and posteriors to polish, he failed to notice the approaching postal van. Neither rain nor snow nor post-yuppie flotsam… The force of the impact knocked him right out of his tie.

"This may be the sign you've been looking for, Libby."

I can almost hear Daniel say that. I imagine him and Ahlene, sitting across from me in my office.

"Yes, I quite agree." Ahlene would arch her back slightly, lean toward Daniel and speak to me.

"People rarely have the opportunity, except in hindsight, to recognize the turning points in their lives. You have come to your fork in the road…and it's a tie."

"And some people say there is no God!" Daniel smiles, and reaches for his wife's hand.

I sit in my office, and I think like this, now. This is what they've done to me.

Ahlene said she wanted to meet with me, briefly. Alone.

"I suppose this has something to do with finding meaning?" The tone in her voice indicated a statement rather than a question.

"This? What is, 'this'?"

"This counseling. To help us find meaning in our lives. To help us help *you*, I thought, was reason enough. That's the reason Daniel gave me for participating in these sessions."

"Help *me*?"

"In your thesis. To be part of the case studies for your new counseling therapy, modality, method, whatever it will be called. We're looking forward to a certain amount of notoriety, should you turn out to be something of a new Young Turk in the field. Do you know if *Psychology Today* is still being published?"

"I don't know," I said, although I did.

"Even though it seems rather…contrived, sometimes, I enjoy being in a control group. I like the idea of being considered part of the normal standard to which others will be compared."

I laughed. "Who said anything about normal?"

"Not allowed to use that word?" Ahlene raised an eyebrow. "Too judgmental, I suppose. Anyway, that's why we're here."

"You mean, that's why *you're* here?"

"Sorry. I didn't mean to speak for Daniel. Wouldn't dream of it, in fact." Ahlene picked up a pamphlet on my desk and read the title. "'Evangelical Lutheran Church in America. ELCA: Come Share the Spirit.'"

She tossed the pamphlet on top of my "In" file. "I realize that they—whoever was in charge of the denominations' merger—were trying to come up with a catchy slogan, but did they have to pick one that sounds like a diet soda commercial?"

"It didn't get my vote," I said.

"I should hope not." She shuddered, and her faux-southern twang resurfaced. "A bunch of Lutherans getting together in Southern California, trying to come up with something really hip. If that don't put the fear of God into ya… So, why are *you* doing this?"

I admired her confident disregard of conversational transitions.

"Why are *you*?" I countered. "Your coming here was, initially, Daniel's idea, wasn't it?"

"Why do counselors always answer a question with a question?"

"How should we answer?"

"Touché." Ahlene picked up a pen and a notepad from my desk and handed them to me. "We're in the directory; I can give you directions if necessary. Three-eleven Cane Street. Wednesday nights, seven o'clock."

"I should be writing this down?" I asked as I wrote.

"You like 'Hearts'?"

"The card game?"

Non-verbal affirmatives usually involve some sort of head nodding, but when she inclined her chin toward the pencil sharpener I knew I was to take it as a "yes." I reminded myself to take notes, some day, regarding her distinctive body language.

"We, a group of friends, get together every Wednesday at our place. Potluck. I choose the wine, Daniel makes the coffee and you can't beat the company. Or me, at Hearts."

"Sounds like a challenge."

"No more so than…" Ahlene flicked her fingers at a folder on my desk. I glanced at the file, which contained counseling session notes. "You're an excellent pastor," she said. "Isn't that enough?"

I shook my head, aware that, without my permission, a quizzical flush was replacing my Serene Counselor countenance.

"Say yes, if you like. It's easy." Ahlene leaned back in the rocker and crossed her hands behind her head. "A few friends getting together. Daniel says you'd fit in."

This is what they've done to me. I noticed it at the library, when I went to check on some interbranch transfers I'd requested.

"Counseling texts always seem to be in high demand," the library assistant said.

"Since it may be a few days until the books are back in, could you help me with this cross-reference check?" I asked.

No, she couldn't. She could, in that she had the capability, the knowledge. But not the permission. That duty falls under the job description of Reference Librarian, and she is a Library Assistant, Grade III. She knew the answer, but couldn't tell me.

"Just this once?"

"No. They're very serious about job duties around here."

"This is hard to believe," I said.

"I know." She blushed.

"So, if you help me, will library goons throw rocks at your car when you come to work the next morning? Will there be a strike? 'Unfair to Reference Librarians—Answered a Reference Question'? Not the most exciting picket sign I can imagine."

"Let me try to explain." She hesitated, and sputtered a couple of girly-giggles. "See, 'Reference Librarian' is a professional position. Me, as an Assistant Librarian, that's considered…"

"No, I don't see. Don't tell me *you* see. Don't tell me you could restrain from breaking into thigh-slapping laughter when you were told this, during the job interview. They *did* tell you, didn't they?"

"Frankly, I don't think about it much, 'cause I might lose what little self-respect I have." She shrugged her shoulders. "I may know the answer, but I can't give it. The guy at the Reference Desk, he'll answer. It's his job. Besides, he gets paid more."

"How do you know what is or is not a reference question? Are you given a list? Aren't you, by referring me to the Reference Desk, using the powers of reference in some way?"

"You're torturing me." She grimaced. "'Yes' to everything you've said. It's a rule, and I'm a library—and therefore city—employee and believe me, you don't want to argue with those people in Personnel. It's downright frightening how they can defend any rule or regulation, like they actually believe in it."

She donned a "What can you do?" happy-face smile, and I almost felt guilty for teasing her. How friendly, how accessible she seems, when she's out of that car, I thought.

She knows me by name and I know her by sight. She drives her daughter to church, sits in the car and reads until Sunday

School lets out, and then drives her daughter home. Neither she nor her husband are members of the church, nor do they attend. Nor does *she* attend; I don't know if there is a "they." She never answers the parent surveys we send out, never talks with anyone at church. Those who try to strike up a conversation fail to penetrate the soundproof newspaper she holds in front of her face. Yet her daughter is there, every Sunday, and she offers a cheery, "Good morning, Pastor Elizabeth," when she sees me at the library.

I stopped pressing her for assistance, for reasons of comfort rather than principle. The morning coffee had found its way to my bladder and insisted I find my way to a bathroom. No more coffee before counseling sessions or meetings, Elizabeth. Remember, in seminary, Pastor Arden's overwhelming java breath?

I think like that, now. This is what they've done to me.

The library eliminated the problem of restroom graffiti a few years ago when some clever librarian put up a chalkboard in each stall. That morning, the board in the middle stall had been wiped clean, and was missing both the eraser and chalk. Perhaps it was the lack of chalk or the urgency of the dispatch that compelled its author to vandalization.

The message was written in forest green ink, in a loopy, flourishing script, on the back of the stall door:

we all deserve to die

Who is she, I wonder, and how does she know?

So Much Not Neither

Some speculations are best left to philosophers and poets, of which I am "so much not neither," to quote my sister, Susan. Hence my reluctance to determine why Susan had decided to use disposable diapers with her new baby. On that portentous, bracingly October morning, I was certain that my only motivation was for everyone to do the right thing.

When I dumped the coffee grounds I discovered the telltale plastic wrapper in the kitchen garbage can. A bag of Pampers, scrunched beneath the *Times-Register*'s sports section…and since when had Susan started throwing recyclable newspapers into the trash? But I am not a man without pity. The circles under her eyes mollified me; I considered that even one admonition might be pushing it that morning. Nevertheless, Susan *had* used cloth diapers with her firstborn. That required no little commitment to the entire concept, I gently reminded her, seeing as how Sean, despite his abilities in other areas, was not completely housebroken until a week before his sister was born.

"It's not a *concept*," Susan said, "it's combat. Day after day, the ammonia smell…hmmm." She dumped another teaspoon of sugar into her coffee. "Toxic fumes. That could explain a lot. And those Bide-a-Wieners, I bet *they're* in on it."

Susan launched into a passionate denouncement of Bide-a-Wee-Wee, the home delivery cloth diaper service I'd hired for her, as a baby shower gift, when Sean was born.

"You leave the bag of dirty diapers on your porch, the delivery guy takes it and leaves a bag of clean diapers. Take dirty; leave clean. How complicated is this? The ability to discern between the two, plus drive a van—it's not like they have to recruit at MIT, you know?" Susan twisted her fingers, as if she were crushing a cigarette against the tabletop. "But this driver, he takes the dirty diapers and then *leaves* a bag of dirty diapers. And, get this: he leaves *other* dirty diapers; it's not like he's returning our batch from the previous week. He leaves a load from some other house, some other baby. This happened *twice*. When Bide-a-Wee-Wee Didee hired that guy, somehow, somewhere, some village was deprived of an idiot."

"Wait a minute," I said. "Maybe they *were* your—well, Sean's—dirty diapers. How do you know the driver didn't simply miss the pickup and leave your bag on the porch?"

"Number one," Susan clicked her fingernails, "I heard the van. Wednesday, eight a.m. The doofus is nothing if not punctual. Number two, I could tell that the number one and number two in those diapers were not Sean's number one and two. Number three…"

"You could tell? You checked a bag of dirty diapers?"

"I had to confirm my suspicions."

"You *looked*?"

"Of course I looked. Any parent would."

Exhibit A. Susan rarely pulls rank with the "I'm-a-parent-and-you're-not" rubbish. With the zeal of the recently converted, she explained her newfound preference for disposables.

"Better absorbency, not to mention less rash…" She made that peculiar, finger-crushing gesture again. "And, let's face it, convenience. It's not the F-word, you know."

"I understand not wanting *in*convenience, but isn't that a large part of having a family?" I paused for effect. "What if there were no disposables, like in the olden days? What if the rest of us get tired of having our landfills glutted and ban 'em?"

"Obviously, that would be too much for me." Susan drained her coffee in one gulp. "I'd abandon the kids in the desert, to be raised by a pack of wild javelinas who'd lick their little bottoms clean." Susan gestured toward the sink. "It's been at least three weeks since I washed the dishcloth." She leaned back in her chair and studied her kitchen. "There must be more of my bad habits to correct."

I grimaced. "You trying to tell me you're smoking again?"

"No!" Susan sounded genuinely hurt. "And stop that sniffing thing." She reached across the table and slapped my nose. "All right. Go ahead, then." Susan crinkled her own nose. "You won't smell anything, except if you get too close to the dishcloth. Sam, you'd know if I was. Remember how I'd try to hide it? Day and night, that damn potpourri on the stove."

I nodded, appreciating the olfactory memory. "Cinnamon sticks and orange peels."

"I haven't smoked since Sean was born. I haven't even had the desire to since after I had Sheila."

"Does that means you wanted to *before* Sheila was born?"

"During labor, actually." Susan smiled dreamily, as if recalling a sensual vacation in the tropics. "It was more like the desire to light up so I could blow smoke—not the low tar kind, mind you—up the ass of that obsequious resident, whom I saw no need for in the first place. Who cares if the doctor was stuck in traffic! The nurses were doing just fine; they were perfectly capable of catching the baby and besides, they wore more...uh, *pleasingly-colored* scrubs." She rubbed her eyes. "That is *not* an insignificant issue, by the way. If you've ever had to pick a focal point you'd know what I mean."

Little by little, creeping across her face, like the shadows preceding a daytime lunar eclipse: that *look*. I knew she craved a slow pull from an unfiltered Marlboro. How ragged she seemed, behind the caffeine cloak. Her hair had the dull-matte sheen of blond going gray. She's only, what, twenty-nine? It must be true, how parenthood ages you. I've always admired my sister's curious lack of vanity, but at some point even she must care.

"You think I *like* looking like this?"

"Aha!" I exulted. "It returns!"

"Yeah." She sounded none too pleased.

I wanted to ask about the university study, but I'm sure she never went back. She's not a see-it-through-to-the-end type.

During her sophomore year in college her Abnormal Psychology class professor obtained a corporate grant to study paranormal mental abilities. Two weeks into the semester he surmised what I had known for years, and asked Susan to be in the study's control group. She sat in an isolation booth and tried to guess which geometric shape a person in another booth was concentrating on. She failed spectacularly, which didn't surprise me. Her ESP, clairvoyance or whatever the hell it is can't be coaxed into performing like a trained seal for some dubious scholastic circus.

I offered her an out. "I thought the new baby situation had stifled those…feelings."

"No such luck," Susan said. "Remember the Paranormal People? They told me that the mind, when stressed, allows its barriers to slip, which is why psychic abilities often seem strongest when you're exhausted. Isn't that special?" Susan grinned. "Useful thought processes take a hike. I can't make sense of my bank statement but I pick right up on it when someone thinks I look like a bag of cat shit run over by a truck." She pouffed her hair with her hands. "It's a gift, really. A blessing."

My sister periodically asks me if I am on the road to getting what I want. Not, do I *have* or even *know* what I want; Susan is one of those "It's-the-journey/not-the-destination" people.

The road to getting what I want? Increasingly, it seems that I pull over and watch my fellow commuters zip by. What is it that those around me pursue with such premeditated dissatisfaction? Everyone seems to be after *something*, but God forbid my co-workers, kinfolk or the general human flotsam show an iota of unguarded enthusiasm in their pursuits.

I'd settle for even *wanting to want* something. And so I look to my sister, whose mind is involuntarily privy to the passions of others…and sometimes even those of her own. I look, and say thanks, but I think I'll pass.

Some rise before dawn to pound the pavement with fellow endurance enthusiasts; I prefer the morning java jive workout, and Susan is a willing exercise buddy. Here is one thing I *do* know: although I'm not the only person who enjoys such company, surely I'm the only sap in history whose out-of-the-blue sister says, one sweltering summer morning over round two of the Seattle Breakfast Blend, "Ever thought of having a sperm count done?" She said this as if she were suggesting I have a pedicure, merely to find out what one feels like.

"Day in and day out you sit at a computer, with all of that radiation zapping your gonads..."

Before I could suggest that perhaps *she* might consider having a brain cell audit, Sean materialized. I never actually hear my nephew enter a room; he's suddenly there, as if he beamed in a la Star Trek minus the cheesy audio effects.

"Hello." Sean's solemn, gray eyes drilled a hole through my coffee cup. "By the way, Mom, what does my imagination look like?"

A child's precocious verbal ability is probably something to be cherished, but frankly, it gives me the jumpies to hear a not-quite four-year-old preface a question with, "By the way." I don't trust *adults* who use that phrase. And then there's how Susan reacts to him. No gleeful, gushing, "Isn't that adorable?" No discernible maternal pride. It was as if he'd asked her to describe his spleen.

"Your imagination?" she replied. "It's long, purple, shaped like a big tamale and sits below your left lung."

That seemed to satisfy Sean. He beamed out of the kitchen and Susan winked at me. "Like anyone can dispute that?" she said.

"'Morning, Sam. One more for the road?"

I turned in my chair, toward my brother-in-law's voice. Erik stood behind me, holding the coffee carafe above my head.

In the years since Susan's marriage I've learned not to take life's soundtrack for granted. My father and I both generate the normal sounds of bipeds in motion. Somehow, the males in Susan's new family have evolved silencers on their feet.

Erik poured me a warm-up. I glanced at my watch; Susan stifled a smile when her husband looked up at the ceiling.

"Did you hear that?" Erik put his empty cup in the sink and sprinted for the stairs.

"Fifteen seconds," I tapped my watch.

Susan shook her head. "Must be something you said."

The mysterious lure of the vertical. Erik is always going upstairs, for something. A child cries, a child *breathes*, and Erik runs upstairs. I never hear Sean or baby Sheila make a peep when they're up in their rooms, but Erik tilts his head like a collie who's heard his master's whistle and races up the stairs.

The closest I've come to having an actual conversation with my brother-in-law was around a year ago. I'd stopped by to drop off some mini-cinnamon rolls, Susan's favorite. Susan was in the bathroom. I dumped the oil-slicked concoction that was in the carafe and started brewing a fresh pot of coffee. Erik somehow surfaced in the kitchen and mumbled something about being envious of people whose jobs allow flexible start times.

"What brings the bakery boy this morning?" Erik picked up a cinnamon roll, turning it in his hands as if he were a frosting application inspector. "You and Susan are...close?"

It was not a statement, yet not exactly a question. I felt as if he had asked me to confirm an obscure hobby: So, you collect yak femurs? Then, the sound of a flushing toilet no doubt prompted one of Sean's silent, dog whistle cries. Susan entered the kitchen and Erik scurried upstairs.

Erik never participates in the topic du jour. Of course, he can talk to his wife any time. There's no antipathy between the two of us; then again, it's not like you can have a high regard for the back of a guy's head. Susan says Erik understands our mutual need to keep up family ties since Mom and Dad retired to Florida. I drop by; kids silently call out; Erik hastens upstairs. Susan solicits my opinion on yet another subject and pretends to consider my suggestions. And the band plays on.

But I digress. As for Susan's overly intimate intuition on that hot August morning, an hour after I'd left she went into labor with Sheila. That's the only excuse I'll allow her. And despite my indignation at her suggestion I did find an excuse to visit my doctor. Sure enough, El Grande Nada. Susan sensitively summarized the situation when my doctor gave me the numbers: not only are my seminal marines incapable of mounting a beach head invasion, there aren't even enough to form a scouting party.

"Here's a list of other diaper services in the area." I'd anticipated her flaking out on the issue and had looked up the competition. "Also, the number for Green Baby, Incorporated. They have information on everything from pesticide-free foods to compostable wet wipes."

"Umm." Susan smiled wanly.

"You don't really want my help," I said.

"I know you're going to advise me, on diapers or whatever. It's inevitable, so I ask. Gives me more control over the situation." Susan tapped her coffee cup. "That's my priority, since going through two labors. Control, when and if possible."

Susan's attempt to change the subject was not a ruse to cover her guilty, landfill-contaminating conscience. She wanted to address a more timely topic; namely, the upcoming holidays, and where to spend them. We discussed our respective plans and I caught her in a major psychic lapse. It was obvious to me, after their last phone call, that Mom and Dad wanted us to visit them for Christmas. How could she not have picked up on that?

"They said no such thing," Susan huffed.

"It's not what they said; it's what they *didn't* say. It's what they meant. You, of all people, should know that."

I had blown it. By criticizing a lapse in her ESP I had given weight to the same. *She*, with her proven extrasensory track record—and she recounted several examples from over the years, most of which I'd rather forget—if *she* didn't sense it, we should then heed the impressions of her intuitively-blind brother, who can't sense what's for dinner even when overcome by the stench of burnt spaghetti sauce?

Susan's chronic facetiousness seemed intact behind her indignant facade. She never admits to dissatisfaction, with the kids or life in general, but she came close that morning. Seeking a reprieve from her Great Moments in Clairvoyant History recitation, I'd asked if she wanted to discuss Thanksgiving plans. From anyone else, her answer would have been a non sequitur.

"There are times," she replied, "when I want to slouch in the pizza parlor with the pepperoni-faced delivery boys. Lose myself in a cloud of clove cigarette smoke and adolescent apathy. But this isn't about me, is it?"

"Not directly," I chuckled. "Although you figure prominently in Joe and Ruth's Thanksgiving invitation."

"What's to discuss?" Susan yawned.

"Oh, that's right," I said. "You claim to enjoy their company. Erik, however…"

Susan's arched eyebrows transmitted an unspoken, "Oh, yeah?"

"I overheard you two, last Thanksgiving," I explained. "Erik said that one day he'll open the newspaper and read about the sudden appearance of the largest sinkhole west of the Rockies. 'Investigators in the town of Simper, Oregon, found what appeared to be the remains of a two car garage and twenty years' worth of *Trailer Life* magazines…'"

Susan laughed wistfully. "I don't know which was more pathetic: Aunt Ruth dreaming about what would never be or the fact that her fantasies were so low."

"*Are* so low," I corrected her. "She's subscribed for years, and they don't own a tent, much less a trailer. I don't get it."

"Yes, you do."

I nodded. "The trips she'll never take. Joe will never go."

"And look at her house," Susan groaned.

"*Her* house!" I gloated. "Of all the post-feminist…"

"Post nothing!" Susan snapped. "It was another generation. The house, the decor and all, was hers. *Is* hers. Why do I always refer to them in the past tense? And it's not just the house. It's the magazine piles, and the miniature spoons with names of national parks on the handles—she must have ten racks of 'em, hanging in the hallway. She gets them at garage sales and thrift shops. Imagine, buying souvenirs of other people's travels."

"I'm amazed she sneaks the bucks to get 'em," I said. "What does Joe plan on doing with all the money he never spends?"

Susan shook her finger. "Don't you know you gotta…"

"…save for a rainy day!" I finished Uncle Joe's decrepit dictum in tandem with Susan.

Whenever Ruth begs to go somewhere or do something, Joe says that it can wait 'til later. They must "save for a rainy day." It doesn't occur to Joe, even after Susan pointed it out, last Christmas when Ruth forgot the topping for the pie and substituted a Jack Daniels 'n Karo sauce, that this is the Northwest.

"The Pacific Northwest, Joe. That ring a bell?" Susan had barely managed to stifle a whiskey-syrup belch. "It's always a rainy day. Your beloved, one-horse town smells like that horse's sodden butt because it rains *all the time*; it is, in fact, raining *this very minute*. Hey, Joe!" Susan rapped her knuckles against her forehead. "It's Oregon! You live here, remember? It rains every damn day from October to June and then some. Now, is it some *particular* rainy day you anticipate, and if so, how in a soggy saint's ass will you be able to tell?"

"Are you going to bring her to Thanksgiving?"

"Her? Ellie? I haven't even decided if *I'm* going."

Susan knew that I'd go, and that I'd bring my new girlfriend. I hadn't yet used that word. "Ellie is my girlfriend," I'm back in the seventh grade. Joe, Ruth, mind if I bring a friend?

Susan loaded the dishwasher. "An awkward stage, isn't it?" she chirped. "Time to meet your quaint relatives, but not quite ready for, 'FYI, my sperm count is lower than mole dung.'"

The table's oak laminate felt surprisingly cool against my forehead. Aunt Ruth will ask; she always does. Susan's new baby will rekindle her concern. Will Sam ever settle down and bounce his own babies? I assumed Ellie had had prior dealings with a date's nosy family. But at what point does one reveal intimate...

"Mislead her."

"Come again?" I lifted my head.

"Not the most original tactic," Susan continued, "but proven to be effective. Drop some well-placed hints; let her think you've got this deep, dark secret."

"I don't follow you." *Liar Liar, you-know-what on fire.*

"A deformity, perhaps. Let her think you've got a crooked or malformed testicle. Oh, wait!" Susan flapped her hands like a first time Bingo winner. "You've got only one testicle, shaped like a cashew, and it moves—it *vibrates*—when the weather changes. It reacts to variations in air pressure, like those old men whose bunions ache before it rains. Embarrassing in social situations but handy when it comes to predicting those Pineapple Express snowstorms."

"You've outdone yourself."

Susan ignored my compliment. "I assume Ellie likes you?"

"Yes. A lot, I think."

"Excellent. Then when she finds out the truth, she'll be relieved. She'll feel guilty about what she'd been thinking, wondering if she subconsciously withdrew from you or withheld herself because of what she thought was your...misfortune."

I felt a rare twinge of jealousy regarding Susan's mind-reading ability. I'd have given good money to have known if she was being serious.

"'Oh, silly me!'" Susan fluttered her fingers in front of her teeth. "'He's really got *two*!' And then you reassure her—it's important that you sound casual—that your parts are normal in both quantity and performance, merely, uh, *dormant* with regard to reproductive capacity. You said she'd been a geology major?"

"Minor, actually." I'd learned not to question such conversational leaps. "Biology or some pre-med major."

"With rocks to fall back on, eh? Anyway, what I'm getting at is that she'll probably pick up on the volcano terminology— the 'dormant' classification. Subliminally, she'll picture volcanoes, in all their seething, hot magma, manliness. This'll make up for a lack of virility she might confuse with lack of fertility, which is a common error. And, voila!" Susan triumphantly hugged herself. "With a sigh of relief, she'll rush into your arms."

I raised my coffee cup in respectful salute. I had to love it. My sister conspired, even if in jest, to mislead a Sister.

How do I get whatever it is I want when I don't, thus far, even want what I get?

If Susan and I don't go, Uncle Joe and Aunt Ruth spend the holidays alone. Jill, their only child, pitched a priority fit three years ago when her parents refused to move the *Trailer Life* mountains so that she could park her Lexus in their garage. She gave an ultimatum: see a shrink for obsessive-compulsive disorder or stop pack-ratting those magazines. It's the RV rags or me.

Fine literature triumphed.

"Four blocks to go." I heard myself make that idiotic, blank-filling comment. Glancing at the occupant of my car's passenger seat, I realized that after four months of lunchroom chats, three months of company soccer team scrimmages and eleven weeks of outright dating, I really didn't know much about Ellie.

I made some lame joke about how she should prepare to have my family check her out. Her response was something about how people in their thirties should expect as much, but one never gets over the uneasiness, which is all right and more than understandable.

I have no idea what she meant.

"Happy Thanksgiving, Uncle Sam and lady friend. A nice day for questions, isn't it?"

I'd warned Ellie about Sean; even so, I think his greeting unnerved her. He seems to have inherited Susan's ESP, but if his genetic acquisitions do not include her associated sense of humor, we're all in big trouble. Twenty years from now I could be seeing Sean's face on the cover of one of those true crime, serial loony books at the supermarket checkout stand.

Introductions were exchanged, and Ruth returned to her mysterious turkey preparations. As always, she resisted offers of help and banned everyone but Susan from the kitchen. Joe offered Ellie his arm and a tour of the house. Baby Sheila was napping upstairs in Ruth's sewing room; there was no sign of Erik, and Sean had disappeared to wherever he disappears to.

I ambled into the family room and looked through the sliding glass door. Susan, a cigarette in one hand and a glass of wine in the other, rested her elbows on the railing of Joe and Ruth's deck and gazed at a once-vintage Dodge Dart which rusted under the mossy oak trees in the northwest corner of the backyard. I tugged at the squeaky screen door. Without looking back she said, "Sam," when the door opened, and motioned for me to join her on the deck.

"Every once in a while, especially with a glass of wine, I still like to hold one." She faked taking a deep, Tallulah-Bette drag from the unlit cigarette. "Some kind of prop obsession."

Faint, fussing sounds crackled from the baby monitor Susan had placed on the deck's railing. She glanced over her shoulder; I looked through the screen door in time to see Erik's backside ascending Ruth and Joe's stairway.

A book lay atop the deck's railing, next to the baby monitor. I opened it to Susan's bookmark and read aloud a passage she'd highlighted. "'Everybody wants the same, everybody is the same: whoever feels different goes voluntarily into a madhouse.'"

"Hey!" Susan's reaction reminded me of when I was sixteen and she caught me sneaking into the bathroom to take a leak while she was in the shower.

"Nietzsche?" I asked. "On Thanksgiving?"

"Pardonez moi." Susan snatched the book back. "Not his season?" She placed the book on the railing and set her goblet atop the hefty tome. "It's not Nietzsche. It's about...*things*, some of which relate to Nietzsche, and don't change the subject."

"We had a subject?"

Susan took another imaginary haul from the cigarette, followed by an authentic sip of Pinot Noir. "When you found out, when I suggested getting checked, you never talked about it. Never mentioned it." She returned her gaze to the oak trees. "Do you, did you, want kids? What tense should I use?"

Sean opened the sliding glass door and spoke to his mother through the screen. "He's showing her the war cutlery," he gravely announced, "and I think she likes it." He slid the glass door shut and slowly stepped backwards, his form seemingly merging into the family room's brown-green striped wallpaper.

"Cutlery." I shook my head.

Susan blew invisible smoke circles into the brittle autumn air. "Perhaps I should rephrase. Do you want *my* kids?"

"Do *you?*"

"Most of the time." She dropped the unlit butt on the deck and crushed it with her shoe. "The love is unconditional but not perpetual. No, that's not right. There's no word for it. It's the one thing I can't explain, and it's not one of those parent things. I don't know how to explain it to anyone else, either."

"Anyone else?"

"Other…*muthas.*" Susan smirked. "You know: the ones whose husbos attend those 'Covenant Guardians' conventions."

Susan's Suburban Alienation quips frequently embellished our morning coffees. She's a stay-home mom surrounded by other Stays, yet her reasons and reasoning are quite different from theirs. Susan bristles when recounting her neighbors' smug acclamations of Susan having, as one of them put it, "the resources and inclination to stay." She chokes on the unsolicited admiration of women whose men seldom scurry up a stairway.

Susan took another sip of wine and waved her goblet toward the screen door. Looking through the gauzy-gray filter, I saw Uncle Joe and Ellie standing in front of the family room fireplace. Ellie looked at Joe with undisguised adoration as he held aloft the battered teak box that contained his Korean War mementos. He opened the lid with great ceremony, as if to reveal the Hope Diamond, and Ellie stood on tiptoe to peek inside.

"Poor, dear Ellie." Susan had a salacious spark in her eyes, like when she caught me poring over the Dermatologic Deformities chapter of Dad's medical handbook. "Ellie, as in Eleanor? Such a traditional name. Not the kind who expects you to be a Promise Guardian? Does Ellie expect a man to keep his word, or…"

"I should rescue her," I said.

"It's okay."

There it was, again: the abrupt shift in countenance, with sarcasm replaced by an all-too-assuming compassion.

"She, or someone like her. Or unlike her." Susan lightly touched my forearm. "Someday. Warts and all, as they say."

But, for once, she was wrong. That is not what I was thinking.

Ruth got up from the table to check on dessert, although it was evident to anyone with functioning nostrils that, despite Ruth's obsessive attentions, the pie was toast. Sean fixed his eyes on Ruth when she excused herself for the fourth time. As soon as the kitchen door swung shut behind her he put down his fork, folded his hands in his lap and addressed his dinner plate.

"Uncle Sam has a crooked testicle."

Sean's precise pronunciation—no cutsie, toddler, "tesibul" variation—was more disturbing to me than the fact that my nephew had blurted out what might mistakenly be taken as A Family Secret. Even more unsettling was his mother's out-of-character reaction. Susan's laughter was much too quick and far too shrill.

"Crooked testicle; isn't that precious! Sean knows that Sam likes bent, hooked and curvy vegetables. Japanese eggplant, crookneck squash—Sam just loves 'em, and Sean thinks that's funny. He says, 'Unca Sam likes crooky vestibles,' or 'kooky tegebles.'" Susan turned to Erik. "We thought we'd heard it all. 'Crooked testicle!' That's one for the baby book."

"I brought it with us." Erik folded his napkin and started to stand up. "It's upstairs, in the sewing room."

Susan placed her hand on Erik's thigh. "Later, babe," she murmured.

"Don't stop chewing on my account!" Ruth cooed. She fluttered into the dining room, dabbing at the perspiration beads that dotted her plump, pink brow. Joe had taken no notice of Sean's remark, but then Joe tends to ignore conversations which lack even the most obscure connection to his war anecdotes or his opinion that financial counselors are shamefully lax in promoting U.S. Savings Bonds to young investors.

Ellie, seated next to Susan, displayed no outward reaction to Sean's allegation. She complimented Ruth's table setting and asked Erik to please pass the crescent rolls. Encouraged by the nimble if obvious change in subject, I maintained my composure, even when Susan took the bowl Joe passed to her and, following his example, topped her serving of Jell-O salad with a dollop of mayonnaise. "Well," Susan whispered conspiratorially to Ellie, "if I didn't suspect *before* that we were white folks…"

Ellie took a sudden interest in the Ma and Pa Turkey salt and peppershakers. Susan segued into her holiday food ritual. She removed the mini-marshmallows from her portion of sweet potatoes—the marshmallows she had so painstakingly helped Ruth top the casserole with—and placed them in a row-by-row design on her plate, between the creamed onions and mashed potatoes.

It has to do with attitude, she'd explained to me, back when I still asked for explanations. The casserole needed an attitude; the marshmallows provided that. God forbid she should be so low rent as to actually consume the "runty, sugar turd puffs."

I find it amazing that someone who is supposedly in tune with the thoughts of others can be so thoroughly self-absorbed.

"Sean keeps Susan and Erik on their toes, that's for sure."

Driving Ellie home, I attempted to explain what seemed beyond explanation. I thought it important to at least try to appear unconcerned. I did not tell Ellie that, after dinner, Susan had wrangled a confession out of Sean. The miserable midget had been eavesdropping for weeks, hovering in the hall just outside the kitchen doorway during our morning coffee klatches.

"Sean is a progressive little boy," Ellie said. To demonstrate my agreement with her statement I told her a couple of "My Unusual Nephew" stories, during which she inspected my car's automatic door lock switch. When I pulled over to the curb in front of her apartment she offered a quick "Bye-thanks!" and promptly exited the car, skipping our usual exchange of lenient kisses and vague vows to get together again.

Therefore, I've no explanation for why, two weeks later, Ellie agreed to attend Joe's funeral. I *can* justify inviting her. Somehow, it seemed proper. She was the last person to whom Joe had shown his Chinese gutting saber collection.

The ceremony was what Joe had been: somewhat lackluster and just shy of dignified. The minister was a squat, balding fellow, whose egg-shaped nose sported a bouquet of gin blossoms. A holy hired gun who'd never met Joe or Ruth before the service, he gave Joe's middle name as Bart instead of Bertrand and mistakenly though respectfully referred to Joe's many acts of heroism in the Crimean War. Jill, still evidently pissed off about *something*, sat pouting in the pew behind her mother and seemed oblivious to the ministerial miscues. Nothing fazed Aunt Ruth. With a Seconal smile on her face and Joe's Purple Heart pinned to her cardigan, Ruth sat Miss America-straight throughout the service, fingering the Spring issue of *Trailer Life* that lay in her lap.

Two days after the funeral Ruth had a trailer hitch welded onto the back of Joe's truck. She'd bought a used trailer—one of the shiny kind that look like they've been plated with meticulously ironed aluminum foil—and joined a senior-ladies-only RV club.

"I think some of them are lesbians!" Ruth gleefully confided to Susan and me. She sounded both shocked and fascinated, as though even having that suspicion gave her a bohemian quality previously unimaginable to a resident of Simper, Oregon.

Ruth put the house up for sale the day after she bought the trailer. Susan and I agreed to jointly handle Ruth's accounts and forward her mail as per her request, which had followed her defiant announcement that she had "disconnected" with her daughter. Jill had threatened to kidnap her mother and have her deprogrammed to break the spell of "those doddering trailer dykes."

She'd check in every month, Ruth said, but don't sit by the phone. She intended to spend the rest of her life on the road, as did many of the Ladies' Leisure and Motorhome Association members. Her new LLAMA comrades published how-to manuals and provided support for those living on wheels. We were not to worry about her.

The Saturday after Joe's funeral I picked up Susan at seven a.m. We skipped the coffee and drove straight to Ruth's, to help with the bon voyage.

"I can't believe she's tossing the Christmas lights," I said. "I thought she'd save at least one string for the trailer."

Susan and I carried the last of the recycling bins to the curb. "Relax, Sam." She patted my shoulder. "The Lesbo Motor Mamas will take good care of her."

Ruth paced in her driveway, tapping her watch and looking up and down the street. "I said eight-thirty," she mumbled. She checked her trailer hitch for the fifth time, then turned toward Susan and me. "Ah, my loves!" She stretched her arms, inhaling as if to devour the entire, crisp December morning. "I am off!"

Ruth reached into the pickup's cab. "This is for her." She thrust Joe's memento box into my hands, hugged and kissed Susan and me, and removed two souvenir spoons from the back pocket of her beige Lady Dockers. "Be happy," she said, handing Susan the brass Yellowstone spoon and me the pewter Grand Teton. "Let the winds of change be the fruit of your loins."

I looked to Susan, and considered asking her if there was anything behind Ruth's inane send-off. Then I remembered the morning of the funeral. I had asked Susan why she hadn't "felt"

Joe's impending stroke. Why hadn't she sensed that he was dying?

"Who says I didn't?" she'd snarled.

"It's safe, now."

"Huh?" I assumed Susan's remark was directed at me, since Ruth was backing the truck down the driveway. Susan shaded her eyes against the morning sun, looked up the street and waved to an approaching car.

"Goodbye, Ruth!" Ellie yelled out the car's open window. "See you later!" She parked her car in front of Ruth's house and joined Susan and me at the end of the driveway.

Ruth tossed a smart salute to the three of us and shifted gears. The pickup truck, spewing exhaust and hauling what Susan said resembled a gigantic, Reynolds-Wrapped bratwurst, turned the corner and headed for the interstate.

"'Let the winds of change be the fruit of your loins.'"

"What's that?" Ellie asked.

"A parting shot." I kicked a piece of gravel into the street. "Meant for me, I think."

I needed to say something. There was, finally, a moment of clarity. I turned to Ellie, and she to me, and we both knew.

No.

That's not how it was, for me. I stood on a curb, next to plastic recycling bins filled with moldy magazines. I knew nothing and sensed even less.

Susan acted as if Ruth's departure was the most natural step in the world. Ellie stood beside Susan. Both women waved to the ever-shrinking trailer, and from what I could see Ruth threw those nonsensical salutes out the window all the way to the interstate.

And so I stood. When in Rome…when in *Simper*, for God's sake.

After thirty years Ruth so readily forsook the obsessions by which we'd defined her. Jesus, Mary and Joseph—and Buddha, Mohammed, the Gemini twins and thirteen Druid goddesses on a raft! Why even pretend to know someone; what's the point? If Erik ceases running up stairways I'd like to see Susan be as go-with-the-flow-ish about *that*.

"Ruth wanted you to have this." I gave Joe's memento box to Ellie.

What is she doing here?

Who is this person, who knows that I do *not* have a crooked testicle? She stands beside me, waving to my widowed aunt, from whose house she couldn't wait to escape a mere month ago. Is this the one, years from now, whose haggard face I will behold across a coffee cup or an attorney's desk? The one whose vows to love, cherish and recycle will evaporate like so much auto exhaust once the going gets tough and the Bide-a-Wee-Wees get mis-de-livered?

How did it go: Everyone who wants the same…goes volun-tarily into madhouses? My brain hurt. Again, I looked reflexively to Susan. I could ask her, I thought. One of these day she might even deign to tell me.

"Have you ever seen Old Faithful erupt in the winter?" Su-san tapped the Yellowstone spoon against her palm, sighed deeply, and handed her spoon to Ellie.

"Keys, please." Susan reached into my jacket pocket. She grabbed my ear and pulled my face down to hers. "Find a ride home," she whispered, then headed toward my car.

"'Whoever feels goes voluntarily'…nah. It's nothing. Again," I reassured Ellie. The befuddled expression on her face morphed into one of skittish expectation.

"Here." I gave her my Grand Teton spoon. "Now you've got a set. Do you want to get some coffee? I know a place where…"

"…where you have to bring your own spoons?" Ellie giggled like a parochial school fifth-grader, and ran for her car. I caught up to her and slid my arm around her shoulder. I was only slightly unsettled by how quickly she in turn slipped her hand around my waist. Her face was flushed, as if she were both embarrassed and emboldened by her cheeky riposte.

"It's funny," I said, pulling her tightly to my side. "I *knew* you were going to say that."

How Heavy is Blood

Is he gone? Where is he? Footsteps? Blood, pumping; I hear it, to my head, my jaw. I can taste it. No pain; it must have just grazed... Still, hold still. Blood, remember first aid—face and hands bleed profusely with surface wounds—but he must think I'm dead, hold still. I am dead. If he looks, I am dead.

Concentrate, think. Stay conscious, look dead. Jamaar must be near, next to me. I was in front. Did he mean to shoot Jamaar first, to make me watch, because I am a traitor—what did he call me—a race traitor? No. Eyes like that have no meaning behind them, he didn't mean anything, it was so fast he did not allow time for me to watch, just pop pop, first one and then the other.

Dirt, salt, cold. We were so hot after the hike and now I'm cold, so thirsty. Think of something. I can taste the dirt with the blood, smell cement, this guy has a log cabin with a cement floor. Bill, he said, when I asked to use his phone, please, we went for a hike and got lost, they'll want to know we're all right, what kind of a counselor gets lost I'm in trouble. I'm Susan, this is Jamaar, I'm a counselor at Camp Shalom and he said Bill, my name is Bill and why didn't I notice did he glare at Jamaar? He must have but all I heard was Bill. He probably made it up on the spot and did he sneer when I said Camp Shalom?

What is he doing now, I can't hear anything, I should be able to hear if he's moving about inside. I'm so cold, thirsty, just one drink. Lie still, I'm right here, Jamaar can you hear me thinking to you? Remember details, they will ask for details. He, Bill, doesn't sweep often. I taste dirt...and salt, blood. My blood. Jamaar's blood? Don't. Stay conscious, look dead.

Jamaar was late for our hike, said it was his turn to clean, he traded with another boy. He swept his bungalow floor and we went for a hike just a walk in the woods and we lie here now on this floor and I'm trying, Jamaar, I'm trying. I send you thoughts, hang in, I know you're alive, I feel it. Be alive, look dead.

Boots on gravel, listen, he's outside, why didn't I hear the door? Leave, leave, please make him leave. Why didn't I know, I didn't say what Camp Shalom was but he lives here, he said isn't that a camp for, how he paused when he said, the underprivileged, drawing out the words, and I laughed nervous and said they don't call it that anymore and why didn't I know. Distracted, embarrassed, what kind of counselor gets lost on a hike, take a new path because Jamaar wanted to I'm supposed to be in charge but he pleaded and looked at me with those eyes, what did they see, eight years old, what did he see. Remember details for the police, remember, pray, Jamaar's memory is not of a gun barrel, a flat voice saying it's niggers what killin' this country, niggers and Jewbait race traitors and it happened so fast, we're leaving now, I say to Jamaar, feeling ants, ants crawling up my neck and I brush them off and look around the cabin but there's nothing there. No ants, no nazi flag posters slogans except for the spiders in Bill's eyes as we back up and a smell, like sewage, and Bill says words and I put my arms around Jamaar and he's coming, where did he get that gun.

"I called Camp Shalom and they confirmed the descriptions, said they were reported missing after going for a hike. The camp director is on his way. I gave him directions to the hospital, but he insisted on coming here first.

"Excuse me, my dispatcher's out and I got two lines going. Lemme put you on hold, just a minute."

So tired I want to sleep, a moment, no, listen. A car door slamming. Truck, it's a truck. Yes, go, please God make him go.

The pickup next to the airplane, remember, Jamaar pointed at the plane and I said look at the little Cessna. We walk out of the woods and there's a cabin and a gravel road and a truck and a plane and Jamaar says where's he take off, in the driveway and I laugh and call Jamaar a city boy. The motor, he's starting the truck, don't move, oh God how it feels to take a deep breath, hold on, Jamaar, I can start the plane if we can get to it. Please let there be a key, and it sounds like tires on gravel now the sound is in back of me.

Prime, throttle, switch on, ignition. Remember.

He's gone, could be a trick, lie still. The sound fades, tires on gravel, he didn't answer when I said this road must lead to the highway, the highway on the map we forgot to take what kind of counselor goes hiking without a map my fault, my fault, we're here. You with the pigtails, do you know why you're here the director asked at opening sing-along. We learn about our environment and to get along with all kinds of people the girl said and 'cause we never see big trees in the city. Jamaar's here for what he is we're here because I got lost, shot for what he is, me because of what I am a white woman with a black boy I don't know but they start young, Bill said, remember what he said, police will want to know but I tried not to listen, to back out the door it happened so fast.

He's gone, if it's a trick I can't hold still any longer and pain, it hurts now because I can't move my head I'm still for so long, slowly, turn, he's next to me. Jamaar, Jamaar, listen, I know you can't talk, hang in there, you're all right, he's gone, I'll get us out of here. Concentrate, remember, prime throttle switch ignition.

"It'll take a while for the local reporters to get here, and if the story gets out an AP reporter will call and I want to keep those lines open. The hospital said they'd call with an update on the boy. Now listen, I'm not trying to stymie anybody, but the families haven't even been contacted yet. I don't care if they've interviewed Mary. I'm not telling you to deny anything, just play it down. Tell 'em we have no detailed information at this time, which is in fact the truth. They love that 'Neo-Nazi Nuts in the Northwest' angle, and they'll jump on it if they get a whiff."

My voice, sounds like some drunk but it has to be me no one else only Jamaar breathing, rattling lung sound not good but he's alive. My stomach, keep it down, deep breath must stay conscious. Jamaar I can get us to the plane I can get us out of here put your arms around my shoulder I'll try not to hurt you. Remember teasing you at dinner now I am glad you didn't finish your dessert aren't eight year old boys supposed to weigh more, how heavy is blood, no don't think like that.

He Bill left the door open he lives alone, out here expects no one when will he be back. Must move fast, I'm okay Jamaar is light fifty yards to the plane count them. Fifty steps, mother may I have fifty big steps. I'm sorry, Jamaar, a moan, you're alive I'll try not to jar you, we're almost there I'm going to be sick no, slow down breathe deep, remember how to start it Jamaar did I ever tell you how I used to ride in my uncle's airplane?

Take off in a corn field in Tennessee that was the runway on his farm, and he took me up every day when my family visited, he loved to fly but not alone everyone else was scared of flying or bored so he took me and I watched him thinking I could do this. If he had a heart attack I could take over, must have seen it on TV the pilot has a heart attack someone has to take over. It's just an overgrown lawnmower he said, the engine. Not many dials altimeter speedometer tach gauges I watched I thought I could land this if I had to, some day get a pilot's license I never did but I watched him every day. And now I have to I will I promise Jamaar.

"Okay, sorry about the interruption. The word on Will is that his truck was spotted heading south on the highway, toward the lake. The roads are blocked; one of the state units should pick him up soon. Two troopers are headed for his cabin; I expect to hear from them any minute.

"I always knew he was crazy, but he kept to himself. Jesus, I don't see how she managed to get herself and the boy in the plane and taxi up the highway with her face half-blowed off."

The door open the key in ignition, yes, who locks airplane out in the woods. Hope this doesn't hurt you too much more we're almost there why can't I remember my first aid no time anyway. Lean you this way against the seat so you won't choke Jamaar can you hear me, it hurts when I talk.

It's like I remember God please God let me remember, oil pressure gauge altimeter airspeed, parking brake, pedals brakes rudders dark gauge, steering wheel red and slippery moving dark spots, no, not now. Head down breathe slowly. Just a bit farther almost there, stay awake breathe breathe don't look at the dials. It's okay Jamaar up the gravel path to the highway right is north, there's that town near the river we'll taxi all the way there or maybe we won't have to someone will report a plane on the road and the police the rangers there's a station near here, remember when they came out and gave the campfire talk on trees and forest fires.

"It was like this: I get a call from Mary down at the Quick Stop. She's frantic, says Will Covey's plane just drove into her garage—drove, not flew, she says—then she yells 'Call an ambulance' and hangs up. I got there in under three minutes. The woman and the boy were in the plane, all I could get out of the woman is a guy named Bill in a dirty cabin shot her and the boy. He left, and then somehow they took his plane, and Tennessee, something about Tennessee. I could barely understand her. She passed out before the rescue crew arrived. The kid wasn't hurt bad, I don't think. He was unconscious, but moaning.

"No, I don't know if she was a pilot or what. What I don't know would fill the lake at this point. All she had on her was her camp I.D. badge.

"'Exsanguination' is the preliminary report; their 'best guess at this time,' the doctor said, like I was pressuring him.

"Now, don't write that down. Nothing's final, not until the coroner takes a look. Nine years, and I can't remember the last time we had to have a coroner up here. Wait, my help just arrived.

"Get that other line, would you? I'll talk to the hospital or to the state troopers' office—no one else."

Mixture rich, carburetor heat cold, prime prime prime, throttle open switch on turn ignition. Every morning Tennessee I watched him are you ready honey he said, shall we go over the lake today. No Jesus God don't think it but what if he Bill comes back and sees us he took his gun I don't know, if he has one in his cabin he has one in truck. Mountain people they are different in small towns what if they all like him and his brother is the sheriff and so maybe he shot us but we stole his airplane.

Don't try to talk Jamaar moan it hurts I know. Don't open your eyes lie still. A counselor is responsible, a counselor is responsible for her prime prime throttle ignition listen, Jamaar it's a big lawnmower my uncle told me do you ever want to fly Jamaar would you like to fly. What would you like to do what do you like, you were so shy you never talked when we were hiking you just smiled I quizzed you on tree names and birds and at dinner you wouldn't eat your peas I teased, you said I don't like peas and we're moving, God, we're moving we're going Jamaar can you hear my thoughts be strong. I'm sorry not talk more it hurts and I have to stay awake. Going back we're getting out we'll be safe back to things we love what do you love Jamaar, blood on my shirt and I don't know you, are you dying beside me and all I can tell them police hospital is that you won't eat peas, I won't either.

Dust gravel and pine…the smell, take the salt out of my mouth it's got to be it's got to be here soon what kind of counselor goes hiking without a map but it's here the road is here. Can you hear me Jamaar don't talk we're turning right the road yellow stripes traffic both ways then. North, go north we'll get there please God let him have gone south please a truck a car a someone.

The Burghers of Troutdale

Merciful heavens and whatever may reside therein! Lawrence moaned to himself. He donned a facade of casual curiosity, and concentrated on smoothing out the cringe muscles that had begun to tighten around his forehead and eyes. *Did they* have *to begin the exhibit with this particular piece?*

"Iris, Messenger of the gods." Lenore stood at the bottom of the stairway and gazed at the image in front of her. "Iris…*Iris?*" She reached down and brushed a piece of lint off the toe of her purple suede boot. "It doesn't suit her."

The sculpture sat atop a wood laminate column to the left of the stairway. A large white banner, undulating in the air currents produced by the museum's air circulation system, hung from the ceiling above the stairway.

"'Rodin: Portland Art Museum November 22 through January 22.' Now, I ask you, is this necessary?" Lenore jabbed her reedy forefinger toward the banner and cast a desultory glance over her shoulder. Her son, Lawrence, stood three feet behind her, his hands clasped attentively behind his back.

"Why isn't the banner outside?" Using her pinkie finger, Lenore slid her cultured pearl-encrusted bifocals up the bridge of her nose. "Do they think we need to be reminded about where we are and what we came to see?" She reread the title plaque on the display stand. "'Iris, Messenger of the gods.' Yes, this is she. Lawrence, what does it say in the pamphlet? Never mind; don't spoil it for me." She removed her eyeglasses and patted her son's shoulder. "But that *is* your calling, isn't it?"

"My lady." Lawrence made a deep and ungainly bow, as if he were an over-eager, apprentice butler. He clicked his heels together and swept his arm toward the stairway. "Shall we?"

"Not so fast. Tell me, you of the recently completed Art Appreciation class, about the protocol of such an exhibit. Are we to pause here and speculate on what message the agile Miss Iris was delivering to, or perhaps for, the gods?"

Lawrence pivoted on his left foot, away from the stairway. He took two steps back, then one forward, and tried to recall the focus formula: was it one step for depth perception and two for perspective, or vice-versa? He pushed up the sleeves of his calfskin bomber's jacket, cupped his right hand around his chin and contemplated the small bronze figure. Iris was a nude, headless female form, perched precariously on her left leg, her buttocks balancing a mere inch or so above her left heel. Her left arm reached out and away from her body, as if for ballast. Her right hand grasped her right foot, splaying the leg at a ninety-degree angle from her lumpy groin.

Lawrence emitted the ubiquitous sigh of Artistic Contemplation. He'd had high hopes for the exhibit as a whole; nevertheless, he admitted to himself, this particular icon held little personal appeal.

She looks good, Lawrence thought. He slowly circled the statue, surreptitiously glancing at his mother while pretending to scrutinize Iris's backside. Try not to sound surprised, he reminded himself, and do remember to say *something*. The ruby pantsuit she wore last month when I took her shopping downtown, and now today. Bold, heavy colors suit her. Since she got the idea about filing her candidacy statement she's definitely paid more attention to her appearance. When she stopped the coloring, Miss Clairol Sienna #87 gave way to a radiant, fiery white. It may have been that way for years, I told her, and you never knew it. Good in dark purple; I should tell her. It sets off her hair quite nicely.

"Is she any less demure from behind?" Lenore fingered the silver chain around her neck.

Lawrence turned to face his mother. Her perusal of the statue was intense yet dispassionate. He'd seen that particular look before, many years ago, when he was home for a visit and two Jehovah's Witnesses came to the door. Although she'd claimed to be annoyed by the intrusion, Lenore had engaged the JWs in conversation. To this day, when recalling the facial expressions of both his mother and the Witnesses, he was uncertain as to whether she had attempted to rid the proselytizing strangers from her porch or invite them in for coffee and canasta.

"Well?" Lenore eyed her son. "Would Iris make a suitable bridge partner?"

"What can I say?" Lawrence raised both hands, as if petitioning the gods. "It is what it is."

Lenore flicked her fingernails together, flinging a crisp, *click-click-click* at the statue. "Apparently, gynecology was a bit more acrobatic in Rodin's time," she sniffed. "Nowadays it is customary for the patient to assume the lithotomy position for her pelvic examination."

How nice it would be to be able to take off a pair of spectacles, Lawrence thought. I could remove them in one swift and seamless display of disgust; or, with a subtle nod of my head they would slowly, sophisticatedly, slide down my nose.

Lawrence envied the bespectacled for having the means to acquire such habits. When I escort my elderly mother and she says…those *things*, he mused, I could remove my bifocals and rub my eyes. Passersby would nod sympathetically, adjusting their own eyeglasses in gestures of solidarity.

"Tell me, Lawrence, is the curator responsible for the placement of this piece? Is this objet d'art intended to lure me up yonder stairway to the-gods-know-what other wonders?"

"Effective, you'd agree, in that it caught your attention." Lawrence grasped his mother's elbow and gently but firmly ushered her up the stairs. "Spurs the imagination, and such. You'll find the symbolism present in Rodin's works to be…"

Lenore halted midway up the staircase. "Whatever my aesthetic reservations regarding that piece, I can still appreciate style and nuance. And intent. Using Iris as the example—and it *is* placed at the entrance—tells me the artist is representational, not abstract."

Lawrence's "How so?" escaped before his better judgment could sense the setup.

"A gymnastically-inclined, headless nude? Oh, come now." Lenore removed her arm from her son's grasp. "No doubt the old guard on the city council would understand. This is how Rodin and his ilk preferred their women?"

Dismissive labels and/or diagnoses are not helpful, Lawrence reminded himself, no matter how gratifying it would feel to make a withering comment about the onset of Alzheimer's disease. Don't fool yourself for a minute. Alzheimer's, feebleness— they're pejorative, not descriptive. She's not delusional, merely (and deliberately) outrageous.

He put his hand in his pocket, jingled his keys and briefly contemplated one of life's great mysteries: Women Who Stayed in The Home. Get a job, Mother, I used to say. Learn to crochet, find a hobby, a purpose in life, after a life of…an After-life. After what? What *did* she do, besides raise me? A task quite necessary and time-consuming in the early years, but at a certain point a son raises himself.

However, to *consider* entering politics—even the small-pond machinations of Troutdale's city council—at her age and circumstance? At most, one might hope for a diagnosis of mild senility, hardening of the arteries, or something. That's it; she's hardening. Fitting, for a would-be political dilettante.

Son and mother silently ascended the stairway.

But hardening leads to brittleness, Lawrence cautioned himself. And the *appearance* of brittleness is often…only that.

"Adieu, Madame Iris." Lenore tossed a crisp salute down the stairwell.

"There's so much to see." Lawrence led his mother to the center of the rectangular Main Exhibit Court. He pivoted slowly, gesturing toward the corners of the Exhibit Court with both hands, as if he were directing a 737 to its arrival gate. "Each corner has a hallway that connects to additional exhibit rooms," he said. "For an overview, we could start with the sketch room."

"Back in the days of Elde and I was doing fine, or at least managing, when during labor I made a noise. One little noise." Lenore again fiddled with the chain around her neck, the clasp of which had caught on an edge of her blouse's neckline. "Yet another inconvenience to the doctor, who was already irritated by my interest in my own bodily processes. You see, he never forgave me for asking, in my seventh month, what exactly does the placenta *do*? And what will you do with it after the birth, as in the afterbirth? A jest! There was no appreciation or even acknowledgment of my attempt to lighten his load: the cumbrous burden of preserving the ignorance of pregnant women."

"Yes; well, that was then." Lawrence opened his exhibit pamphlet. "We could skip the sketches and…"

"Seeing that man's sour, brine-crinkled countenance completely eliminated any trite craving for pickles I might have otherwise experienced." Lenore tucked Lawrence's shirt collar point under the neck of his jacket. "And I made a noise, one little noise. I cried out, and so they put me out, as they did back then. However, unlike our dear Iris I was able to keep my head and most of my clothing so perhaps I shouldn't complain. Still, they put me out. You had a baby and they put you out."

And when I woke up, Lenore said only to herself, you were in the first grade, somehow having learned to tie your shoes and slick back that pestiferous, hamster-brown cowlick. She felt her arm reaching out, as if manipulated by a puppeteer, but she was able to master the immanent urge. Her hand arced back toward her face and smoothed her own white curls behind her ear, as if that had been her original intention.

He'll be thirty-nine next month, you maudlin matriarch. He combs his own hair when and how he likes. And if he won't do it here, then he won't do it in Los Angeles.

"We can follow the tour suggested in the pamphlet, which is organized by theme and chronology. But even that order is fluid. Notice how the exhibit is set up?" Lawrence circled the pamphlet above his head. "Here's where I'd say the curator's design is certainly intentional. This hall," he said, pointing toward the northwest corner, "leads to 'The Gates of Hell.' Smaller works from that major piece are excerpted, so to speak, along the hallway. Or you can do a 'best of' tour, if you like. See what you want, skip the rest. After all, it's your birthday."

So it is. And here I am, with my own private Elder Hostel host. Last year it was the theatre matinee. Next year, another field trip: music theory or wildflower identification.

Lawrence, hands clasped behind his back, toured the Main Court. Lenore followed faithfully and listened sporadically. Lawrence encouraged her to explore and observe, but Lenore had already given herself that permission. She was interested in the edifice that engulfed her; she felt more attracted to the museum's structure and layout than to the exhibit itself.

"Notice the sketches, the studies from which Rodin created his final pieces." Lawrence meandered about the room, speaking of fluidity, angle, curves.

Odor, noise, vibration: Lenore was intrigued by their absence. She closed her eyes and concentrated on the lack of sensory stimulation. Submerged in a sea of warm Nothingness, save for an infrequent echo of footsteps bubbling toward the surface, the surface of... Lenore opened her eyes. An amalgam of blue-gray sunlight, angled and distilled through the ceiling's translucent glass panels, blended with the effluence from the museum walls' fluorescent light fixtures.

Lenore looked around for her son. Lawrence stood before a large statue that appeared, to her, to be a cross between a centaur and a tugboat. Lawrence stared at the piece as if he intended to estimate its displacement.

"We shouldn't stand so long in one place." Lenore tugged at the sleeve of her son's jacket. "Our shadows don't belong; they might disrupt the other patrons' appreciation of…" she flicked her fingers at the ceiling, "…of all this visual fluidity."

"Why are so many of his people naked?" Lenore caressed the strap of her purse. "Did the models pose *au naturel*, or did Rodin omit the clothing later, when he sculpted?"

"Why do some people get stuck on that?" Lawrence sighed.

"'Some people' as in old people. Like me, my generation?"

"That is not what I said."

"For your information, I did not fall off the rutabaga truck on the way to art history class. Neither am I one of those AARP behemoths whose taste starts and ends with Norman Rockwell. The Troutdale Chamber of Commerce acts as if the city charter mandates decorating—if you can call it that—with nothing but those prints. One of my first acts as council member will be to send dear, doddering Norman into retirement, along with those Leroy Nieman-Marcus, splattered vomitus sport posters." Lenore shuddered. "Have you seen the city council facilities? You know what they'll say: 'You want highbrow? Go to Portland.'"

Lawrence jingled his keys.

"I was born the year Rodin died," Lenore said. "I'm sure you're surprised that I know such a thing."

Lawrence turned to the back page of the pamphlet and cleared his throat. "Rodin died in 1917."

"Well, it *seemed* like 1920." Lenore took her son's hand and led him toward a statue of two entwined, embracing nudes. "I want to see 'The Kiss.' You probably feel we should see his lesser-known works, while we have the opportunity."

Lawrence chuckled. "I'm surprised you want to subject yourself to more bare bronze behinds."

"You think you see more; is that it?" Lenore tapped her fingernail against her temple. "They are unclothed, therefore exposed? You think you see more, but I say we see less. We see less but fail to realize it because we're distracted…by their privates and such. And you *are* distracted, no matter what you say. Because this is how we were raised. You; me. This is not France," Lenore sniffed. "This is not even Los Angeles."

"Speaking of which," Lawrence pointed straight ahead, "'The Gates of Hell' beckon." He laughed heartily and nudged her with his elbow. "I thought you might appreciate that."

They beckon indeed, Lenore thought. She held her breath for a silent count of ten, and considered the promise she had made to her husband.

Yes, Raymond, if Lawrence is determined to sabotage his life he shall not hear about it from me. He could easily find another dead-end job in Portland; nevertheless, he shall not hear it from these lips. Just as he will not hear about how, if his life continues on its present course, he will surely pass into his dotage, sharing a tin of dolphin-safe tuna with a decrepit, neutered tomcat. An old bachelor is far more pitiable than an old maid, in whom one often detects more of a sense of freedom from encumbrance than loneliness. An old maid has a license to abide, eccentrically solo in this two-by-two world. A man without a woman, however...

"Many of Rodin's most famous individual works, 'The Thinker,' for example, are from this larger piece."

Lawrence chatters afresh, Lenore mused. *Still.* "*Entwined yet separate motifs within 'The Gates of Hell'?*" Lord knows where he gets it. His father was so constrained—wouldn't say prunes if he had a mouthful. I agree, Raymond, that discretion is the better part of gratitude. I shall graciously enjoy the outing. What good, anyway, my counsel? I no longer hear his exasperated, "Get a job!" or the like; nevertheless, the retorts remain. They are in remission. They lurk behind the results of the $3,500 orthodontia to which he vehemently objected, behind the now-perfect dentition he so dazzlingly displays when dismissing me with his, "*Really, Mother*" smile.

You just want him to be happy.

Raymond had flung that banal bromide at her as if it were an accusation. Yes, Lenore had admitted to her husband, it is possible that I do wish my son contentment. However (and this she confessed to herself alone), the plain, parental truth is that *I* desire grandchildren. Lawrence's happiness is his own affair; I learned that long ago. My adult education is ongoing, and far more illuminating than the Senior Ceramics classes into which my son would dump me.

There must be places, still, somewhere upon this earth, where a parent's counsel is treasured instead of tolerated; where it is acknowledged that the years do indeed bring wisdom and not merely declination. My current events readings suggest that, while the strip mall culture of the West is everywhere encroaching, contamination is still far from widespread in the East. The rural isles of Japan. I shall emigrate and become a venerable, if adoptive, Mama-san.

Son and mother passed through Hell and back. Lenore reminded herself to focus on the here and now as Lawrence's omnipresent voice-over became more specific. He intermixed seemingly ad-lib comments on Rodin's technique with general observations on late 1900s sculpting. Lenore pretended not to notice his covert glances at the museum's pamphlet. She donned her eyeglasses and read the plaque from yet another differently-abled statue.

"'Meditation without Arms.' Female, of course."

"Note the hands," Lawrence suggested. "Uh, that particular meditation excluded. Rodin has many studies of hands."

Son led mother through a labyrinth of small bronze images, which nested on top of low, white and gray marbled columns. Lenore held on to Lawrence's elbow, fearing she might slip on the room's highly polished, blond hardwood floors.

"This is my favorite." Lawrence paused in front of a small bronze. "'The Hand of God' is a Creation study. Note the vaguely spherical, black mass emanating from a hand—from *The* Hand, I suppose."

Lenore clasped her hands together. Her fingers caressed the leathery age spots on the backs of her hands, spots which, she had lately come to think, resembled the brown blemishes on the lefse she had eaten as a child. Aunt Kalma had been her family's maker of lefse, which was considered by many fellow Minnesotans to be the culinary exemplar of their ethnic heritage. Lenore's mother, a second generation Norwegian-American, scorned the bland, floury potato flatbread as "An insipid icon for those herring-heads who mewl about how life was better in the Old Country." Lenore, although she adored lefse, had never learned to make it.

I should not have let her intimidate me. Mother's disdain, for nearly everything, grew exponentially with age. She took every opportunity to remind Raymond and I that we had Lawrence too late in life and then gave him no siblings. "Had you not waited so long to have a child, you'd have been able to have another one who might have been more…normal." Lefse, schmefse! How Old Country, indeed, of Mother; how trite in any country—to assume that Lawrence is gay when in fact he is occasionally priggish and often boring. Such traits are hardly mortal sins, although I realize they decrease his likelihood of procuring a family. And whatever was I thinking, to voice the longing for such? To let it slip out, over tea with my kindly, widowed neighbor, also of Norski heritage, who speaks longingly of better and healthier times, back in Wisconsin, feasting on her mother's lefse and krumkake. "Yes, that is the way of life, is it not?" we commiserate. No time, back then, to learn the proper ways, and now with the time there is neither energy nor desire.

"I'm hungry," Lenore said.

"It's still early." Lawrence tapped his watch. "I'll try to speed things up." He led her past "The Three Shades," a piece consisting of a man-woman-man trio, toward another entwined bronze couple.

"I don't see any mothers," Lenore said.

"What do you mean? There are many women in Rodin's works."

"But no mothers."

"How can you tell? I'm sure he…"

"You misunderstand me," Lenore said. "I am not faulting Rodin. A woman, a female form, is one thing. A mother is not. You can't capture that, in stone. Now, which way to the cafe?"

Lenore marched ahead of her son, into another exhibit room. A large sculpture of six bronzed, male, life-sized figures was set on top of a low wooden platform in the center of the room.

"'The Burghers of Calais.'" Lenore spoke softly, as if to a confidant.

"You know this one?" Lawrence opened his pamphlet.

"No. Not in the sense of…yes." Lenore removed her glasses and approached the piece. "I know this one."

The six figures were hostages: a thick rope, wrapped noose-like around each Burgher's neck, bound them to one another. Five Old Burghers faced forward in a variety of postures; a younger sixth was turned to the side, looking back, with his hands passing before his eyes.

"Military annals furnish few cases of more determined, noble resistance than that maintained by the Burghers of Calais," Lawrence read. "Calais…uh, French village, some general history…was beset by both famine and the soldiers of King Edward, who demanded the town's unconditional surrender. At last mercy was promised to all but six of the chief Burghers, who were to come to the king bare-headed, bare-footed, to be put to death." Lawrence put the pamphlet in his jacket breast pocket. "Burghers were leaders of some kind—elder statesmen or committee members?"

"Citizens of stature, such as members of the mercantile class," Lenore said. "They assumed civic responsibilities via their status, rather than by being elected by their peers."

Lenore stepped back and walked in a slow circle around the sculpture. Each of the figures was visible from any point of her circle. She approached one of the Burghers, raising her hand as if to touch the curly hair on his forehead. "Look at their faces," she murmured.

"Ah, yes." Lawrence coughed. "You like it because they're all more or less fully clothed."

Lenore faced the platform, her hand clasped to her bosom. He can't possibly understand, she thought. These are the most exposed of all.

"See how heavy he made their feet." She pointed at the platform. "They volunteered, didn't they?"

"So it seems." Lawrence indicated a large plaque on the floor in front of the work. "Here's more of the story."

Lenore's hand fluttered, tracing an imaginary line up from the feet and one by one to the six faces. "Have you ever seen such…such noble desolation? They are so sad, so infinitely sad, so *majestically* sad. And yet, the greatness of what they are about to do fills them, and they go forward."

"It says here," Lawrence pointed at the plaque, "that they were not, in fact, killed. A woman of stature in the King's court pled for mercy, and they were freed."

"But they didn't know that, not when they walked, bound together. *They* believed that they were being led to their deaths." Lenore inclined her head toward an elder Burgher. "They *knew*, which is why they do not turn back. But he," she indicated the younger Burger, "see how he looks back?" She removed the pamphlet from Lawrence's pocket and waved it in front of his face. "This won't tell you what he was looking for."

Lawrence snatched the pamphlet from his mother and opened it. "A point of interest," Lawrence read. "This work was controversial amongst many of Rodin's contemporaries, who wanted a more heroic presentation. Rodin answered his critics: 'I intended to show my Burghers sacrificing themselves as people did in those days, without proclaiming their names.'"

Lawrence stuck the pamphlet under his armpit and folded his arms across his chest. "I suppose one can make such a sacrifice, if one believes that by doing so, the village will continue." He checked his wristwatch. "Are you still hungry?"

"No." Lenore resumed circling the statue. My only child, what could he know of such things? He offered to help pay for his braces, and we didn't even let him do that.

"See how the young one looks back? Look at the Old Ones. They know what it is they carry; what awful, final burden they have agreed to bear."

"But, remember, they *were* spared." Lawrence willed himself not to check his watch again. "Rodin knew that. The young one who turns back, perhaps he represents the promise of hope?"

"Rodin knew that *they* did not know," Lenore insisted. "The young one, what could he know? *Look at his face.* There is no hope. All he knows is what he thinks he will miss."

The sound of crinkling paper broke Lenore's concentration. Lawrence crammed the pamphlet into his pants pocket and mumbled something about eating. She gazed upon her son and marveled at the peculiar pride she took in his full head of hair; it was as if her maternal resolve had given him the follicular fortitude that so many other men his age lacked. She'd read that balding was determined by the mother's side, but such determination was not through strength of will or content of character. No, 'twas the random transmission of a genetic mandate.

What is a mother? The young Burgher who turns back…it is something else he's missing. Whatever he's looking for, or to, it's not his mother.

Yes, Raymond, I am overly concerned about Lawrence's chances for love, children, a good job. About my son's chances for a life. But what is a mother? A custodian of childhood and expectations, fear and ambition; a docent of doubt, a prurient pedagogue; the frail holder of a leash, the rebelling against which provides the parole into adulthood.

What good is a mother, past the probationary years? With his father, at least, there was the feigned camaraderie of career. Their distance was bridged by kvetching about bosses present and past, and shall I transfer the 401K or rollover the IRA? Best wait to see the new options. And so we are one.

There is no severance pay for the job I was given. The product was produced, the factory closed, and I am expected to divorce myself from quality control. Nothing to retire from, save remembrance, obligation and finally…indifference? What is, what was, a mother? Once upon a time I bore him, and now I simply bore him. And now, it seems we trade places, as it becomes plainer and plainer that I am the one to be borne.

And so, then: this. What can remain from this time of after-birth? You tug and pull at what refuses to emerge; you persist beyond hope or reason. Headlines extol a 63-year old woman's pregnancy; truer miracles happen daily, and surpass the fleeting wonder of autumnal fertility. The struggle is to push out, at great cost and in even greater pain, and with cries of both despair and triumph, that which will love you and leave.

"Mother?" Then, more gently, "Mom?"

The persistent tug of tender words. Time to go.

There were no mothers in that ancient council, no mothers among the Burghers, Lenore thought. If there had been, she knew that they, like Lot's wife, would have looked back. They would have turned for a final look at the children left behind, the village to be spared. Their looks would have been brief, yet not entirely despairing. "Do you see me? Will you see what I freely do for you?" Resigned and resolute, you turn and march on to whatever awaits, knowing that you are privileged to comprehend what is expected of you; acknowledging that gratitude is in the past and that remembrance can be its own, regrettable reward.

Lawrence followed his mother on her measured, resolute trek, back through the maze of hallways and exhibit rooms. He winced when, just outside the museum entrance, she headed for the nearest ashcan and lit up a cigarette.

"Wouldn't this make a lovely campaign poster." Lawrence struggled to keep the disdain out of his flat tones.

"You know full well I quit years ago. This," she took three short puffs, "is affirmation. And *this* is my birthday present to myself." Lenore snapped the cigarette in half and tossed the butt into the ashcan. She dropped the other piece on the ground, crushed it with the toe of her boot, then daintily picked up the still smoldering tobacco sheath as if it were a tea time canapé and dropped it into the ashcan.

All these years, Lawrence silently chuckled, and she still performs that odd ritual. Some habits die hard…including our perpetual tardiness. He glanced at his watch.

"Come; it's late." Lawrence held out his hand. "Sorry about lunch. It was a nice espresso booth but scones hardly qualify as a birthday feast."

Lenore waved off his apology. "I'm not complaining."

"I know." Lawrence took her hand in his, gallantly bowed, and kissed her fingertips. "We'll visit Dad another time. We forgot the flowers, and I couldn't find the whiskbroom after our last visit. His stone will get a thorough cleaning before I go down to LA, I promise. But we do need to get going. I'm already in the dog house with the manager, after our last outing."

"So I heard," Lenore said. "The night security guard had to set aside his copy of *Northwest Militia Digest* to press the main entrance's lock override. Having to buzz us in an hour past our estimated return time—merciful heavens!" Lenore clasped her hand to her forehead.

"You'd think they would appreciate the diversion," Lawrence laughed.

"Certainly the staff has never before experienced such inconvenience." Lenore sighed. "I'd best concentrate my campaign efforts elsewhere. No doubt I've lost the influential retirement home workers vote."

Lenore walked down the street, arm in arm with her son, toward the parking garage. "I had hoped to get to the LaserKopy while we were out, but I *am* getting tired. I wanted to run off a mockup of my campaign flyer. I may not have the time again, before you leave. Shall I send you one? The final version will be nothing fancy: the usual position statements, plus a candidate's portrait. Fully clothed, I promise." She turned back to look at the museum. "Nothing that might sway Miss Iris's constituency."

"Yes, Mother; please do." Lawrence touched his index finger to his lips, then smoothed a lock of Lenore's hair across her temple, tucking the wayward ivory curl behind her ear. "Send me your flyer."

Landscape

"You gotta be kidding." Jim read from an identification tag that hung from one of the tree's twisted branches. "'Norway Weeping Spruce.' Uh-huh." He grabbed my arm, turned me about face and steered me toward the back of the nursery. "The maples and oaks are this way."

"No." I pulled away, surprised that I could so easily break his grip on my arm. I walked back to the tree and caressed its meandering branches. "Isn't it the most unusual tree you've ever seen, the most…"

"'Unusual' would be a kind description."

"…the most eye-catching," I continued. "I'm not being kind. I *like* it. It looks friendly."

He snickered and shook his head. "Since when have you paid any attention to plants?"

"Never; that's the point. This one caught my eye." I placed one hand on my hip and shielded my eyes with the other. The Norway Weeping Spruce's pine needles were backlit by the setting sun, and they shone red-gold, like the dying embers of a campfire. "I want it for the backyard."

"Wait a minute. *I'm* the one planning the yard, right? *I* called the landscape contractors; *I've* been reading the manuals. I'm also the one who cares for the houseplants." Jim ran his fingers through his hair, up from his forehead and over the crown and then down his neck, urgently, like raking the leaves before it rains. Ever since they told us, he keeps touching his hair.

"It's absurd," I said. "How hard can it be to water a plant? But you know what happens when I even look at them. I think it's one of those things people either have a knack for or they don't."

"Brown thumb," he said.

"It doesn't make sense that putting water into a dirt pot is difficult. Plants don't like me. You've got the green thumb. Mine is gangrenous."

"Exactly," he said. "That's why you agreed *I* would be in charge of the landscaping."

"I didn't agree, I suggested it," I said.

Hands on his hips and his I-am-*not*-irritated look on his face, Jim forced a grin. "As I recall, *you* delegated this task to me."

"I decided to see if I liked it any better, pretending it's my idea in the first place rather than agreeing with your version— your decision—later," I said.

"My *version*?"

"Decision," I said. "Your decision,"

He ran his fingers through his hair again. *Stop it.* I wanted to reach out and grab his hands. *Leave it alone.*

"As far as I can tell," he said, "*my* short term memory is unaffected. You think I don't know that you don't want me to know that *you* can't remember we decided who was in charge of the yard?"

"You lost me," I said. "Anyway, what difference does it make?"

"Exactly. What difference does it make who decides something first, if we both come to the same conclusion?" Jim waved his hand next to his ear, as if shooing a fly. "This way." He walked briskly toward the nursery entrance. I half-walked, half-skipped to catch up to him.

The nursery was one giant rectangle; the layout was probably some efficiency expert's idea. As I followed Jim up and down the ramrod straight, parallel rows of trees, shrubs and flowers I considered the overall design and concluded that the nursery itself could use the services of a creative landscape architect. We walked away from the evergreens, through rows and rows of flowers. It was a relatively pleasant, late autumn afternoon, yet, other than the two attendants and one customer we passed in the hanging plants row, the nursery was practically deserted. Jim marched up and down the rows, his eyes fixed straight ahead, oblivious to the riot of colors on either side of him. Perennials, annuals, bulbs; I glanced at the identification tags as I scurried past pots of yellow, orange and red, trying to keep up with him.

All the information the doctors gave us, running through my head...if I could just slow it down and try to remember. Why does he keep questioning what I say, what I mean? Is paranoia a side effect? There are so many listed in the pamphlet. I remember saying something like, "We should look on the bright side—at least we're not alone. Plenty of other people get this disease. It even has its own information pamphlet." I remember him barking, "That's it, make a joke! It's all one big, fucking joke, isn't it?" And I remember fishing the pamphlet out of the wastebasket after he stormed out of the living room.

"Whoa! 'Scuse me." A panorama of blue and green Pendleton plaid filled my field of vision and interrupted my musings. Jim had stopped so abruptly I practically walked right up his back.

"I figure rhodies along the back fence." Jim pointed to a wall of shrubbery in front of us: mid-sized azaleas and rhododendrons, their olive-green leaves turning swamp-brown after a hotter-than-usual summer, their bulbs shut tight, clenched like angry fists.

"They've got all varieties here," Jim said. "This place has everything. There's samples of fence styles over by the entrance that I want you to see."

"What about the lawn?" I asked. "Seed or sod?"

"Sod's quicker, and we won't have to worry about keeping the Haney's dog from digging up the seeds. What's his name, Frenchy?"

"Françoise," I said. "I wish they'd put *their* fence up."

"The city has a leash law," he said, "and the neighborhood association, too—I checked. I'd be within my rights to shoot the little s.o.b. if I catch him on our property."

He gave the gun to his sister, last year, after she got mugged. He's forgotten. I haven't. He wouldn't really shoot someone's pet, would he? They said the tumor presses on the part of the brain that...*stop it.* He was joking. He was expressing frustration at a situation he can't control. He was joking. He'd never shoot someone's pet. *I'd* like to strangle the ugly mutt.

"I've never actually seen Françoise in our yard," I said. "It could be some other dog."

"No, those are poodle poops," he said.

"Remember the rhodies, Jim. You wanted me to check all the different colors. Let's look at the others. We need to get going."

Jim calls them rhodies. He says it's easier to pronounce. I like the full name, the way it rolls off my tongue. Rhododendron. No signs of aphasia, yet. Maybe the doctors are wrong.

Jim followed me as I walked to the west side of the nursery, back to the Norway Weeping Spruce.

"Oh, no." He grimaced and turned away from my tree again. "I wanted you to see the rest of this place." He swooped his arm above his head, as if to encircle the nursery. "This is where I'll get everything. The price includes delivery..."

"We could fit some of the hedge-type plants in the back of the truck," I said, "and the Norway Weeping Spruce would fit, also, either propped upright or on its side."

"I wasn't planning on getting anything today. I just wanted you to see the selection."

"Why not get some things now, if we know what we want?" I asked. "We're here, it's convenient, and maybe we'd save money." I ran my fingers through the hair at my temples, pushing a few errant strands away from my forehead, using my ears as a makeshift headband. Jim hates it when I do that. I've only a few streaks of gray, but they stand out against the mousy brown. "The sod might not take and we'd have to replant. But whatever we do," I tapped my watch, "let's do it now. I want to take a shower before the group meets."

"If they're truly a support group they're used to contingencies."

"Contingencies?"

"People's lives. We're not the only ones who've ever been late."

"I'd feel funny, walking in on the middle of the meeting, our first time."

"That's not a concern for me right now," he said. "*You* be on time. It was your idea, anyway. I've got things to do."

"It's only two hours…"

"Only?"

"…with a coffee break in the middle. We don't have to stay for the whole thing."

"Look, the surgery is in three days, and we don't know how long the recuperation will be," he said. "Some people react to the anesthesia, they say, so it could be two weeks or more. The lawn could be growing in that time."

He couldn't have forgotten. The surgery was canceled, after the test results were correlated with the scans. Inoperable. It's the radiation treatments that start in three days. He doesn't remember.

"And I don't want to take a Scandinavian bellowing cry-baby tree home today," he said. "Think about it, about how it would look. I can't believe you *really* want that ugly thing. It doesn't go with anything else."

"It won't violate the blueprint to plant one more tree," I said. "There's plenty of room."

"We paid the design firm good money for that plan. Just because it looks like there's plenty of room doesn't mean you fill up every available space. You have to account for growth, and visual focal points and balance."

"Focal points and balance? Are we talking about a backyard or an impressionist painting?"

"Those are landscape concepts," he said.

"I *know*. If you're really opposed to it, if you really don't want the tree, why don't you say so?"

"I really do not want that tree," he said.

"Well, I do."

"I think you want it 'cause I don't." Jim hugged his arms to his chest. "Just *look* at it."

"I did. And I intend to look at it every day, in our back-yard."

"It's misshapen. It looks deformed."

"Its shape is natural for that species," I said. "You're think-ing of the perfectly manicured, Disneyland-type gardening, which is natural to *Sunset* magazine, maybe, but not to reality."

"Natural or not, it's ugly. And uneven. It's not symmetri-cal."

"Neither are you," I said.

"I can't believe I'm actually arguing this," he said. "I may not be symmetrical, but *I'm* not gonna be planted in the yard."

"I'm not going to touch that one," I mumbled. "Jim, I want this *one* thing. You can pick everything else. You can choose all the other trees, the shrubs, the lawn—everything else."

"Does everything else include choosing where it gets planted?"

"You'll pick a spot where it won't get any sun, where you know it won't grow properly."

"How would you be able to tell if it's growing *im*-prop-erly?" He pointed to one of the tree's branches that curled up sideways, twisted in a corkscrew twirl and then drooped toward the ground with a peculiar sort of resignation. "If that kind of spastic limb development is normal, what would it look like if it were dying?"

"You'd be able to tell," I said. "It would look as if it were sick, like any other sick tree. You'll get to know it."

"No, *you'll* get to know it," he said.

"Oh, I see. You'd care for everything in the yard but that tree?"

He nodded.

"How juvenile. Fine. *I'll* take care of it, when it's planted."

"*If* it's planted."

"*When.*" I fingered the tree's looping branches. He doesn't want to look at it. He doesn't want to look at it, and think of me.

Jim raised his hands in supplication. "Your move," he implored of the heavens.

"I vote for a compromise," I said.

"There's a difference between compromise and capitulation." He sighed, and looked around the nursery. "We might as well get some peat moss while we're here."

We walked toward the fertilizer section. "The manager said they can install the lawn next Saturday," he said. "They roll the sod out for us when they deliver it. I'll rototill and fertilize in the morning and schedule the delivery for the afternoon."

"Not Saturday. That's when the group meets again," I said. "You could break it up: rototill in the morning and have the grass delivered on Sunday."

"I don't think they deliver on Sundays."

"Their sign says seven days a week."

"I want to get it all done at once," he said. "Besides, the Saturday meeting is a social thing, right? Just a barbecue."

"It's more than a barbecue."

"Oh, that's right." He smirked. "I almost forgot, they're going to play croquet afterward."

"What are you afraid of? That some of them might unsnap their prostheses and use them as mallets?"

I closed my eyes through his silence, and inhaled deeply of the enfolding earthiness. Mushroom composts; manures; organic mulch blends. I sensed enrichment, not decay; inimitable fragrance, not pungent odor. I should have been a farmer, I thought.

"Jenny, I don't need this."

"And I do?"

"You can go without me."

"No, I can't. This is as close as I'll get to begging."

"I'd really like to get the lawn done," he said. "The group meets every month. We'll go together, to the next one, I promise."

"You're an optimist," I whispered. I bent over a sack of peat moss.

"Wait," he said. "I'll get that."

"I can lift it," I said. "Or if I can't, then I won't."

"That stuff is heavier than it looks."
"I'm not going to *look* at it. I'll carry one bag, not two."
"You might hurt yourself, Jen, if you drop it."
"What makes you think I'm going to drop it?"

Sister Dentia and the Reading List

Sitting on the round leather exam stool, poised, as it were, at the precipice, I reach for an instrument and pause to consider the chasm of spirits laid open before me.

I often marvel at my fortune, that on a daily basis I am privy to such spectacles. And so I cringed this afternoon when, sitting in one of the vinyl, high-backed booths at the pizza parlor, I was subjected to the recollections of a man in the booth behind me. He was fresh from a routine cleaning and bitewing x-ray appointment; his lunch companions alternately guffawed and moaned while he loudly related the horrific tale of how his dental hygienist had "tortured" him.

If I talk to outsiders about my work, if I say anything at all, it is along the lines of, "Most people don't realize the importance of regular flossing." I compliment their son's pleasing smile; I say the expected and change the subject. That I consider my profession a calling more than a vocation is considered at best a non sequitur. Such commitments—to a lifework rather than spouse or family—are neither appreciated nor understood. In my patients, my parishioners, I see the results of years of misunderstandings; I see enough to know I've no wish to solicit the same for myself.

And so I scrape and scale, cleanse and purify, admonish and praise, correct and instruct, always careful to change gloves should I carelessly happen to brush aside one of the silver strands which, with increasing frequency, tumble down my forehead and onto my protective goggles. And over careless words at a pizza parlor I am once again reminded that others consider me a sadistic, glorified window cleaner, if they consider me at all.

There are words I remember…words I first heard in my Psychology of Perception class; a reference used by an anxious, pale blond wisp of a boy with the sincerely ubiquitous black wardrobe to open his term paper on sensory perception: "The eyes are the window to the soul." The quotation's author and source are long gone to me; the words themselves left an indelible (if rather trite, I confess) impression on a romantic, idealistic student. I truly thought it to be the most profound thing I'd heard until the boy presented his next paper.

The words return to me, these many years later, only now I beg to differ. The eyes may be a window, but the soul's door is the mouth. Eyes lose focus when I tilt the chair back and position the exam light; when, contrary to the rhetoric of the day, I am face to face with a monumental *lack* of diversity. Eyes fog and fade into white-yellow dots, betraying whatever sense of racial identity, ethnic pride or gender differentiation their owners may, in their most focused, upright positions, hold dear. The irises are drained of color; cosmetic enhancements dissipate in the ocher beam.

From my vantagepoint, they all look alike.

Over the years I've heard dentists, orthodontists and fellow hygienists mutter a plethora of variations on that observation; I'm certain the majority of my colleagues concur and go no further, and this knowledge ices my veins. This perception of facial affinity leads my associates to the subliminal conclusion that, indeed, their patients *are* all alike, and they treat them accordingly.

I greet my clients personally when they enter the office; I wave off the receptionist and escort them to the exam room. I wish to see my patients before they slip into the chair and blend into The Masses under the pale gold halo. True, I am often lulled by the general sameness of their corporeal concerns; even so, I am sometimes overwhelmed by the singularity of their spirits.

The basics of oral hygiene have become routine for me, which allows for a certain freedom in considering such things. I revel in this freedom even as I feel constricted by the collective distaste for one who attempts to incorporate the existential in her work, although I most certainly understand and even appreciate the skepticism when I see what passes for spirituality these days.

I subscribe neither to the tony obsession with angels nor to the general celestial humbuggery of my era. No seraphim hover over my shoulder, guiding my scaler. Neither do I equate the spiritual with the observance of pedestrian, religious ritual. If God truly is my copilot (as an aeronautically inclined, proselytizing patient once assured me), surely S/He trusts me to check my own altimeter readings.

I have felt called to ministry, perched in my aerie, beholding the canyon of souls below. My patients, the ones whom I consider my parishioners, sense this. Why else the confessional aspect to their conversations? Casually, desperately, they endeavor to chart our discourse into the most personal of seas. They steer my comments and guide my inquiries, even when limited to yes/no grunts by the presence of my hand and a triplex syringe in their mouths.

A brilliant if reserved and reclusive high school senior, whom I had seen from fluoride treatments through molar sealant applications, confided to me that he received radio transmissions through his fillings. Dr. Lettner declared there was precedence for the boy's claim, and showed me copies of several research papers to back it up. Nevertheless, the lad's promising academic career was cut short when several college admissions counselors surmised he was in the initial stages of schizophrenia.

The boy risked ridicule and rejection with such a revelation; he knew instinctively as well as experientially that I would not violate the sanctity of our ersatz confessional. Of course, some instincts are more basic than others. Mirror in one hand, suction tube in the other, mouth mask and eye shield in place—in such a pose, deliberating treatment options, I have been the recipient of

coy glances, suggestive comments, even lascivious leers. Dr. Lettner
ascribes this phenomenon to the reclining leather chair. His jests
aside, there may be something inherently provocative in the situation. I have lost count of how many Tartar Toms, Decay Dicks
and Halitosis Harrys (and even one young woman, whose appearance and demeanor were not as butch as one might expect
from a lady bicycle messenger) have "come on" to me from that
position.

        Phlegmatic Mr. Than claims an ancestral curse of bad gums
and schedules cleanings every other month. Our relationship is
like a dance, with him lightly prodding me to lead. His tales of
life in the Old Country center around his father's refusal to accept his emigration; I think they are, in fact, about his own dealings with his flamboyantly Americanized, teenaged, mall-rat-of-
a-son.
        Alma Carter is a recent convert to international cooking,
and her ardent, middle-aged breath is redolent of herbs and gar-
lic. She "reeks" of exotica, says Dr. Lettner. I suspect she senses his
disapproval, as she utters nary a sound for him but wholeheart-
edly recounts her latest culinary adventures to me. She describes
the astounding successes and the crashing failures, none of which
matter to her husband, who would be content with tuna burgers
every other night. I am invigorated by her exuberance and savor
the aromatic ambiance, secondhand though it may be, of her visits. Her zest for new foods matches her skill at flossing—I've yet
to pick so much as one cracked Szechwan peppercorn from between her molars.
        There was one, a new patient…I've yet to fully consider the
ramifications of her visit. She filled out her dental history form
while I prepared a chart and made the usual inquiries regarding
work, family and hobbies. Her pressing concern was compiling a
suitable reading list for her precocious daughter, Meryl, whom
she described as "seven going on forty." The woman, a voracious
reader of novels, had recently perused the works of several South

American and Asian authors and announced that she had "given up" on both classic and contemporary American and European literature.

She praised the Latin and Asian authors' recognition of the mystical; she described how ever-present in their stories is a sense of the continuity of life. Ghost, spirits and the guiding presence of ancestors are a part of everyone's story, no matter the characters' economic class, educational attainments or religious convictions. The existence of a Spirit World and its interaction with the Living is treated as a physical reality, and she decried what she described as the lack of the same in Western literature.

"There's an incredible world out there," she said, "and I want Meryl exposed to it. I've studied the multicultural aisle of the children's bookstore and I'm convinced, in comparison; well, what I mean is, after reading all that…" She sighed dismissively. "What can I say? The White Man has no soul."

I strapped on her bib and began the exam. Charles Dickens would most certainly disagree, I thought. Yet, as I considered her audacious pronouncement, no contemporary authors came to mind in refutation. Perhaps I am not so well read and therefore cannot offer a rebuttal, although I seem to recall a sense of the supernatural or spiritual in the works of pre-Industrial British and American authors.

The White Man has no soul? Or merely thinks he's outgrown its usefulness?

These are but a few of my flock, and how they might laugh to hear me describe them as such! I think of them fondly, and they come to me. Later in the day they tell friend or family, "I went to see the dentist." True, it is Dr. Lettner's name on the office door. He makes his obligatory appearance five minutes before the exam is scheduled to end; he affirms my cleaning job and bids them adieu "until we meet again." Occasionally, he'll note a spot on the x-ray or the irritated gum flap below the bicuspid— always at my request, and always as though it were his discovery.

My patients by and large leave my chair in an almost insufferably good mood, reveling in their clean teeth and filled with the satisfaction that comes from doing the right thing. They return to home or work, to their empty, meaningless drudgeries, or worse—to lives which once promised fulfillment and stimulation but now fester in inertia. They are drained by pursuing (or in some cases merely occupying space in) what they think is the Good Life.

I profit by their experiences. I live simply and alone, for aesthetic as well as ascetic reasons. I have chosen to empty myself, to be rid of distractions. In my self-styled Spartan life I emulate my parishioners' barren emotional and spiritual lives, and thereby am able to empathize, to understand. I have this option; it is my great fortune to be able to recognize it as such.

Leonard Alan Kane was a welcome respite, an oasis of normalcy on a Friday afternoon. The week had been comprised of a seemingly continuous stream of new patients: tense, anorexic women in their late twenties, whose collective pearly enamels bespoke of an overabundance of whitening gels. Mr. Kane's robust, yellowed incisors (due to the mineral content of the water in Kentucky—Mr. Kane's home state—according to Dr. Lettner) were truly a sight for sore eyes. His chart confirmed what I knew by instinct: it had been a year since his last cleaning. However, I neither reminded nor questioned him about this.

Crimson, Novocain-thickened lips stumblingly proclaim their masters' anesthetized hearts. Patients steel themselves for Dr. Lettner's syringe, unaware that they've been effectively numbed for years. I am not unfamiliar with Such Things. I know what comes of abandonment, of ephemeral promises. I know of anxious, pale youths who speak old words to new loves. I know that those who claim to have found a kindred spirit in the search for Higher Purpose—and who go so far as enlisting the noble thoughts of others in the quest—later venture to find such a spirit in the eyes of another.

The clues are in charts and scheduling books. A devoted Regular misses routine cleanings; the mother, so particular about her child's checkups, cancels and reschedules. She phones one day, tentatively requesting we ignore the phone calls from *his* attorney and by the way, is it a bother to ask about a transfer of benefits?

Mr. Kane sank into the chair without his customary "So, how's my favorite Keeper of the Pearly Gates?" A surreptitious check of his wife's chart confirmed my suspicions—fourteen months since her last visit. Ruthann Kane was obsessively conscientious with her checkups: every six months; every other month during the last pregnancy when, despite her meticulous hygiene (she was the most effective lay flosser I've ever encountered) her gums became inflamed. We had seen their older child for the initial child's exam, to ensure the deciduous teeth are in: Such a fine boy; it's not so bad at the dentist's, is it?! You may choose your own toothbrush—Dynamo Super Ranger or Sesame Street character?

The usual small talk seemed more minuscule than ever. The cleaning, which according to the clock flew by, seemed to drag. I picked and scraped, scaled and sprayed and "Rinse, please"-d. When he leaned over to spit I stared at the bowl of swirling water and let my vision slip into its comfortable, out of focus mode.

"Watermelon?" Mr. Kane lifted a shaky hand. He pointed at the vial of tooth polish I had opened. "Didn't it used to be cherry?"

"Peppermint, the last time you were in." I smiled, warmed by the memory. "Then it was strawberry. We're experimenting with new flavors. Everyone likes the watermelon, although you're the first to guess the aroma before I even got it near your teeth. Is your vision as strong as your sense of smell?"

"No," he said. "Not any more, at least. But, now that you mention it, I do remember the peppermint."

I nodded. "It was my favorite. Reminded me of my father's aftershave lotion." I held the polish in one hand, adjusted the exam light with the other and looked down, into his eyes, which transformed under my gaze into his very own. No seething broil of humanity; they had their own shape and size—the bluest brown eyes I had ever seen, and they were increasing in water content with each microsecond.

"He switched to Old Spice or some sea-faring scent when I was around ten years old, but I'll always remember the mint one." I spoke fondly and rapidly. "One whiff and I'm back in the garden, with my father. Smell is the most evocative sense, according to the medical studies I've read. I'll do the upper molars first. Open wide, please; close slightly; good."

"Do you remember what new babies smell like?" Mr. Kane raised his right hand almost imperceptibly from the exam chair armrest.

"Yes." I paused, holding the polishing drill an inch above his tongue. "I know what you mean. I love the smell of baby shampoo."

"No," he said, "not that."

The polisher quivered, ever so slightly.

"Not only the fresh-from-the bath smell. When you hold her close, and rub your nose in her hair and around the back of her neck." He closed his eyes and turned his head away from me. Before the tear could roll down his cheek and into his ear I let my hand slip, and gave him just cause.

"Oh, I'm sorry! That smarts, doesn't it?" I reached for a gauze pad. Mr. Kane lay silent and motionless under the hypnotic yellow beam, and faintly emanated gratitude while I dabbed at the blood on his gums.

The finger pointed from the grave to him, and back again.
"No, Spirit! Oh, no, no!"
The finger was still there.
"Spirit!" he cried, tight clutching at its robe, "hear me! I am not the man I was. I will not be the man I must have been but for this intercourse. Why show me this, if I am past all hope?"

Leonard Alan Kane thanked me for his new, angled-head toothbrush and samples of unwaxed, cinnamon-flavored dental floss. I think of Mr. Kane, of how he looked as he departed, promising to be more faithful in his appointments. I think of what would be in a book he would write, and of the reader who would dally between its covers and then claim the author has no soul. I load another set of instruments into the autoclave, take my lunch break and am subjected to secondhand, vapid yarns of dental abuse.

This is how I come to be in my kitchenette, sitting at my breakfast nook table, reading Stave Four—The Last of the Spirits—from *A Christmas Carol*. The open windows of my second floor apartment offer little relief to a static, sultry, July midnight.

Tomorrow I will return once more, to scrape, clean and dig, to query, encourage and absolve. Then, when one would think I am alone, I will offer a prayer to That Which May Be Listening, for all who clutch tight the tattered hem of a Spirit's robe.

Rescheduled

"I commend you for not smirking."

I stood in front of the magazine rack, gazing at the selection of last year's headlines. Since I was the only other person in the waiting room, the white-haired, well-dressed woman sitting in the leather armchair must have spoken to me.

"Excuse me?" I said.

"Is it that we've heard it so many times before, and know the outcome, that we no longer even bother to protest that it will, in fact, be more than 'a few minutes' before the doctor will see us?"

She spoke with a smile that began and ended at her mouth; her lips angled upward, exposing her teeth. The lines around her eyes and on her forehead remained fixed in bold, horizontal strokes.

I chuckled. "Oh, is *that* what the receptionist said?" I picked a copy of a weekly newsmagazine and sat down on a couch, across from her. "I really wasn't listening, past the 'have a seat' point."

"The collective unconscious, or rather, conscious, experience of the waiting room." She made fluid, rolling motions with her right hand, alternately moving it around her head and then smoothing her hair back behind her ear, as if she were caressing an invisible wave that lapped at her hairline. "The patient announces her arrival, the receptionist responds. It is a dance sans choreography, since we all know the steps."

She must be waiting for a friend, I thought, and I scolded myself for the ageist addendum that immediately sprang to mind: "Old people aren't usually bothered by allergies."

She was a striking figure. Her shiny, silver-white hair framed her reddish-brown face and forest green eyes. She wore no eyeglasses, and no makeup that I could see; nothing distracted from those dark eyes, whose color seemed accentuated by the olive-colored, paisley patterned scarf draped across her shoulders. Her alligator purse matched her shoes, both of which were just a shade darker than her silk dress.

All that green, I thought, would make *me* look like a peeled grape. I repositioned myself on the couch, and, under the guise of retying my shoelaces, tried to pull my pants legs down to cover the gap between the hem and my knee socks, which were slouched around my ankles.

"I'm just happy to finally be here," I said. "It took me a while to get this appointment."

She looked inquisitively at me.

"It's not like it's an emergency or anything," I said. "But I've already been rescheduled twice. Most of the appointments are reserved for return patients or special cases, and I'm just here for a general workup, to find out what makes me sneeze."

"Not that you'll receive any more attention, emergency or no, once you get into the examination room," she said. "Unless, of course, you embellish your symptoms, beyond the routine."

"What? Like, make myself more interesting?"

"Precisely," she said.

"This works for you?" I laughed, a tinch too loudly. I wanted to find out why she was there but didn't feel as though I could ask her directly.

"I've never deigned to do so, though I've been tempted." She adjusted her scarf and sighed. "The Downtown Clinic…you are familiar with HMOs?"

"Yes, I've got one of those plans. Preferred Provider."

"We've all been roped into those, haven't we?" she said. "At the main clinic, the specialists are rotated through the routine internal medicine ward. For two days each week, each oncologist, cardiologist, endocrinologist and the like must work in the general medicine clinic, seeing aches and pains, influenza and rashes, and what have you."

"I didn't know that."

"It is something you may wish to consider, should you require their services. My experience last winter is, unfortunately, indicative of the attitude such a situation fosters in the physicians. While waiting in the examination room, I noted that the doctor who was to see me was an otorhinolaryngological oncologist, board certified, and quite active in his professional associations, as indicated by the diplomas and certificates adorning the wall."

"I read those, too," I said, "just to make sure it says 'doctor of medicine' instead of 'registered cosmetologist.'"

She murmured, "Yes, of course," and clutched her purse to her bosom. "When the physician finally came into the room, looking harried and bored although it was not yet ten a.m., he barely so much as nodded in my direction. He mumbled a few cursory questions, which, apparently, comprised his diagnosis. Had I exhibited symptoms of throat cancer rather than a mere viral infection I might have had more of his attention."

"That's so frustrating." I shook my head, thinking of the times when I had received similar treatment. "But, it's understandable that doctors, or anyone for that matter, might get bored with the same old thing—just another runny nose."

"I am not 'the *same old thing*,'" she said, sharply enunciating the words, "and neither are you. No one must ever be treated as 'just another' anything. Mortal illnesses often produce the same initial symptoms as 'mere' viruses, and simple viruses which go untreated can progress from the mere to the mortal."

"That's right." I leaned forward. "My college roommate's friend got sick. It was strep throat, and he never really took care of himself; I mean, no one ever convinced him, and the virus settled in his heart, and two years later he had to have a heart transplant, at age twenty-seven!"

"Yes." A warm smile illuminated her face. "Such stories abound. The medical profession is a service profession. But," she lifted her hand toward me, "since the present system can afford to let needy, though not outwardly suffering, people wait weeks for an appointment, they have little incentive to remember that *they* are here for *us*."

"I think it's 'cause most doctors are men. They don't listen to what we—what women—say. I choose women doctors whenever I can."

She dismissed my comment with an imperious wave of her hand. "It makes no difference. They are all trained in the same way, by the same teachers. It is a mistake to link sensitivity with gender in the medical profession."

"I hadn't thought much about that."

"Well, now you have something new to think about." She crossed her legs at the ankles, aimed her icy smile toward the reception window, and raised her voice just as a nurse opened the reception office door. "If they would simply treat us as human beings…it is a simple complaint, with a simple remedy."

The nurse called my name; I glanced at my watch and stood up. "Only fifteen minutes late," I said. "That's not so bad. It was nice talking with you, Mrs.?…"

"My friends call me Mrs. Castillo, though it seems I go by Elizabeth here. No titles other than for the doctor, you see." She waved me off in the nurse's direction. "Good luck, my dear."

I sat, fully clothed, on the examination table. Although it had been twenty minutes since I was brought back to the exam room, I was only on page five of the seven-page "Allergy History" form I had been asked to complete.

The nurse returned to the room and caught me frowning at the "Composition of Household Items" page.

"Whiz through that last part," she said. "Dr. Sorenson needs to review this before she sees you, and most people don't know what their furniture is stuffed with, anyway."

She stuck her hand toward me. Under "type of carpeting" I wrote, "ugly," and handed the form to her.

"The doctor will be with you in a minute," she said.

"Thank you, nurse…" I meant to ask her name, or at least look at her nametag, but she was out the door. I checked the floor for skidmarks; none were visible on black and white checkered vinyl. "Do I have time to use the bathroom?" I said to the door.

Ten minutes later I heard a soft rap on the door, and a slight, pale, salt and pepper-haired woman came into the room. I started to offer my hand, then pulled it back when I noticed that she held my open chart in both of her hands.

"I'm Dr. Sorenson." She gave me a quick smile and returned her eyes to the chart. "I'm sorry about the wait…Jaclyn?"

"Yes, Jaclyn Moran. 'Jackie' is fine."

"I've been reviewing your history form. I see you've been reading some of our patient information brochures."

"I picked these up in the waiting room," I said.

"As you can see from the information, you have a lot of company." She placed my chart on the counter next to the sink and began to wash her hands. "Millions of people suffer from allergies of one sort or another, usually experiencing the classic 'hay fever' symptoms you describe in your history form."

"I didn't know what else to call them," I said. "I've never had trouble, like some people do, in the spring, but I had a real bad attack of *something* last month…"

"First, it is important to determine the allergens; that is, the substances to which you are allergic, if, in fact, you *are* allergic, which your symptoms would seem to indicate."

Her voice wavered as she washed and rewashed her hands. She must be trying to scrub off that pesky first layer of skin, I thought.

"Right." I angled my head toward the sink, and tried to make eye contact with her. "I don't want to get into a routine of shots or medication unless it's absolutely necessary. But it's weird, whatever it was, it hit me so suddenly, so hard, and when I sneeze, it's like machine gun fire—ten times or more in a row—I can't stop. The pamphlet said there's a name for that…"

"We'll find the allergens," she broke in. She methodically dried her hands, then pressed a red button on the wall next to the sink. "That is, we'll find the things you're allergic to…"

"Right, they're called allergens." I figured it was my turn to interrupt. "I mean, I literally could not function. There wasn't enough room on the form to go into great detail, but it seems to me, compared to what I've heard from people I know who have allergies, that it was…"

"We'll identify your allergens by performing a series of skin tests, followed by laboratory tests."

The door opened, and the nurse stuck her head in. "You rang?" she said to the doctor.

"We'll need the skin testing tray," Dr. Sorenson said, "plus a lab order form, for…" she glanced down at the chart, "for Jaclyn, at the front desk, with a return appointment in two weeks." The nurse nodded and left the room.

"Most of what is called 'hay fever' is in fact an allergic reaction to tree, grass or weed pollens, or some combination thereof. It sounds as though you have a common…"

"How can I sound like anything?" I heard the exasperation and disgust in my voice and thought, for a moment, that someone other than myself was speaking. "You haven't listened to me. I have questions. And I want to discuss how those things work before I get punched with any testing needles."

I felt my face flush as Dr. Sorenson looked up from my chart and in my direction. Though looking directly at me, she seemed to focus beyond, or through, my body. Her gaze was so strong that I turned my head to see what was on the wall behind me: a Norman Rockwell-ish painting of a troupe of ballerinas.

She lowered her eyes and whispered, "Please excuse me." She left the exam room, shutting the door behind her.

I remained on the table until my face returned to its normal color and temperature. I walked to the exam room door, started to open the door, and paused, thinking, *now* what do I do?

The door opened on its own, and I was face to face with the nurse who, thirty minutes earlier, had called me back to the exam room.

"Oh, oops." She seemed embarrassed, and I saw that she held a scheduling book in her hand. "There will be no charge for today's visit. Dr. Sorenson apologizes…"

"No, she doesn't." I felt the muscles in my jaw tighten. "You're apologizing for her." I pushed past her and marched down the hall. "I just want to get out of here," I said to the nurse, who followed behind me. "I'm late for work and my bladder is full."

"You're going the wrong way," the nurse said. "The reception area is back the other way. The restrooms are next to the entrance."

I did an about face and walked back down the hall. "How about this one," I said, as I opened a door on the right marked "lounge."

Dr. Sorenson sat on a reclining sofa in the lounge. She was leaning forward, bent over at the waist. Her head was in her lap, her hands covered her ears, and her back quivered. She moaned softly and rhythmically with each ragged breath she took, and did not look up when I burst into the lounge, nor when I backed out and shut the door.

"Excuse me," I mumbled, to no one in particular, and walked back toward the reception area. I wanted to leave even more than I wanted an explanation.

"I'm sorry," the nurse said. She still followed, a few steps behind me. Something in her voice made me stop and turn around.

"She shouldn't be seeing any patients," she said. "There was a death, deaths, in the family. An auto accident; her daughter and son-in-law." She looked up at the ceiling. "Two weeks ago…we thought it best, we tried to reschedule all of her appointments for the month…"

Her voice, thin and shaky, trailed off into silence, and she wiped at her eyes.

"I suppose she shouldn't be seeing anyone right now." I stumbled for words of sympathy and understanding. "Her, uh, professional judgment would be off."

"She insisted. She said that her on-call group couldn't see everyone, and that it's hard for the asthma patients, especially the elderly ones, to wait. And as long as she's seeing them, she might as well see others. She thought it would take her mind off..." The nurse shook her head and rubbed her nose on her shoulder. "I could reschedule you," she whispered.

I nodded. "That would be fine."

"Maybe something next month?" She opened the schedule book and turned the pages.

"Let me call from work, so I can check my schedule."

I walked through the waiting room, down the office stairs, past the blooming rhododendron and azalea bushes that lined the sidewalk, out to the parking lot. The warm spring sun reflected off the top of my car into my eyes, making me squint as I opened the car door. It's going to be like an oven in there, I thought. I sat in the driver's seat, rolled the windows down, took a deep, floral-scented breath and sneezed until I cried.

Sound No Trumpet

I no longer believe in the infallibility of body language, Mary Catherine thought, as she watched her father pick up the newspaper from the secretary's desk. She watched, and walked behind him, while he marched through the reception area, into the office of Harold Deale, Attorney at Law. Her father's blue-collar demeanor belied his pin stripe ensemble, and he glared at the massive black headline which proclaimed the acquittal of his daughter's rapist.

"Tabloid *shit!*" Ray Donovan threw the newspaper at their attorney, who sat behind his desk. Mr. Donovan quickly turned to his daughter. "Excuse me, Mary Catherine."

"One of the paralegals must have brought it in." Mr. Deale picked up the newspaper and tossed it into the wastebasket beside his desk. "My apologies. You shouldn't be subjected to..."

"It's not a tabloid," Mary Catherine said. "It's the *Times.*" She sat down in one of the two plush velvet armchairs that faced the dusty mahogany desk and extended her slim, pale hand toward Mr. Deale. "I'd like to see it, please. I always read the paper with breakfast, but it wasn't there this morning."

Harold Deale reached into the wastebasket, and looked up at Mary Catherine's father. Ray Donovan nodded curtly, then paced beside the desk while his daughter read the front-page headline.

"'Not Guilty Verdict in Robert Armstrong Murphy Sexual Assault Trial.'" Mary Catherine folded the paper on her lap and rested her chin on her palm. "At least they don't use his nickname. I hated it when his relatives called him that, in court. 'Robbie.' Like he was some roguish schoolboy."

"Honey, don't." Mary Catherine's father placed his freckled, gnarled hand on her shoulder. He gently took the newspaper from her lap and dropped it into the wastebasket. "Did you see this, Hal? I read it this morning. They interviewed his family yesterday, after the verdict was announced." He resumed pacing beside Mr. Deale's desk. "At a party, like an afternoon tea, can you believe it? His aunts and uncles and cousins talked about 'poor Robbie' surviving the ordeal. The *ordeal*. Ten minutes after the end of 'the ordeal' a catered victory reception miraculously appears! The press was invited, naturally."

Ray Donovan looked at his daughter. Mary Catherine sat, ramrod straight, her hands folded across her lap. She flinched imperceptibly when he reached over to brush a strand of her curly, auburn hair away from her forehead.

"Honey, I need to speak privately with Mr. Deale." Her father took a ten-dollar bill from his suit pocket. "Why don't you have his secretary run downstairs and get you coffee, a Danish— whatever you want."

Mr. Deale stood up and cleared his throat. "Yes, it's about time for her break, and I'm sure Sherry would appreciate the company. And the chairs really are more comfortable in the conference room. We'll join you in…"

"No, thank you." Mary Catherine reached into the wastebasket. "I'd like to finish the article. It mentioned something about them praying for me."

"One of his uncles said that." Ray Donovan put his hands on his hips and looked up at the water-stained, acoustic ceiling panels. "Said that, the night before the verdict, the family got together and prayed for 'his accuser.' They *prayed* for her." His mouth quivered, as if he was being forced to recite an obscenity.

Mr. Deale shook his head.

Mary Catherine closed her eyes and pictured a group of people kneeling in a circle. Even with her eyes open she could still conjure up his face. Glistening jowls, like a mantis' mandible;

piercing, glacial, cobalt blue eyes. *He'd look like Satan, if it weren't for those enormous teeth. The devil historically assumed the form of a serpent, a goat, a satyr—not a rodent. Eight men and four women, blasphemously referred to by both the defense and the prosecution as 'my peers,' looked at him and saw an impish rodent. They saw a mischievous beaver with an electric, electable smile. Beavers will be beavers. And naughty girls should be silent, grateful for their prayers. A family of kneeling rodents, insects; a coven of praying mantises, their vermin supplications rising to the heavens...*

Mary Catherine shivered. She turned toward the sound of muted, distant thunder. Her eyes remained closed while she listened to her father's hoarse tirade. *He sputters and roars,* she thought, *yet it is as if he bellows from under a sea of feather pillows.*

"I went to school with the sons of bi—with people like them. They didn't all go to academies. You can't claim to be a man of the people if daddy sent you to prep school while your constituents waded through garbage at Southie. Even back then, someone was thinking ahead. Every move was for the future. I'm surprised the press wasn't invited for a photo op during their prayer rally. That musta been quite a sight, don't you think, Hal?"

Mr. Deale smirked. "That's a group I'd certainly enjoy seeing on their knees."

Mary Catherine opened her eyes. She watched her father run his hand over his head. He combed his fingers from his forehead to the nape of his neck, a habit he'd retained long after he'd ceased to have a full head of hair.

"They trot out their religion for their annual Easter egg hunt photos; for their campaign launchings. For their rape trials."

"I share your frustration, Ray," Mr. Deale said. "But right now we need to decide whether or not to proceed with the civil suit."

Mary Catherine stood up. Shielding her face with the open newspaper, she gradually backed away from the desk. She feigned reading the *Times* and withdrew to a corner of the attorney's office.

Leaning back against a bookcase, she peered over the top of the newspaper.

Ray Donovan slowly lowered himself into an armchair. "I've had enough of courtrooms to last the rest of my life. And I don't know if Mary Catherine can stand…"

Mr. Deale's intercom buzzed, and he held up his hand. "One moment, please." He picked up his telephone. "Yes, I see," he murmured into the mouthpiece. "Are they staying…uh huh. Thank you, Sherry." He hung up the phone and tapped his pen against the desk blotter. "There are quite a few reporters outside."

"So soon?" Mr. Donovan glanced at his wristwatch.

"This office is private property. We've informed building security. I don't want you to worry about them getting inside."

"Goddamn vultures." Mr. Donovan swore under his breath. "What about the press—can we get a restraining order? I thought it would get better after the trial but it's gotten worse."

"You may have to hang tight for a while," Mr. Deale said. "Eventually, interest in the story will fade. They'll go onto something else."

"As will he," Mary Catherine whispered.

"Something else," Mr. Donovan snorted. "You mean fresh meat. What are we supposed to do until then? I'm worried about my granddaughter. Katy's only four; she doesn't understand why she can't go and play with her friends. All those photographers…we've had to keep her inside. When one of us walks by a window, the reporters yell. They're even there at night; they must trade off shifts. One tried to scale the trellis. Katy thinks bad people are trying to do something to her mommy."

She knows already. A bad person did something to Mommy, and so Mommy did something, and now there are even more bad people. She hears the noises at night—don't worry, it's just rats, I tell her. The house is infested. Grandpa will call the exterminator, soon.

"It is possible that…if you grant an exclusive interview to one, the others will back down," Mr. Deale said.

Mary Catherine dropped the newspaper and walked toward the desk.

"If you decide to do that I could be your intermediary. Sherry and I would make the arrangements. You won't have to deal with any of them until the interview."

"I don't know." Mr. Donovan removed his glasses and rubbed his eyes. "It's hard, saying 'No comment, no comment,' when I really want to—if I felt I could *trust* one of them, it would feel so good tell our side of the story." His broad shoulders sagged, and his stomach heaved and strained against his vest. "No one believes the truth," he choked. "Nobody hears the truth."

Mary Catherine knelt beside her father's chair. "Thank you for all you've done," she said to Mr. Deale. She put her arms around her father and he buried his face in her shoulder. "Dad, you stay and finish up here. I've got to get back to Katy."

"No, honey, wait." Ray Donovan pulled out of his daughter's embrace and stood up. "Let me go with you."

Mary Catherine shook her head. "Don't worry. I'll walk right past them."

"At least let us, let me call you a security escort," Mr. Deal stammered. He picked up his telephone. "We can have one or two…"

"No." Mary Catherine waved her hands in front of her face, and Mr. Deal hung up the phone. "I appreciate the offer but I've had enough of all that. I'll go out the back door."

"But they'll…"

"Please, Daddy; both of you. I have to do this."

I will go down to the river, and the waters will part.

"Honey, you're not strong enough," her father sobbed. He sank back down into the chair.

"I know." Mary Catherine kissed the top of her father's head. She nodded to Mr. Deale and walked toward the door. "Pray for me."

People Like You

"Why didn't you tell me on the way over?" Callie moaned. "I knew you'd jump out of the car." Margaret hoisted her shoulder bag onto a counter top and plunged her arm into the maw of the wheelbarrow-sized purse. Her hand surfaced, clutching two fashion magazines. "Look for styles you like," she said.

"A makeover." Callie surveyed the various cosmetic and skin care booths which infested the department store's ground floor. "My present is a *makeover*? I asked for socks."

"You can buy socks any time. Birthday presents should be special."

"Agreed. How about a new life instead?"

"This is close."

"I was kidding."

"This is *new*, for your life. It'll make you feel good."

"Margaret, I really was kidding. But not about the socks."

"Give it a chance. If you don't like it, I'll buy you ten pair of socks." Margaret smiled at her sister. "It'll be fun."

"For you, maybe, watching me get painted like a clown."

"I see. People who wear makeup look like clowns." Margaret checked her reflection in the mirror on the counter. She rubbed her finger against a lipstick smudge on her incisor, then placed her hand on Callie's shoulder. "I wanted to do something special for you. You've been down for so long."

"About my job, not my face." Callie folded and unfolded the magazines she held, avoiding her older sister's sympathetic gaze. "Rick's attorney called yesterday. I let the answering machine get it…again."

"I know." Margaret lightly caressed the back of Callie's head, then ran her fingers through her own hair, flicking strands of frosted blond bangs away from her forehead. "These are growing out, finally. I say it's good to pamper yourself now and then."

"Now and then," Callie echoed. "You *are* good to yourself. Believe it or not, I admire that."

"Be nice to yourself, that's what I say. Because, ultimately, you can't count on others." Margaret picked up a coverstick tube from a display rack on the counter and rolled it back and forth between her palms.

"The papers are ready," Callie said. "That's what Rick's attorney wanted."

"Look and feel good for yourself—not to impress others." Margaret picked up a sample lipstick and looked into the counter mirror.

"I'm not going to sign."

"And in this economy people have to present themselves, market themselves, in person as well as on paper." Margaret paused, mouth puckered in anticipation of the lipstick application. "*What?*"

"Don't get excited." Callie said. "I'm not going to contest the divorce. I'm just not ready to sign any papers right now."

"Oh." Margaret snapped the lipstick tube into its cap. "I'm sorry, Callie. I keep hoping…"

"Please, don't. I lost Rick…oh—listen to me! Like I misplaced a set of keys. I didn't *lose* anyone. And I lost my job because I lacked seniority, not because I didn't wear makeup."

"I'm not saying that. Why are you reading so much into this? Look." Margaret motioned toward the end of the long display case, where a tall, pale woman stood, arranging mascara tubes. "She's the one I made the appointment with. See how smooth her skin is? No wrinkles or laugh lines and I'd say she's twenty-nine, at least."

"At least." Callie furrowed her brow. "Of course there aren't any wrinkles. Prove to me there's even *skin* underneath all that.

Natural light can't penetrate. I bet her face hasn't seen the atmosphere in years."

"Very funny."

"Tunneling through those layers would be an archeologist's dream. You might find artifacts from 1986 which could explain the evolution of espresso cafés."

"Go ahead, make fun," Margaret huffed. "But remember, she'll have the last laugh on us when she's sixty and looks forty."

"Huh?"

"Try to be civil to her when it's your turn."

"Sorry." Callie flipped through *New You* magazine. "My acid tongue lowers the pH of my mouth, which could lead to lip line cancer unless I use anti-carcinogenic lip emollients."

Callie fanned her face with the magazine. "Phew. I usually avoid this part of Cartwell's. Remember those salesladies who used to spray perfume samples on you when you walked by? Aunt Erva slapped one."

"Erva *slapped* a saleslady?"

"Not hard. On the wrist."

Margaret groaned. "Don't get any ideas. I made the appointment, I'm probably liable."

"Then she complained to the store manager." Callie hunched her shoulders and mimicked her aunt's whiskey-and-cigarettes growl. "Dousing me against my will is an assault upon my bodily integrity."

"I can just hear her." Margaret laughed. "I understand being annoyed, especially if you're wearing a conflicting scent."

"People who are allergic to perfumes could really get…"

"I know where this is headed." Margaret waved her hand, trying to get the attention of the woman at the end of the counter. "I was assured Dermatage products are hypoallergenic."

"Hy-po-al-ler-gen-ic." Callie drew out each syllable. "Mere cosmetics? No, it's science! Twenty bucks says my makeover artist wears a lab coat. If she doesn't, I promise to smile through the whole thing and purchase every product."

"It's just a uniform, to look professional."

"It's more than that, Margaret. It's to imply some pseudo-scientific legitimacy. But it's losing effect; too many people wear them. That NutroPlan diet quack wore one, remember?"

Margaret sighed. "Two hundred dollars down the drain and maybe two ounces off my thighs."

"Manicurists wear them. *Barbers* wear them. My friend, Ginnie, went to one of those anti-abortion centers—you know, the kind that masquerade as clinics?—for a pregnancy test. Her 'counselor' looked legit, wore a lab coat with some medical-type title. Ginnie asks for a referral, Madame Lab Coat locks the door, says, 'This is your preborn baby two weeks after conception,' and shoves pictures of third trimester stillborns in Ginnie's face."

"Can we change the subject?" The words hissed past Margaret's clenched teeth, past the broad smile she aimed at an approaching saleswoman.

"You're the ten-thirty?" the saleswoman asked.

"*She* is." Margaret nodded at Callie.

"Fantastic! Come have a seat." The saleswoman pointed to a chair on the employees' side of the display case. "These pamphlets describe the products we'll use today. I'll tell your facial stylist you've arrived."

Callie picked up the pamphlets and gingerly sat down. Margaret rubbed samples of wrinkle cream on her wrists.

"Welcome." The tall, pale woman glided around the corner of the display case. "I'm…"

"'Andrea Loren, Facial Stylist-slash-Consultant.'" Callie read the name tag on the woman's lab coat pocket.

"An-dr*aaaa*-ah. Accent on the second syllable, long *A*," the woman said. "And you're Margaret Denton?"

"That's me," Margaret said. "I made the appointment for my sister, Callie. It's a birthday present."

"Congratulations," Andrea purred. She fluttered her slim hand against her neck, curving her tomato-red fingernails as if clutching an imaginary choker. "Callie, we'll start with a skin tone and color analysis to help us choose our products. When I do the application, I'll give pointers on…"

"It says here," Callie read from a pamphlet, "your lotions have 'sunscreen properties offering maximum UVA protection.'"

"Dermatage products have the highest SPF of any skin care line," Andrea said.

"This stuff prevents skin cancer?"

"Daily protection significantly reduces the chance of…"

"That's so much easier than changing your behavior or diet, or reducing pollution. Just slather this on every morning and forget about signing petitions against ozone depletion. Will my medical insurance cover this?"

Andrea smiled from her chin to her lower lip. "We're working on it."

"May I speak with your doctor?"

"Her *doctor*?" Margaret gasped.

"The company makes medical claims. They must have a staff MD."

Andrea bent over, picked up a tray filled with small jars and set it on the counter. "Many prominent pharmacists and dermatologists helped with the design."

"Fine. The company 'ologist' will do."

"Did I mention when I made the appointment," Margaret said to Andrea, "that she'd be a real challenge?"

"I enjoy a challenge." Andrea's smile crept up to her nose.

"That's good," Callie said. She pointed to the display advertisement for the wrinkle cream that Margaret had sampled. "These photos are computer enhanced, right?"

"Something like that," Andrea said. "Shall we begin?"

"Don't worry about interrupting her," Margaret said. "Callie is perfectly capable of ranting while you're working."

"I saw something interesting…" Callie picked up *New You* magazine. "Here it is. 'Desert Storm Splendor: Persian Gulf Army Nurse Veterans Get Dazzling Makeovers.'"

Andrea placed her thumbs on Callie's temples and lightly stroked them across Callie's forehead and down her nose and chin. "Oiliness in the 'T-zone' is common. We'll start with an astringent wipe."

"Look at the before and after photos." Callie showed the magazine to Margaret.

"You must admit the difference is dramatic," Margaret said.

Callie frowned. "So's the technique. In the 'before' photos, the women don't comb their hair or smile. They wear drab colors and the photographer uses mortuary lighting."

"No talking while I apply the foundation." Andrea flicked her finger against Callie's jaw. "Tilt your chin; good."

Callie snickered. "The things women do to please men."

"Here we go," Margaret murmured.

"My sister gets going when I say things like that," Callie said. "She'll rationalize by saying that we're really pleasing ourselves."

"Callie, *everyone* wants to look nice," Margaret said. "There's nothing rational—nothing to rationalize, about that. You *are* judged by your appearance. It's not fair, but it's a fact."

Callie grumbled. "It's all about access to power."

"You renewed your *Ms.* subscription, didn't you?" Margaret smirked.

"Women in control of their lives don't even *think* of which 'shades of the seashore' to paint on their eyelids."

Margaret sighed. "Didn't we have this conversation in 1979?"

"I've selected 'Nature's Earth tones' for your palette," Andrea said.

"'Scuse me, Andy." Callie turned her head to sneeze. "Hypo or hyper, I think I'm allergic. Back to wanting the approval of others. Remember that health internship I had in college?"

"Vaguely." Margaret sprayed her wrist with a perfume sample.

"One day, in the pap smear clinic, I saw this woman who'd shaved her pubic hair because her fiancé thought it was sexy."

Margaret grimaced.

"Imagine how it looked, forty-eight hours later; how it *itched*." Callie shuddered. "She had a rash from scratching herself."

"That's barbaric." Margaret shook her head.

"Bingo," Callie said. "You think that woman ever stopped and wondered *why* she made herself uncomfortable? *Why* she catered to the whims of a guy who likes pussy with a five o'clock shadow?"

"Oh, Lord." Margaret's face turned the color of Andrea's fingernails.

"I've read about that," Andrea said. "'Poodle cuts.' *L'Urbane* magazine says they're all the rage in certain European circles." She pumped a mascara wand up and down in its case. "Let's try 'deepest sable.'"

"Try this," Margaret said. She waved her wrist under Callie's nose. "It reminds me of my rose garden."

Callie inhaled deeply. "Not bad. *National Geographic* says ancient Egyptians designed perfumes to be aphrodisiacs. This one mimics flowers in heat."

"That explains Kristin," Margaret sniffed.

"My husband's girlfriend," Callie explained to Andrea.

Andrea nodded and cleared her throat. "Something unorthodox with the lipstick: a flaming scarlet."

"Remember the cologne she wore to Rick's office party?" Margaret arched her back and wrinkled her nose. "You could smell her from across the room. One of those cheap, designer imitations, the kind drugstores sell."

"Yeah." Callie snorted. "'Eau de Do I Fuck Like a Bunny.'"

Andrea jerked her hand, running a deep red lipstick streak across Callie's upper lip and down her chin. "How clumsy of me!" she gushed. "I'll show you how easily it comes off with Dermatage's moisturizing makeup remover."

"She was so *nice* to you." Margaret wrapped her hands around her teacup. "Especially considering the hard time you gave her, not to mention the language you used. And then you wouldn't let me buy you one thing. Not even a lipstick."

Callie drummed her fingernails on the faux marble tabletop. "This is nice, but strange. I wonder who first thought of bringing the outdoor café atmosphere to indoor shopping malls? A little bit of Paris in Oxnard."

Margaret laughed heartily. She gazed across the table at her sister. "You *do* look fantastic."

"I agree." Callie sipped her coffee. "You can start breathing again. Didn't think I'd say that, did you?"

"I didn't think you'd admit it."

"It's a moot point, since I'm not willing, or able, to do this myself." Callie leaned back in her chair. "So bask in my beauteous reflection while you can. Cinderella's pumpkin returns long before midnight."

Margaret glanced at her wristwatch, put a ten-dollar bill on the table and stood up. "Get a croissant or something. I'm going back to Cartwell's. I owe you some socks."

"Bright colors, no polka dots."

Callie thumbed through *Glitter* magazine, reading the advertising copy to herself. "Le Visage's patented moisturizer products are cruelty free…Biocomplex uses its patented 'derma-nalysis' to…"

"Hello."

Callie startled at the sound of her husband's voice. She slid the magazine off the table, onto her lap, and put her foot on the seat of the chair Rick started to pull out from the table. "That's Margaret's. She'll be back any minute…" A rueful light flickered behind Callie's eyes. "But you probably know that."

"Something smells nice," Rick said.

"More like fishy," Callie grumbled.

"This is a new look for you." Rick put his hands on his hips and smiled. "I didn't know you owned a lipstick."

"I'm participating in a scientific experiment. By wearing this makeup I'm helping the environment *and* preventing skin cancer. Cosmetic effects are secondary. And temporary."

"That's too bad—the temporary part. You look good. I mean, you always do, but…"

"It's tougher than it looks, helping science. It'd be easier to take a pressure hose to my face and then send a check to

Greenpeace."

"O-ka-y." Rick pivoted in a slow circle, making exaggerated sniffing motions. He pointed at Callie's wrist. "The source! That's nice. What's it called?"

"Eau de do...dah day." Callie rested her forearms on the table. "Whatever Margaret did to get you here...ouch." Callie clawed at her wrist, then vigorously rubbed her paper napkin over the back of her hands, where Margaret had sprayed the perfume. "I must be allergic," she mumbled.

"If this was planned, I wasn't in on it," Rick said. "She's friends with Susan, my marketing assistant. Susan knows I get lunch here every day. Best sandwiches within walking distance of the office." Rick adjusted his tie. "Say, did your attorney call about..."

"No shop talk outside the arbitration room, remember?"

"Sorry." Rick unbuttoned his suit jacket. "Go easy on Margaret. She has good intentions, assuming this was intentional. Don't you believe in coincidence?"

"No, I don't. Margaret does, though." Callie's burst of laughter was a bit too quick, a bit too loud. "She believes in a lot of things. She thinks people want to be happy."

"Protective sisters." Rick chuckled nervously. "What can you say?" He rested his hands on the back of Margaret's chair.

"Pickup, number seventeen," yelled the café countergirl.

"C'est moi." Rick put his hand in his pocket and jingled his change.

Callie looked over her shoulder, toward Cartwell's.

"Turkey on wheat, to go. My order." Rick sidled away from the table, all the while looking at the back of Callie's head. "Guess I'm going now. Say hello to Margaret for me."

"Ta-ta." Callie flicked her hand dissuasively toward Rick's fading voice. She waited a minute, then turned back toward the table and picked up *Glitter* magazine from her lap.

"'Do it yourself makeovers: A Matter of Confidence.'"

"May I warm that up for you?"

Callie looked up, her eyes focusing on the words "Java Express Manager" which were embroidered on the shirt pocket of a man holding a coffeepot who stood at her side. He refilled her coffee cup and lasered a smile at Callie. The beam of caffeine solidarity, she thought, and feigned reading her magazine. Java Man stood beside her, radiating geniality.

Callie sipped her coffee. "That's warm, all right. Thanks."

"My pleasure." Java Man stood, smiling and unwavering, as if he'd been planted.

"So, the manager helps out?" Callie broke the silence.

"When the days are slow," he leaned toward Callie, "and the customer is gorgeous. You must be waiting for someone."

"Why must I?"

"Well, I...ha!" He placed his free hand on his hip. "Believe it or not, I almost said, 'What's a pretty woman like you doing alone. In a place like this?'"

"I'm not."

He slapped his thigh and guffawed, tilting his head to the side, like a robin trying to get an angle on a worm.

"Yuk it up, birdneck," Callie said to herself.

"Not what?" he chortled. "Not alone, or not a woman? Might as well ask; you can't be too careful these days!"

"Not pretty. I have horrendous facial scars from an acid tongue—acid *tong*—accident. A Hollywood stunt cosmetologist taught me to apply makeup. It takes three hours, every morning."

"Really?" He shifted his weight, moving his legs for the first time since he came to her table. "It doesn't show; I mean, it's..."

Callie took pen and paper from her purse and scribbled a note while Java Man stammered.

"It doesn't...well, you can't tell. I mean, you look fine..."

Callie stuck the note and the ten-dollar bill under her coffee cup and stood up.

"...you do a fine, *fine* job. It's marvelous, just incredible, inspirational, in fact, what they can do nowadays."

"Isn't science grand?" Callie ran her fingers through her hair. "Please see that my sister gets this note. She'll be the short blond returning to this table in a few minutes. I've got to run. Important papers to sign; you know the business world! Looks like you've got customers up front."

He looked toward the café counter. "Duty calls. It's been wonderful talking to you. Uplifting, even."

"Yes, I know." She dismissed him with her deft and dazzling smile. "People like me are an inspiration to people like you."

Hope

"Volunteers needed at Hope Adult Care Facility (formerly Sunny View Convalescent Hospital). See Pastor Bricker or Mary Sutherland for details."

I nudged Ahlene during the opening hymn and pointed to the announcement in the church bulletin. "Which name is more euphemistically incorrect?" I whispered. "A nursing home called 'Hope,' or one implying the residents have a nice view?"

I did not receive the anticipated kick under the pew. My wife's reply came via Pastor Bricker, who hailed me after the service.

"Ahlene says you're interested in volunteering at Hope." Bricker beamed a ministerial "Gotcha!" smile and shook my hand.

Before I could comment on my wife's peculiar sense of humor, Mary Sutherland materialized. Mary chairs the Social Concerns Committee; merely thinking "volunteer" around SCC members is tantamount to dangling a rotting possum in front of a vulture's nest.

"Got one, did we?" Mary swooped to my side and put her arm around me. "I'll take over from here." She winked at Pastor Bricker and steered me away from the coffee cart.

"Redeemer Lutheran has always supported Sunny—oops, make that Hope!—financially," Mary said. "We also recruit volunteers. I'm sure you've questions; such as, what exactly does a volunteer do?"

Well, yes, if I *were* to ask a question, that might be…

"That's the beauty of it—there are no exactlys!"

During Mary's exhortation of the virtues of volunteerism I looked around for Ahlene. My beloved stood at the far corner of the church courtyard, biting the edge of her Styrofoam coffee cup in a vaguely successful attempt to temper her amusement vis-à-vis my situation.

"Many patients—oops again! I mean *clients*. They want us to use 'proactive' terms... I like 'residents' better and I do think it's more descriptive, don't you? Anyhow, many have no visitors. Seek them out. Read to them or listen while they reminisce. A college student plays piano in the recreation room every Tuesday afternoon, show tunes and the like. Whatever your special talent or interest...well, you don't even have to *have* a talent. Just be there, one half hour a week. Are Monday evenings all right?"

"It's nature's tradeoff," Ahlene said later that morning, when I expressed admiration for the intensity if not the uninterruptibility of Ms. Sutherland's presentation. "The stamina of post-menopausal women should not be underestimated."

"You're in big trouble." I tried to sound surly, lagging behind Ahlene as we walked toward the church parking lot.

Ahlene smirked and tossed me the car keys. "You drive. Stop at the mini-mart; we're out of bread."

"*You're* the one who works in gerontology."

"Which is why I shouldn't volunteer," she said. "I know what you're going to say next."

"Do enlighten me," I sighed.

"You know nothing about old folks and even less about health care, etcetera. Which is *exactly* why someone like you should get involved. Your chromosomes may have something to do with it. Or, rather, the way someone with your chromosomes was raised."

"I'll probably regret asking, but chromosomes as in the XY pair?"

"Bingo. People in 'nurturing' fields are always expected to do double-duty...except for the men. You never hear Dr. Anson being asked to do anything extracurricular, do you? Look around, the next time a similar request appears in the bulletin. Everyone expects Ellen or Mrs. Karl to volunteer."

"They're nurses. It's only natural to expect…"

"And not to discount the big bucks those gentlemen may offer, but it's not the same as donating your time. The Social Concerns Committees of the world should target engineers and businessmen. The ones who get away with saying, 'I've no aptitude for that,' or 'I'm not a people person.'"

"You don't have a bone to pick with this issue, do you?"

"Can you honestly say that that's not the case?"

I let silence indicate acquiescence as I steered the car into the mini-mart parking lot.

At five-thirty the following evening I pushed through the swinging double doors of Hope Adult Care Facility. A sign on the wall directed me to follow the painted lines on the floor: yellow to the administrative offices. I followed the yellow line down a lime-green hallway, turned right, and the smell hit me.

Don't try to ignore it, I thought. I closed my eyes, grabbed one of the handrails which ran the length of each wall, inhaled deeply through my nose and concentrated on identifying the once familiar odors: sour milk; ammonia and/or urine; disinfectants. I continued down the hallway, turned left and nearly collided with a wheelchair.

An ancient woman, the translucent skin on her face covering an atlas of broken veins, crept along in her wheelchair by pulling on the handrail. She stopped but did not look at me. I squatted so that I was eye level with her. She mumbled something, and her withered hand tugged at the crocheted comforter that covered her lap.

"Going my way?" I tried to sound cheerful. "Can I give you a lift somewhere?"

"Hail Mary blessed Jesus help me, help, pray for us sinners…"

She repeated her fractured Rosary over and over. I touched her hand and asked her if I could take her somewhere or get her anything.

"Hail blessed among women, pray for us at the hour, the hour..."

I stepped to the side and she continued to pull herself along the handrail, keening her endless Hail Mary loop.

"Mrs. Kennedy, *there* you are!"

A young man in a white uniform sashayed past me and up to the rosary woman. "It's dinner time." He gently loosened her grip on the handrail. "Gather up your beads, honey, and I'll take you to the dining room."

He flashed a tired smile at me. His nametag read 'Edwin P., Attendant Manager.'

"Hello," I said. "I'm looking for the administration office. I may be a new volunteer."

"You look like a fresh one." He bent over the wheelchair and folded Mrs. Kennedy's comforter on her knees. "I get to recognize all the visitors. There aren't many faces to memorize, and no new ones 'cept for around Christmas."

"I thought she was lost." I patted the back of the wheelchair.

"No way. This lady knows exactly where she's going, don't you, Mrs. K.?" He raised his voice at "Mrs. K.," and pointed to her left ear. She wore a massive hearing aid that was partially hidden by her wispy, yellow-gray hair.

"Follow the yellow brick road." Edwin P. pointed to the painted line on the floor. "I gotta roll Mother Teresa to the trough. See you around."

"Such a treat, to get a male volunteer!"

The Chief Administrator, a plump, smiling, bat-faced woman in her early forties, gave me the mimeographed sheets that comprised Hope's "Official Volunteer Manual." Her secretary wrote the names and room numbers of the residents who had no visitors on the back of my manual while the Chief rattled off some information.

I could come anytime between eight a.m. and nine p.m. and didn't have to sign up for any particular hours unless I needed to reserve the recreation room or other facilities. "Don't commit to anything right now. Walk around, talk to people. We don't mind if you question the staff. Talk to everyone!"

I sat on a sofa outside the administrative office, read a few pages of the manual and then wandered through the halls until my stomach told me it was time to go home.

"Poor old lady," Ahlene said, when I told her about the creeping, keening Mrs. Kennedy. Ahlene refrigerated the leftovers while I rinsed the dishes. "She's not senile, she's terrified. She probably just realized she's in a Lutheran nursing home."

I threw the dishrag at her. She ducked, and it hit the refrigerator. "Don't be so cocky," I said. "You're older than me, remember? I've already got your room picked out."

"Something in primary colors, I hope." Ahlene walked to the sink, poured herself a glass of water and leaned back against the counter. "You know how I loathe pastels."

"The place looks surprisingly cheery, considering what it is." I leaned alongside her. "No peeling paint or dirty floors. The colors are garish, but bright. The halls are decorated with bulletin boards announcing activities…it's not what I expected."

"Or remembered," Ahlene said. "They're not all alike, you know."

"It looked different, but the…*aroma*…was the same."

"You're going back, aren't you?"

It was more statement than question. I looked for a clue in Ahlene's expression; she averted her eyes and picked up the stack of mail that lay on the counter.

"I'm not sure I want to be in a place full of people who don't want to be there. Even for a half-hour a week. You went with me a few times to see Grandma."

"She didn't know who I was." Ahlene placed her drinking glass in the dishwasher. "That I was little Danny's wife."

"She didn't know who *I* was. She thought I was one of her cousins." I followed Ahlene into the living room. She sat at one end of the couch; I stretched out on my back and laid my head in her lap. "Dad said she was stuck in her early twenties, back at her family's cabin at the lake. I was Cousin Fred, and Dad hadn't been born yet. Sometimes she thought Dad was her brother. He stopped visiting her. 'She can't miss me if I don't exist,' he said.

"I got him to go with me one more time before she died. I said, 'Gram, guess who's here to see you today?' She motioned to me and I leaned over the bed and she whispered, 'Tell that strange man to leave so you and I can talk.'"

"It'll be different." Ahlene stroked my forehead. "Ask them how they like the food or what they think of the weather. I bet they're starving for someone to ask their opinion, about anything. Ask the staff, too."

"Good idea. One little favor, though."

"No way."

"Could I ask first?"

"Oxygen is a precious resource. If you want to waste your allotment, be my guest."

"Go with me?"

"Later. I don't think I should, at first."

"But you handle things like that better than I do."

"Uh-huh."

"There may not be a later."

"I'll chance it. You're the one with the score to settle."

"Come again?"

"If you think I'm going to spell *this* one out for you..." Ahlene shook her head and poked my stomach with her foot.

"Come with me. Obviously, I need your emotional strength."

"Hmmph." She reached for the stereo remote control. "I hope you noticed my restraint: no audible retching sounds."

"That's what I mean. You're *so* in control. You're my idol, my one and only adult role model."

"Nice try." Ahlene stood up, tossed me the remote and sauntered into the kitchen. "Find something classical. I feel like dessert."

I went back to Hope the next day, after work. At five forty-five p.m. I sat at a table in the dining hall, sipping a cup of coffee for which I'd been charged twenty-five cents ("A nominal fee for non-residents," the kitchen attendant explained). Two packets of non-dairy creamer and three spoonfuls of sugar couldn't mask the coffee's institutional flavor. I have proof our church supports this place, or at least supplies the coffee, I thought. I'd recognize that janitor-in-a-drum strength brew anywhere.

"Hello again." I waved to Edwin P., who pushed a man in a wheelchair into the dining hall.

"Hey, it's Mrs. Kennedy's boyfriend." He wheeled his charge over to the table where I sat.

"Daniel." I offered my hand. "If you've got a minute I'd appreciate it if you'd let me ask you some questions."

"You a reporter?" He pulled a chair out from the table, turned it around and sat across from me, straddling the chairback.

"No, just nosy."

He laughed. "Sure, shoot. I'm on break. But I gotta warn you," he pointed at my coffee cup, "that stuff'll rot your insides. Drink it fast, before it eats through the Styrofoam."

"They serve the same stuff at my church." I took a sip, and grimaced. "Anyway, it says in the volunteer's manual..."

"You really gonna volunteer?"

"I'm thinking about it." I looked around the dining room. "I have a lot of questions."

"Such as?" He stood up and walked to the giant coffee urn that sat on an aluminum cart near the kitchen service window. "Lemme get some java for Methuselah." He jerked his head toward the tiny, bald, snow white-bearded man he'd wheeled to the table.

"Here's one thing I noticed." I opened the manual. Edwin placed a cup of coffee in front of the old man, who stared at it with watery, blue eyes. "Most of the residents, eighty percent, in fact, are female. Yet the 'unvisited' residents…"

"'Solos,' I call 'em," Edwin nodded. "Lonely old bastards."

"…are mostly men. I figured it out." I reached for the notepad in my pants pocket. "Only twenty percent of the residents are men, but *nine* of the twelve—that's seventy-five percent—without any visitors are men."

"Sounds about right."

"Don't you find that interesting?"

"Not especially."

"What I mean is, that seems rather skewed."

Edwin shrugged his shoulders. "When I end up in a place like this I'll have so many visitors they'll have to make reservations."

"I don't quite follow you."

Edwin reached across the table for the sugar dispenser. "Ever know anyone in a nursing home?"

"My grandmother. She died two years ago."

"You visit her?"

"Yes."

"Regularly?"

"As often as I could."

"Mm-hmm."

"I *could* have come more often…"

"It's the grand*daughters*." Edwin poured a hefty amount of sugar into the old man's coffee. "Wives, daughters, sisters, even aunts and nieces—they're the ones what visit. Their menfolk drag along, maybe on a holiday, and act like they can't wait to leave. Or they put on their high and mighty Pope face…"

"Like they're incredible martyrs for coming?"

"Made that face yourself, a few times?"

"I hope not." I laughed nervously. "So, are you—do you think those men, the 'Solos,' deserve to be lonely? That, somehow, they got it coming to them?"

"Close enough."

"Isn't that a bit harsh?"

"Sure."

"Don't you feel sorry for them?"

"Sometimes. But you can look it up," Edwin pointed at my manual, "most of them *have* families. Their kids pay the rent and don't visit. Those old dudes are reapin' what they sowed and one day it'll be their sons' turns, unless they get lucky and die first.

"Another thing, in case you're taking notes. Those churches that support us, now that a couple of 'em have women preachers we get them visiting a lot more than the others ever did." He leaned back in his chair and put his feet up on the table. "I haven't been to church in I don't know how long. I didn't know they *had* lady preachers. We saw the men preachers at Christmas, when they bring their kiddie choirs to sing carols, and then again to give last rites or whatever they do when someone dies."

He put his feet down and leaned forward, elbows on the table. "I'm no Dr. Sociology with a research grant. I was raised to call things what they are. You look around, you see things, you know?"

"Yeah, I know. Do you mind if I ask another question? I don't mean to hog all of your break time."

"I don't punch a clock. Besides, this is kinda fun. I like to talk, and they," he gestured around the room, "have nothing better to do than listen. But it's good to do some communicating with someone who's got—I'll give you the benefit of the doubt, here—a full set of furniture in the upstairs guest room."

"Thanks for the compliment, I think." I scratched my head. "I take it the visitors don't talk much to the staff?"

He nodded. "Except to ask for directions to the bathroom or to their aunt's room. But then," he smiled and traced his index finger along his jawbone, from ear to chin, "not every staff member is as gracious and articulate as myself. Take Maria." He pointed toward a scowling, young Hispanic woman who leaned against the wall behind the coffee dispenser. "She'd as soon bite your head off as speak to you, staff as well as visitors. She shows up every day and does her work but it's like she's always pissed off at something."

"Maybe she hates her job."

"Then she should quit."

"Maybe she's got nothing else to go to."

"That's what everyone thinks, right?" Edwin's eyes scanned my face. "You work in a nursing home because you can't do anything else. Or you're working your way through school or on to something else."

"Are you?"

"Not me." He smiled. "I like what I do, and the other staff, they don't bother you. Everyone has different attractions, different limitations. This is better than the head trauma ward at the hospital, I can tell you that."

"Better, how? Less depressing?"

"Less *dangerous*. Those brain damaged dudes'll toss their shit and stuff at you, and my reflexes aren't what they used to be." He ducked an imaginary projectile and we both laughed.

"Your coffee's getting cold. Trying to cut down on the caffeine, eh, Mr. C?" Edwin pushed the coffee cup closer to the old man, who still hadn't touched it. "The therapists say he's stone deaf. Eyesight too poor to lip-read and no brains to learn Braille." Edwin sighed, and turned to me. "Now, Maria, there, if she's doing this for the money, she's wrong. And stupid. There's other jobs for that. You can have a purpose here. You should have. Or you should get out.

"It's not that I'm not ambitious." He picked up the sugar dispenser and tossed it back and forth between his hands. "People don't know the meaning of that word. This job could be the most important thing in the world, 'cause you are the most important person to some of them." He gestured toward Mr. C. "Not many situations in life where a person can be...*necessary*, you know?"

He put the sugar dispenser down. "Man, you got me going. You sure you're not a reporter?"

"Positive. You sure you're not a politician? Not running for something?"

"Who knows. The future's wide open."

"Back to another question. About Maria, for example. It seems like all the residents are Caucasians, Anglos. You know; white. And from what I've seen, besides the administrators, the staff is mostly Hispanic or Black."

"The majority are minorities," Edwin hummed. "That's got a ring to it. Am I supposed to agree or disagree?"

"It's just an observation. You can't really disagree with those numbers, can you?"

He shook his head. "There's a Chinese dude in the room at the end of the north hall. Other than that, you're right."

"Any thoughts about that? About the, uh, proportions?"

"Not really." Edwin drummed his fingers on the table. "When I first came here, about three years ago, there was this guy in 112, this old southern dude. We called him 'The Colonel.' His family brought him bed sheets with the confederate flag on them."

"You're kidding."

"His wife embroidered his pillowcases with the state flag of Virginia. He's what my momma used to call a genuine, dyed in the wool, fried in the head, Dixie dude. How he ended up in Sacramento's gotta be some story."

"What happened to him?"

"Same room." He jerked his thumb over his shoulder. "He should be on your list. No visitors since his wife died, over a year ago."

"What happened to his sheets?"

"They didn't last long. Didn't clean as well as the plain ones. After five or six soilings, we tossed 'em. He never noticed."

Edwin P. stood up and pushed his chair back against the table. "Now I help him to the can and wipe his sorry redneck butt and he's grateful. He'll talk your ears off if you give him a chance, but," he put his hands on his hips and laughed, "he won't say a word to Mr. Wong, the Chinese dude. 'I don't talk to Japs,' he says."

He glanced at his wristwatch. "Mr. C.'s gotta get back for his dinner. Nice talkin' to you."

"Thanks; me too. Okay to look around at dinner time?"

"Absolutely. Most of them eat in their rooms. This might be a good time to catch one of those on your list."

With a wave of his hand, Edwin left, pushing Mr. C. in front of him. I tossed my cup into a wastebasket and looked at the first name on my list of "Solos." Jacob Nadert, age eighty-seven, room 209.

A tall metal cart blocked the hallway in front of room 209. The cart held about twenty-five meal trays, stacked in individual horizontal slots. I took a long look at the food: baked fish, yams and peas, in a variety of textures, according to, I surmised, the diner's chewing ability.

The door to room 209 was open. It was the standard nursing home room: two hospital beds, one by the door and one near the window. Across from the beds between two closet doors was the door to the bathroom. Next to each bed was a chair and a portable television set on top of a nightstand. Stitchery samplers and family pictures hung on the walls.

I knocked lightly on the doorframe. "Anybody home?" I cringed when I heard myself, and thought, what a stupid thing to say.

The bed near the window was unoccupied. An old man lay in the other bed, which was cranked up into a sitting position. A young, petite female attendant placed a dinner tray across the man's lap. She practically had to stand tip-toe to set the tray on the bed, which, being a hospital bed was taller than usual, but still… I couldn't imagine her helping someone to the bathroom, or doing anything physical. Her nametag read Angie Nguyen, Asst. Attendant.

"Hello. Is this Jacob Nadert's room?"

"Yes." The attendant smiled at me, leaned over the bed and spoke loudly into the man's right ear. "Mr. Nadert, you have a visitor."

Mr. Nadert picked up his fork and poked at his dinner.

"I said, you have a visitor."

"Who's that?" He looked up from his plate and stared at me with liquid, gold-blue eyes.

"Daniel. Daniel Spangler." I walked to the side of his bed.

"It's strawberry tonight." He picked up a plastic cup from his tray. "Have some."

"Oh, thank you." I hesitated, thinking that refusing his offer might be rude. As I raised the cup to my lips Ms. Nguyen frantically shook her head and mouthed, "No!" I faked taking a sip and put the cup back on his tray.

"That's good," I said. "Too bad I already ate dinner."

"You can go now." Jacob Nadert pushed at the food on his tray with his finger. "This is halibut."

"He likes to eat by himself," Ms. Nguyen said to me, and then loudly, to Mr. Nadert, "I'll be back for your tray." As we left the room she said, "Good thing I caught you in time."

"I didn't know what to do. I was going to sip, to be polite. Is he on a special diet?"

"No. Their medications are in their milkshakes. His has a laxative and a sedative in it."

I rolled my eyes. "Thank you *very* much. I'm not constipated, and I sleep just fine."

She blushed, quickly turning toward the stack of trays. "Why don't you come back when he's in a better mood? Like in another century." She giggled. "You know how he is."

"Actually, I don't. I've never seen him before."

"You must be the new volunteer," she said. "I thought you were lost, at first. Mr. Nadert never has visitors."

"He does, now, if he wants one."

"Now, there's a question," she said. "Remember to speak into his good ear. He has forty percent hearing in his right and none in the left. The partially deaf ones, sometimes they hear and sometimes they don't. Or they act like they don't. I think they tune out on purpose." She pushed the giant serving cart, which towered almost three feet above her, down the hallway. "Give him fifteen minutes to finish his dinner and maybe he'll talk to you."

I did. He wouldn't.

"Fine," was my reply, later that evening, when Ahlene asked about my visit to Hope. She smiled enigmatically and murmured, "That's good." I girded my loins for the questions she didn't ask.

I don't know why I didn't feel like talking about Mr. Nadert, about any of it. I don't know why I didn't tell her that I left work early the next five nights in a row, stopping off at Hope for an hour before going home, and that for four nights, while attendants served and then removed his dinner tray, I watched Jacob Nadert ignore me.

On the fifth night Ms. Nguyen suggested that I read the newspaper to Mr. Nadert. Sports, business, travel, politics, arts? She didn't know what his interests might be. His chart said he was a retired dairy farmer.

"Most of our residents are originally from the Midwest," she told me. I followed her into the hall when she returned Mr. Nadert's dinner tray to the cart. "Strong, Scandinavian farming stock. They live forever, the poor souls."

I returned to room 209 and sat in the chair next to the bed, close to Mr. Nadert's head. Looking at his leathery, freckled scalp, I imagined what color his hair must have been, when he had hair. As on the previous nights, I had a one way conversation with a geriatric mannequin.

"Angie says you were a farmer, in Wisconsin?"

There was no indication he even knew I was sitting next to him. I asked him a few more questions and got no response, so I talked. I talked about Ahlene, my sister, my parents, my job. I talked about the children I wanted to have some day, and the grandchildren they would have, and…

"He's going to die."

I startled at the sound of his loud, shaky baritone.

"Mr. Nadert?"

"He's going to die." He looked straight ahead, staring at the closet door.

"I *knew* you could hear me." I reached over to straighten his pillow, which was bunched up under his neck. "There. I bet that was uncomfortable. Can I get you anything? I could call…"

"He's going to die." His milky eyes looked right through me. "Is that you?"

"Well, yes," I stammered. "It's me, Daniel, I mean, if that's what you're asking…"

"He's going to die." Mr. Nadert's voice rose. "And I said, is that you?"

"Are you asking about me, about when *I'm* going…"

"When?" He sat straight up in his bed and jabbed a spindly, withered finger toward the closet door. "*When?*"

"I don't know." I looked around the room. "When the time comes, I suppose."

"Ha!" he snorted. "What do *they* know." Mr. Nadert raised his wavering hand toward me. "Where's my robe?"

"You want your robe?" I stood up and walked to the closet.

"Who *are* you?" he roared.

"You remember." I turned around. He was staring at the empty bed near the window. "Daniel, Daniel Spangler." I opened the closet door and yelled across the room to him. "I've visited you, the last few nights." A pair of brown leather slippers were on the closet floor, and a dozen empty wire coat hangers hung on the rod. "There's no robe here," I said.

"He said I'll be buried in my robe," he bellowed, "because it's *comfortable!*" He lay down and turned his face to the wall.

I walked back to the bed, sat on the chair and placed my hand on his shoulder. He turned his face even further to the side, and then reached out and put his hand on top of mine. Though wrinkled and knotty his hand was as soft as a newborn's.

"He told me who you are." He whimpered, and patted my hand. "We know who *you* are."

Ahlene had been right, but only partially. I went to Hope with the intention of losing faith. And I tried, I really tried.

Kiss Me I'm Irish

It was one of those days I'll never forget. I guess it started out normal enough, but it sure did end strange. Are you sure I didn't tell you this before?

We were practicing in the girl's gym. Volleyball season was officially over so we'd all gone on to our other sports: field hockey, swimming or basketball. However, the Orange Invitational Volleyball Tournament was coming up in two weeks, so those of us who'd tried out and had made the team were excused an hour early from our other sports to practice for the tournament.

So, there we were one afternoon, doing our spiking drills—yeah, right, everyone except K.C., who was doing block-jumps up against the wall as a punishment for removing her bra. She always complained that it got in her way, so whenever she felt like it she'd just take it off, right in the middle of practice. It cracked me. She'd pull her arms back up in her sleeves, do these epileptic belly-dancer contortions, then just whip it out from under her jersey and kick it over near the end line to use as a marker so she wouldn't do a foot fault on her serves.

Yeah, to continue, there we were when lo and behold, Mr. Mierda, the boys' Athletic Director, walked in. Mierda was puny, about 5'6", with a mealy, pastry-tart complexion. He looked like an albino earthworm, and in profile his nose resembled Florida.

Mr. Mierda shuffled on over to Mrs. Mouton, our coach. We kept practicing, speculating about their little chitchat. Mierda was always bitching about something the girls were doing. Either the hockey players were tearing up the football field or the girls' track team was messing up the track (where else were they supposed to run?)…somehow, in some way, we females and our petty concerns were screwing up the honor and glory of male athletic endeavors. I swear, if the junior varsity quarterback developed jock itch it was the fault of females in athletics. Of course, we always had to give in to his demands. You see, this was before girls' athletics went into organized, statewide competition like the guys' teams, and boss hogs like Mierda could get away with anything.

Anyway, in a couple of minutes Mrs. Mouton called us together near the center net. Mierda stayed over in the corner near the door. Mouton said she had bad news: the volleyball team could no longer practice in here. The freshman boys' basketball team needed our gym to practice.

I couldn't believe it! At first, we all thought it was a joke. There was dead silence for maybe thirty seconds and then the whole team started yelling. The old chickensh—uh, shucker—was still over in the corner. While the rest of the team jumped around, howling and swearing, our captain, Gina, called out, "Hey Mr. Mierda, could you please come over and explain the situation? Perhaps there's been a misunderstanding."

He ambled over and Gina started posing questions and stating facts. She was the perfect diplomat—move over, Henry K.—logically and politely explaining to him how unreasonable the whole thing was, and, not in so many words, showing him what a flaming, weasel-surfing butthole he was to do this to us.

"Mr. Mierda, have you forgotten that this is the *girls'* gym, and that it was finished just this September? Where did the freshman boys' basketball team practice last year? On the outside courts. They have done so every year before this. Why must they now practice inside? This volleyball team will be competing against other seasoned teams; it is an honor to be invited, and our team is composed of upperclasspersons, not just ninth graders. We can't practice anywhere else; the few outside courts and nets, unlike those for basketball, are not regulation tournament size. And this *is* the *girls'* gym. Why should we have to be put in a position to defend our use of it?"

It was pridefully awesome; I mean, she was *so* and *way* cool. No wonder she was the first Junior ever elected as Student Council President. Anyway, while she delivered her speech, the rest of us nodded our heads in agreement, trying to look vital and serious and worthy of terms like "seasoned teams" and "upperclasspersons." Surely, Mierda could have no choice other than to capitulate when confronted with such brilliant diplomacy.

Hell no! He just scratched the southern end of Florida, pulled his diarrhea-gold colored golf cap lower on his forehead, cleared his throat and said that he understood, but that the boys would have to have priority. That was it! Then he turned around and walked toward the door.

Understood my ass-ignation! Mrs. Mouton looked at us and shrugged her shoulders. A nice coach, but what a wuss—no help at all. She asked Gina to collect the volleyballs and help take down the nets; the rest of us were supposed to go back to hockey or swimming or whatever. But K.C. picked up a volleyball, and WHAM! A perfect, hardbody knuckleball serve—shimmied across the net just so too much; she really had something on it. I swear it hit the wall no more than two feet from Mierda's head. Well, maybe three or four feet, but you should have seen his face! Veins, all purple and red, bulged underneath his skin—his neck looked like a road map. He glared at all of us for what seemed like forever, then turned around and stomped out the door.

A few girls giggled nervously; me, I was scared. But Mrs. Mouton didn't blow up. She said nothing, just kept collecting the volleyballs and jamming them into the ball bag. And off we went, out to our other practices.

Hockey lasted longer than usual that afternoon. All of the coaches had some league organizational meeting to attend, so they left us to work out on our own. We got a nasty intra-squad scrimmage going; I guess it was about four-thirty or quarter to five when we finally came in to the locker room.

Gina and I went over to our lockers and started peeling off our smelly sweats. Basketball must have come in earlier, 'cause Erin was already out of the showers and getting dressed. I remember Gina staring with fascination as Erin put on the layers.

"Okay, Erin," Gina sighed, "fill me in. Every day I see you get dressed. It's either a bra and no underwear, or underwear and no bra. Don't you ever match; I mean, neither or both?"

Erin giggled. "Do you really want to hear why, Gina?"

Gina cringed and said, "From previous experience, probably not."

Erin was diff, but I liked her. She was the first person to offer me drugs: some chalk-white pills before a volleyball game one day when I wasn't feeling energetic. I declined, but appreciated the offer, as it was my first (one look at my Four H ankle bracelet and no one even tried. I think I was considered developmentally challenged in that regard).

Anyway, Erin kept giggling and pointed at the sucker Gina was licking.

"Left over from lunch," Gina slurped. "Want some?"

"Oh, no, it's just that suckers remind me of, of…popsicles."

I swear Erin was practically on the floor, she was laughing so hard. It cracked me. I had to ask what was so funny about popsicles. So she told me.

"Well, one night when Peter and I were—excuse me, Gina—and he was eating a popsicle, a cherry popsicle, and you'll never guess what he did with it!"

Gina started hiding under her towel, moaning, "No, Erin…"

"It was *sooo* cold!" Erin chattered her teeth for effect. "Peter also likes bananas, but they get too squishy."

By this time Gina was unsuccessfully trying to stuff herself into her locker, yelling, "Enough, Erin, *please!*" Gina then grabbed a towel and fled to the sanctity of the showers, only to return shortly after, grumbling about the swimmers who, as usual, had monopolized the entire shower section. And once they got in they'd stay in for hours…well, practically. They'd soap the front of their suits and have belly sliding races under the shower partitions, then the suits would come off and go flying in the face of any landlubber who dared to scurry by.

I guess this is when it started. "I need an accomplice; come, oh worthy woman!" Gina roared. She grabbed my arm and pulled me toward the shower stalls. We went down the towel rack line, collecting all the towels from the hooks, and then threw the entire load into the last shower stall.

We scampered back to our lockers with the outraged protests of our waterlogged sisters ringing in our ears. I had started to get dressed and suddenly got a feeling of impending doom. You can't imagine what it was like to turn around and see a convoy of six naked and leering chick-jocks trucking bathing caps full of water in your direction. My locker was open; everything got soaked. I escaped, but the swimmers captured Gina and dragged her, fully clothed, into the showers. I sneaked back; Ruth's locker was open and her civvies were inside. I grabbed them and headed for the head, where I crammed them into the first toilet.

I ran out of the bathroom—psssst!—straight into a near-toxic, ozone-depleting fog of aluminum chlorhydrate. Ruth proceeded to chase me around the locker room, shrieking, "A sprinkle a day helps keep odors away," and other odoriferous jingles. I managed to make it back to my locker and armed myself with some Lady Right Guard, and we became embroiled in a full-scale pit spray fight.

It cracked me. Within seconds, everyone—and I mean everyone—was involved. The battle quickly spread down the aisle; hey, it's not like *I* doubt the Domino Theory. Soon there were no innocent bystanders. The artillery consisted of pit spray, towels, waterlogged underwear, toilet paper…it was excellent. And no coaches to scream, "Ladies, remember we *are* LADIES," over the intercom. The only people in the coaches' office were the two teachers' assistants, who wisely locked the door and observed the skirmish through the office windows.

I don't know how long the war had been going on—maybe ten minutes—when K.C. and three other girls decided that they wanted to streak the pool area (the guys' water polo team was having practice). They put on bathing caps, swim goggles, field hockey shin guards, and nothing else. Alas, foiled! The door to the pool area was locked from the outside. A minor setback. Not to be discouraged, they began to streak the locker room. It cracked me: four chicks streaking a girls' locker room, brandishing hockey sticks and singing "I Am Woman" at the top of their lungs. K.C. was in the lead, and to this day I can't figure out how she could run so fast built the way she was and not get a couple of black eyes, or even a bloody nose.

It was at about this time—let's see, they'd done about four laps of the locker room and were on the final verse—when who should round the corner but Mr. Mierda! Sure, he usually dropped by every Tuesday after everyone else had gone home, to talk with Mrs. Gras, our athletic director—but he must have known she was at that coaches' meeting. And, besides, the doors were locked. Of course, he had the master keys, but you'd think he'd have checked to see if the coast was clear.

Maybe he just wasn't paying attention, but, whatever—he came in through the front door and walked by the hall trophy case just as K.C. and company went streaking by. And then, well, I don't know, everyone was so hyper and in, shall I say, such good spirits...

Mierda, the jerkface, just stood there. His jaw dropped down so far you could have driven a train through it, and his face was the color of Erin's pills. He stood there; he just stood there!

So on the next lap, they—the four streakers plus a few extras—half-chased, half-pushed him toward the showers and then threw him in. Yeah, they *threw* him in. And then everyone (well, practically everyone, what with Gina and Ruth cowering in the first stall) started bombing him with ammunition. We tossed towels, toilet paper, underwear and verbal abuse galore: "Shove it high and mighty, you old lech. EEEK, it's a man...*that's* a man? Take that, you sexist pigdog!"

It was kinda cool; like...*solidarity*, you know?

Anyway, that seemed to take away our fighting spirit. Hostilities ceased; everyone returned to their lockers and started dressing...and coughing. The pit spray still permeated the air, like atomic fallout. I kept glancing behind me, toward the showers. Where was the old fart? It was ten minutes—okay, maybe two or three but it seemed like a long time—before Mierda peeked from behind the shower partition and tried to sneak out. It cracked me. He had a wet bra hanging by its strap from his ear, and around his right shoe was a pair of green and white panties that had "Kiss Me I'm Irish" embroidered on the front. He shook his finger, as if he were getting ready to deliver one of his "You Girls" speeches, but then his face flashed deep scarlet and he flicked the bra strap off his ear.

The girls ignored him and kept dressing. K.C. casually took her clothes out of her locker and started talking rather loudly to no one in particular. She looked at her shoes, like she was inspecting them for dust or something, and said that it would be a shame if word got out about the shower incident. But then, she yawned, she knew none of the girls would say anything, 'cause if parents heard about an adult male employee of the high school running around in the girls' locker room there would be a scandal, not to mention lawsuits and demands to have the afore-mentioned person fired or at least castrated, and what with homework and sports and all it would be such a hassle to find the time for depositions...

Mierda must have sneaked out during K.C.'s soliloquy, 'cause when I took the sock out of my mouth (laughing would have been tacky) and turned around he was gone.

So, that's about it. I suppose I should add an epilogue. Nobody really said much about the whole thing. All the girls just dressed and went home, and the next day we—the volleyball team—got to practice in our gym. K.C. said it would be okay. We got there before the boys' basketball team and there were no hassles. We had the gym to practice in, every day, until the tournament.

We never had any more real conflicts with Mierda. He kept complaining about the girls screwing up everything for the boys, but he mumbled his protests and never made us get off the field like he used to. And whenever he had to talk with Mrs. Mouton or any of the other girls' coaches, he seemed real...*calm*. The hockey team would make a point of chasing the hockey balls or running our laps where we'd have to pass by him, and we'd all wave and say, "Yoo hoo, Mr. Mierda!" Without fail, his face would glow like a red pimento and he'd stare intently at his shoes and pick at his ear with his hand.

Leave It Up

In the month of May, the May of my fifteenth spring, my sister, Amy, took a twenty-dollar bill from our mother's purse. Amy was ten, Mom was thirty-eight or -nine, however old Daniel Cullen was he was definitely younger than Mom, and Dad's headstone was almost two.

Amy and I still visited the cemetery on a regular basis back then. On Sunday afternoons we climbed into the back seat of the Buick. Our mother hummed along with the songs on the radio (she drove with one hand on the dial and changed the station constantly) as she chauffeured us the eight miles to Hilltop View Memorial Park.

Mom went to the cemetery with us every Sunday, the first eighteen months after Dad died. She always parked in the blue-lined, "Handicapped Only" spot. Using my scornful, "You are *so* ignorant, Mother" tone of voice, I'd try to make her feel guilty by lecturing her on the rights of the disabled. No dice.

"This is the space closest to the mausoleum," she'd say.

The walkway that led to Dad's grave started in front of the mausoleum. Mom insisted we use the concrete walkway and not shortcut through the grass in the other burial areas.

"A cemetery is private property," she'd say. "There's no meter maids to ticket us for parking violations. Besides, how many wheelchairs or blind people have you ever seen at a cemetery?"

After Mom parked the car, Amy and I would fidget in the back seat while Mom looked at her reflection in the rear view mirror and methodically arranged and rearranged her hair. She'd then douse herself with a cologne that reeked of what she said were flowers ("nasturtium blossoms; those were his favorites") but smelled to me like those essence-of-citrus bathroom deodorizers.

"You know he can't smell that, Mom," I often reminded her, "even if every *living* thing from here to the freeway can."

As Amy and I walked toward the grassy knoll where our father was buried, Mom hung back. She'd stroll up the walkway, methodically and rhythmically placing one foot in front of the other, as if she were part of a processional. Dad's grave was the middle of three plots that lay between two towering eucalyptus trees on the top of the knoll. I would brush a week's accumulation of eucalyptus leaves from the headstone while Amy replaced the flowers in the headstone vase with a fresh bouquet.

Mom lagged behind, perfectly timing her arrivals. We'd smell her coming up the hill just as Amy would be finishing arranging the new flowers. Mom said she didn't like to see dead flowers on Dad's grave, though she seemed offended when a friend suggested that, if wilted blossoms upset her, she could have a plastic arrangement placed in the headstone vase and save the live bouquets for special occasions.

Amy would talk to Dad, or rather to his headstone, and also say a few words to the graves on either side of Dad's, "just to be polite."

Mom stopped going to the cemetery with us every Sunday not long after she started going out with Mr. Daniel Cullen.

"I met him through a friend at work," she told us, during one Sunday afternoon drive to the cemetery. She hadn't been out to visit Dad's grave with us for four weeks (Amy and I had been taking the bus), but she steered into the handicapped parking spot, as usual.

"He's a marketing representative," she said, "for one of the companies that…"

"What's a 'marketing representative'?" Amy asked.

"That's a nice way of saying he's a salesman," I said.

"A *nice* way, Andrea?" Mom raised her eyebrows and pursed her lips; I could see her face from the back seat by looking in the rear view mirror.

"It sounds more respectable." I turned toward Amy. "Like how Mom's not a secretary, she's an administrative assistant."

Although hardened by the power I thought my rapier-like wit gave me, a part of me cringed at the cruel words that were forming in my mind. I spoke them anyway, directing my next comment toward the front seat.

"How come we're not choking for air like we usually are by now? Did you run out of that insect repellent—oops, I mean, perfume?

"Now, let me explain something about salesmen." I resumed enlightening my sister. "Salesmen make their living convincing people to buy things they don't want and can't afford."

"Huh, Mom?" Amy asked.

"Listen to your sister," Mom said. "She knows everything."

Our mother tried, during the next few weeks, to let us know she'd be spending more time with Mr. Cullen. She never told us so directly, but instead dropped what she obviously thought were meaningful hints. I got the impression she was reading a lot about divorce and stepfamilies and second families—the "How To Introduce Your New 'Mate' To Your Kids"-type articles in women's magazines—and had decided to be subtle about her new relationship. Circumstantial evidence replaced direct confirmation, as Daniel Cullen started spending more and more time at our duplex.

I admit I made no attempt to get to know him. It seems as though he was a shadow, a benign, obsequious shadow, passing through our lives. Daniel Cullen seemed nice enough. He reminded me of cottage cheese: inoffensive, innocuous, bland and white. I told myself I had no opinion of him, or of my mother's dating him, one way or the other. She was clearly delighted by his attentions. I was deliberate with my indifference.

After they'd been seeing each other for almost two months, Mom invited Daniel over for dinner. "We'll have a 'Family Night,'" she said, when she told Amy and me that instead of going to the movies like they did every Saturday evening, she and Dan wanted to spend some time with "the girls." Dan barbecued steaks and chicken and, after dinner, attempted to teach Amy and me how to play bridge.

"Isn't it nice to have a man around the house again?" Mom said, after Dan had gone home.

I sniffed. "I don't see how whether or not he's a man makes the house any nicer."

"He leaves the toilet seat up," Amy said. She counted the piles of quarters and dimes that were stacked next to her dinner plate. Amy had won six dollars from Dan after she'd refused to even hear the rules of bridge ("That's an old ladies' game," she whined) and insisted on playing poker instead: "Seven card stud, like my Dad taught me."

"We had a deal. He has to leave the seat down, like it's supposed to be, in the 'ready position,' like *you* taught *us*."

"Well honey, he *is* a man, and he lives alone, so it's not second nature for him." Mom winked at me. "Since it's important to you, Amy, I'll mention it to him, tomorrow."

"Yeah, you talk to him." Amy pocketed her winnings and started clearing the table. "Don't worry about us," she muttered, as if to herself but loud enough for Mom to hear. "We'll take the bus and be back before dinner."

Mom bought two bouquets of flowers every Saturday when she went grocery shopping. One was for the kitchen table, the other was for Amy and me to take on the bus the next day to the cemetery.

It happened in the spring, in the May when I worried that my ten-year-old sister was starting to sound like me. I was fifteen going on forty-five. Mom was thirty-eight or -nine going on seventeen, and as the end of the school year approached I decided to stop treating her as if it, as if everything, was her fault.

But old habits are hard to break.

Weekends were their only opportunity to spend time together, to get to know each other, to have fun, Mom told us. It wouldn't be fair to Dan, to take him along to visit Dad's grave every Sunday.

"That's a lot of pressure to put on him," she said. "That would be hard for anyone to have to live up to that."

To live up to what? A dead man? To visiting a dead man? To live up to dying from a heart attack at age forty? I never asked her to explain what she meant by the live-up-to remark.

Instead, my sister and I exchanged cheap cologne effluvia for bus exhaust fumes. Amy still insisted upon the weekly pilgrimage; she had my unenthusiastic, though uncomplaining, accompaniment.

Early one afternoon, a Saturday afternoon in May, I walked into the master bedroom and saw my sister take a twenty-dollar bill from Mom's purse. Mom and Dan had gone to put gas in Dan's car and were coming back to get Amy and me for another "Family Night": this time we were going to a matinee before the two of them went out to dinner. Amy didn't see me enter the room. She jumped when I spoke.

"What's that for, Ames? It's okay, they're not back yet."

"Flowers." Amy lowered her voice and spoke rapidly. "Please don't tell. I'm going to get him some good flowers, not the plastic ones, but the pretty dried ones that are sealed in plastic. I've seen them at the crafts store where Mom buys her yarn."

"Why don't you use your paper route money?" I suggested. "Or ask Mom. She'll spring for a worthy cause."

"She doesn't care." Amy looked down at the purse that lay on Mom's bed. "She doesn't have time anymore, and…" she looked up at me, "I know you only go with me to keep me company. I know you really don't want to go anymore."

"Not as much as before." I listened to myself, amazed that I could tell her the truth so easily. Somehow, her eyes demanded it.

"Maybe not every Sunday, like at first, but I still want to. Maybe every other week, or once a month, like Mom. You can still go whenever you want to, Ames. It doesn't mean that we, that I, don't care, you know?"

"I know." She put the twenty into her pocket, dumped the contents of Mom's purse onto the bedspread and walked out of the room.

"What are you doing?" I followed her into the bathroom. She raised the toilet seat. I started to put the seat down.

"No, leave it up," she said.

"This is stupid, Ames."

"Shut up, Andy. You promised you wouldn't tell."

"I didn't promise, I merely *said*. All right, I won't tell on you. But I *will* tell you she's not gonna fall for it."

"She'll think it's a robber."

"No, she won't." I put the seat down and sat on it. Amy sat down across from me, on the edge of the bathtub. She batted at the roll of toilet paper, unrolling and re-rolling it.

"You're trying to get Dan in trouble. You know Mom knows, we all know, he's the only man ever here, the only one who'd..."

"It could be a robber," she said.

"A thief is going to break in, take her money, and then use the bathroom?"

"When you gotta go, you gotta go," she said. "Even robbers have to pee. You can't plan stuff like that."

I heard a car horn honking. "That's them." I stood up; Amy reached behind me and raised the toilet seat again.

"Let's go," I said. "Don't you think she's gonna come in to get her purse?"

"Dan's paying," Amy said.

"Did you remember that tomorrow is Memorial Day?" I locked the front door and walked with Amy to the curb, where Mom and Dan waited in the car. "She'll probably go to the cemetery."

"Maybe," Amy said.

We got into the back seat of Dan's car.

"Do you know anything about this?"

Mom stood in my bedroom doorway, holding her wallet. She turned it upside down and shook it.

I shrugged my shoulders.

"That's a rhetorical question, of course, lest you think I forget that you know everything," she said. "My only question should be whether or not you'll tell me what you know."

She sat down at the foot of my bed. I was sitting cross-legged, leaning against the headboard, with a textbook in my lap and some homework papers at my feet. I looked out the window and saw Amy sitting in the driveway, folding advertising inserts in preparation for her newspaper route.

"Andrea, please don't lie to me."

"Mother, please don't accuse me of lying when I haven't even said anything yet."

"Andy…"

"Mommie…"

"Good Lord, Andrea! Is everything I say so stupid that you must mimic it?" She lowered her voice. "It must be hard to be so smart so young and still have to live with your stupid mother."

"I get by." I flipped through the pages of my algebra book.

"I went to visit your father this afternoon. There was a twenty-dollar bill in my wallet yesterday, after grocery shopping, and now it's gone. Enough money for some laminated dried flowers, and bus fare to and from the cemetery."

She looked out the window and sighed. "She left the price tag on." I saw the corners of her mouth flutter, as if she were about to laugh or cry, I couldn't tell which.

"I suppose I should be mad," she said, in a voice just above a whisper, "but it's almost funny. She made such a big deal, when we came home after the movie and she had to go to the bathroom, about having to put the seat down *again*, and how did it get up when we'd just cleaned house *that morning* and…"

"She misses him," I said. "Dad."

"I know." She paused. "And you?"

"Sure. Of course. But I'm older."

I thought of the wise words we were taught in our Family Life class at school. I thought I should use some of them.

"It won't be long before we're gone, off to college, and you'll have to get your own life. You should find someone for yourself, while you're still not too old. *I* know that's true, Mom. It's just that Amy doesn't have to like it right away, even if she could understand, and she can't. She's a kid; I mean, she's only ten."

"I remember her age," my mother whispered.

"What I mean is, it makes no difference to me, Mom. You should be happy. And Ames—Amy, only thinks she's happy when…"

"They *are* nice flowers." Mom stood up and ran her fingers through her hair. "They'll last a long time. She knows how I hate it when they wither and die. She throws the kitchen bouquet away as soon as *one* petal starts to wilt. I haven't thrown away flowers since I can't remember when." She chuckled softly. "My little protector. My daughters," she smiled at me, "in shining armor."

Mom and Dan stopped seeing each other. There was no specific breakup that we noticed; they gradually spent less time together. When one of us—I think it was Amy but it might have been me, I can't remember—finally asked why we hadn't been seeing Daniel around, Mom said Mr. Cullen had been transferred to the southwest, and that she didn't believe in long distance relationships.

There is a certain moment for me that remains fixed in time, a moment between the cemetery and the driveway. It happened on one of those rare days when spring seems to sneak into summer, into the summer when Amy stopped going to the cemetery.

It was the spring when I was fifteen, when I thought that people had to choose between caring too much, or not at all.

Modus Operandi

The madras dragon with the dog-gold eyes is waving. And so, once again, I go to his table.

The dark-haired young man stood in the back of the restaurant. Leaning against the wall next to the kitchen, he loosened his copper-toned bow tie and smoothed the wrinkles in his matching cummerbund and pleated trousers. He contemplated the restaurant's ubiquitous brown-ness from beneath the dim glow of the wall's torchiere light fixture. If not for his white shirt, he thought, he could blend in with one of the mahogany, faux-leather booths. A complete and perfect camouflage.

"Yo, David! Table six wants you." One of the servers walked past the kitchen, snapping her fingers. David followed her to the drink station and hovered by the ice machine while she poured herself a cup of coffee. Cindee's thick, tri-colored hair was sectioned into six braids which were coiled like cinnamon rolls, three behind each ear, and welded to her auburn roots by an army of bobby pins.

She is my age, and also new. I should ask her opinion.

"I offered to get them more water or coffee, but the man wants his waiter. Waiter—that's what he said. Actually, we're servers, right? I'm not a waitress, I'm a server; I forget all the terms sometimes, not that it matters, right? This is my first week and stuff…there's *gotta* be an easier way to keep hair out of the salad bar." Cindee fussed with her bobby pins and tugged at a link of suicide blonde hair that had escaped its braid. "It's all right for me to do that? I mean, it's casual around here, right? I can help another table if I'm passing by and they need something, right? And it's not like I'll ask you to split the tip or anything?"

"Yes, that's fine. Thank you." David reached into his back pants pocket for his ticket book. "He wants his check."

"Again?" Cindee dumped three packets of artificial sweetener into her coffee and glanced at her wristwatch. "I can take my dinner break in the little girls' room, right?" Not waiting for a reply, she snapped her fingers in a goodbye salute and sauntered toward the employee's lounge.

"Problem, hon?" Angela, the evening line cook, called to David from the kitchen window. Standing on tiptoe, she leaned her muscular, freckled forearms across the stainless steel counter and surveyed the restaurant. "Every time I look you're writing on that pad. I expect ten chef's specials to come back at once."

"I only have one table." David felt momentarily soothed by Angela's chocolate pudding voice and mother's-milk eyes. He exhaled audibly and allowed his shoulders to soften.

"They want their check. I gave it again but now I have to give them another. They keep asking...I know I did not lose it."

"One more reason why we need double carbons; you oughta mention that to Larry, sometime. Order up, Jason!" Angela added a sprig of parsley to a plate of fish 'n chips, set the plate under the counter's warmer lights and hit the call bell. "A ticket's an easy thing to misplace. One time at Jimbo's Hickr'y Pit they slipped the tab under my napkin and I wiped my mouth with it. Barbecue sauce all over the total, which was fine by me."

Angela straightened her hair net and shooed David toward his customers. "Don't let 'em fuss you. Two halibuts, two Caesars, side dressing—it's the only ticket you've sent back this shift."

"Thanks, *again*." The woman at table six parted her lips and bared her shiny, bonded teeth; David assumed she was forging a smile. She picked up the check and waved it casually back and forth in front of her face. "Such a teensy bit of paper."

"Easy to lose track of, no doubt." The man sitting next to her scrutinized David's nametag. "Are you new here?"

"No," David lied. His eyes never left the check; he watched the woman inspect it in the feeble light of the table's votive candle and then drop it in front of the sugar dispenser.

"How about a warm up?" She tapped her wiry, crimson fingernails against her coffee cup.

Thirty seconds later, when David returned with a coffeepot, the man arched his eyebrows and lowered his voice. "Now, if it's not too much trouble, son, we'd like the check."

David froze momentarily, then willed himself to move.

Speak with confidence, not accusation. You are not a deer in this fool's headlights.

David poured the refill and set the coffeepot in the center of the table. He folded his arms across his chest and looked back and forth at his two customers. "What did you do with this one?"

"Excuse me?" The man clenched his massive hands together, cracking his woolly knuckles. The woman sipped her coffee and seemed oblivious to David's presence.

"This is ridiculous. We're gonna be here all night." The man wrinkled his forehead, knitting his eyebrows together into one long, furry, black caterpillar which squatted an inch below his surgically enhanced hairline. "I'd like to speak to the manager," he rumbled.

David held the man's reptilian stare, silently counting to three before he turned sharply on his heel and walked to the front of the restaurant. The manager was crouched behind the check-out counter, rearranging the breath mints and candy bars in the display case underneath the cash register.

"Mr. Dullens?" David stood stiffly in front of the counter, arms at his side, perfectly still except for his fingers, which twitched convulsively. "The man at my table wishes to speak with you. He will complain about me because he wants his check, but I have written it four times and then he asks for..."

"Whoa, slow down." Larry Dullens stood up and ran his fingers through his thinning, curly chestnut hair. "He lost his check?"

"No, he has it… I don't know. I write the check and put it on the table, then they ask for more coffee or water and I return and they ask for the check again." David anxiously scanned the restaurant. "Cindee can tell you, but she's on her dinner break. She saw me. I give it, then they ask again. Now he wants you."

Mr. Dullens locked the cash register and looked around the counter. "Where's that extra ticket pad? Here it is. Lemme talk to 'em. Smartass kids like to jerk you around sometimes."

"They are not children…"

Mr. Dullens' eyes followed David's finger, which pointed to the middle-aged couple at table six.

"That's okay, David. You wait here."

The man and woman at table six stood up and strode toward the checkout counter. Mr. Dullens hitched up his trousers, smoothed his hair again and approached the couple.

"Larry Dullens, night manager. Can I help you with something?"

"We've been waiting on our check." The man ignored Mr. Dullens' outstretched hand. "We finished some time ago. Our waiter, David Nee, n-something, what's his name tag say? I can't pronounce it."

"Nguyen."

"Yeah, I thought he looked Vietnamese."

"Ameras…he's American, actually." Mr. Dullens cleared his throat.

"Just off the boat?"

"I don't know what you mean." The manager placed his hands on his hips.

"That might explain it," the woman purred. "Perhaps they do things differently where he's from."

Mr. Dullens tugged at the elastic waistband of his trousers. "I doubt that. Here in California we bring the check to the table when the meal is finished. You two from out of state?"

The couple exchanged glances.

"We wish!" the woman snickered. "After all the troubles these last years…"

"I didn't mean to get you sidetracked." Mr. Dullens glanced impatiently at the checkout counter. "I've got a register to audit and…"

"We need our bill." The man feigned checking his watch. "Perhaps there's a communication problem. He seemed real busy."

"We're not that busy. He'll have it right away."

"Larry!"

Mr. Dullens turned toward the sound of Angela's voice. "Excuse me one moment," he said to the couple. Angela signaled through the kitchen window for him to meet her at the drink station. She came out from behind the kitchen counter, wiping her hands on her apron.

"Don't you listen to those poker-pullers. David brought their check three times already. He told me, so I watched 'em the last time. He gave it to the lady, and when he went to get more coffee she slipped it in her purse, real casual. Then she and her hairy-ape husband or whatever-the-hell he is cackled at each other."

A server placed a ticket on the kitchen counter and slapped the order bell. "Hold your horses," Angela hollered. She jabbed her finger at Larry's sternum. "You watch those two. She's probably got a purse full of checks," Angela said, hurrying back to the kitchen, "and I'd frisk that jerk in the cheap plaid suit if I were you."

The couple strolled to the front of the restaurant, the woman holding on to the man's elbow. Mr. Dullens walked briskly up a side aisle and reached the checkout counter a few steps ahead of them. David stood behind the cash register, talking to himself as he scribbled on a piece of paper. "Two Caesars, dressing on the side; two halibut specials, one coffee, one decaf."

The man slapped a twenty-dollar bill on the counter. "This should cover it. We never did see the total." He and woman headed for the door.

"Why don't you look in her purse?" Mr. Dullens stepped in front of the couple.

"I *beg* your pardon?" Clutching her purse to her bosom, the woman gaped at the manager in wide-eyed, comic innocence.

"Are they all in there? Or maybe," Mr. Dullens looked from the woman to the man, "you put the others in your pocket?"

David held his breath. The woman looked at her escort and rolled her eyes, and couple headed for the door.

"Someone saw you." Mr. Dullens stepped back and to the side, blocking their way to the door. "Maybe you owe the boy an apology."

David stepped out from behind the cash register and stood at his manager's left side.

You are not a child. You are not in the wrong. Look at her; do not look away. Look at him and do not look down.

"You can't keep us here." The woman's tone was crisp and frosty; David expected to see a mist-puff arise from her mouth, as when one speaks outside on a chilly morning.

But it is always warm, here, even in the winter.

"I'm not trying to." Mr. Dullens sidled to his right, just enough to let them pass. "I'd simply like to know why you did it."

The man buttoned his sports jacket, grasped the woman's elbow and steered her toward the door. "For the same reason my dog licks his balls," he said, winking at the manager.

The couple walked out the door. Larry Dullens shook his head, the incensed embers fading from his eyes. He stifled a conspiratorial grin, placed his hand on David's shoulder and studied the young man's quizzical face.

"What say I help you clear that table, huh, David?"

David followed Mr. Dullens back to table six, listening intently as his boss muttered to himself.

"Because he can," the manager chuckled. "Because he can."

Where Things Are

This morning I found a quotation by James Thurber, written in red ink on a piece of white notepad paper, on top of my dresser. Underneath the citation my wife had written, in her distinctive, left-leaning handwriting, "Daniel—you may find this useful."

"What's that supposed to mean?" I asked her. Ahlene was brushing her teeth; I leaned against the bathroom doorway.

"Figure it out," she said, or rather gurgled, and she spit out a mouthful of foam. "I may not always be around to explain things." She rinsed her toothbrush, wiped her mouth with a towel and patted my butt as she walked past me to the bedroom.

"I don't know about this hidden meaning stuff," Anne mused. Forever the obeisant younger brother, I had telephoned her as soon as I got to work to request her interpretation of Ahlene's note. "You're assuming too much. Thurber's your favorite author. She probably thought you'd find it interesting. Period."

Anne says I need to "get off this man-woman thing."

I meet Anne at one p.m. for lunch, every Thursday, outside her office at the State Capitol Building. It was too windy this afternoon for our usual spot on the service entrance stairway so we ate in the basement, next to the mailroom.

We had the room to ourselves. I sat on a stack of newspapers. Anne sat across from me, on top of an old rolltop desk. She dangled her legs over the side of the desk and swung her feet up and down, like a schoolgirl sitting on a fence, while she ate her yogurt. It felt strange to be there. I hadn't been back to visit since I quit that job, almost seven years ago.

"It's weird, to be down here...again. Everyone out for pizza?"

"As usual," she said. "Al Cramer still asks about you."

She couldn't keep that Older Sister tone out of her voice.

"You're making me feel guilty."

"You want guilt?" Anne said. "Al still reminds me, every so often, about how angry he was when I pulled rank and got you hired. He was determined not to like the wet-nosed college boy who turned out to be the 'best journal sorter this mail room ever saw.' The one who left for greener pastures and never visits his old boss."

"Thanks. I feel better now."

"'How's the Map Man?' he says, when I come down to do my express mail." Anne gestured with her spoon, dropping little blobs of yogurt on the desk. "I told him your National Auto Association nickname; he got a kick out of it. They still call you that?"

I nodded.

"He's due to retire soon. Twenty-six years, the last eleven as mailroom supervisor. He asks me if you own the company yet."

I shook my head and took a bite of my tuna salad sandwich. I tried to say, "Jeeze, that old geezer," but with my mouth full it sounded like, "Jeeshleesolx."

Too much mayonnaise. I reminded myself to ask Ahlene, again, what proportions she uses, and to write them down. Two or three tablespoons per can?

"Seriously. Every time he gets his N.A.A. newsletter he checks the letterhead for your name—thinks you're moving up in the ranks or something." She took an apple from her lunch bag. "I don't know how he got the impression you had any career aspirations."

"Twenty-six years of inhaling newspaper ink fumes, I suppose."

"I didn't even try to explain your pre-incompetency theory to him. I *did* tell him you'd turned down several promotions to remain at the map desk."

"That's '*Pre-level* of incompetency.' And it isn't my theory, it's my addendum to The Peter Principle," I said. "I'm the rare genius who realizes he's reached his level of competency and refuses to be promoted to incompetency."

"I don't think I've reached that level, yet," Anne said. "One more promotion ought to do it. Accounting's not so bad, but managing other government bean counters is not my idea of meaningful public servanthood."

"You can't say I didn't warn you," I said.

"I will never say that. But you got me off track, as usual. You wanted to continue our phone conversation."

"During which you made a loaded remark about 'this man-woman thing,' when all I wanted was your opinion on Ahlene's note."

"Did you like it? Want a bite?" She held her fast-browning, half-eaten apple toward me.

"No, thanks. Did I like what?"

"That quote she left for you. Thurber, wasn't it?"

"Yes: 'I hate women because they always know where things are.' I have to figure out the significance."

"Do you *like* it or don't you?" Anne swung her feet against the side of the desk. "Is this for those counseling sessions? Are you *supposed* to look for hidden meanings in everyday conversations?"

"Not that I know of. Unless Ahlene and Libby are in cahoots. Which wouldn't surprise me."

"I can't get used to that," Anne said. "Your pastor lets you call her 'Libby.'"

"It's her name. Nickname, actually, for Elizabeth."

"I know that. But not even, *Pastor* Libby?"

I shrugged my shoulders. "Not necessary. To her, at least."

"What did you mean about she and Ahlene cahooting?"

"Maybe it was an assignment the two of them cooked up: leave something provocative and see how I react."

"She gives you assignments?"

"Not exactly." I gave up on the sandwich and looked in my lunch bag for the banana I forgot to pack. "We're supposed to give them to ourselves. We have these mini-cassette recorders…I don't know how much of this I'm supposed to talk about."

"It's no secret, right?"

"No, not that we're participating in the counseling sessions, though I get the impression that the *process* is. I don't know, exactly. I'm sure Libby would say, 'Use your judgment,' if I asked her about it. As long as you aren't another theology grad student trying to develop a new counseling method she probably wouldn't care what I told you."

"Here." Anne took another apple from her lunch bag. "I always bring two pieces of fruit. Keeps me away from the vending machines. So, have you and Ahlene resolved any major issues?"

"We don't have any major issues. None that need resolving, anyway." I bit into the apple. It was mushy.

"Yet."

"Huh?"

Anne tossed her apple core and the empty yogurt container into a wastebasket. "You mean, 'yet.'"

"Don't you think I'd tell you if we did?"

"Would you? Do you?"

"Yes; no."

"There are, probably, some underlying reasons you both agreed to do this counseling thing," she said.

"Now look who's going for hidden meanings. Have you and Ahlene been talking?"

"Don't get defensive," she said. "The party line is that you want to help your pastor with her thesis project, that it sounded like a fun thing to do…"

"There are five or six other couples in the congregation— that I know about, so there might even be more—doing the same thing."

"…but deep down you both have things that are bothering you." Anne dismissed my explanation with a wave of her hand. "Of course, neither one wants to bring up something that might seem, on the surface, trivial…I'm rambling, aren't I?"

"Yes. But, hey, thanks for rambling—oops!—I mean sharing."

"I do not consider that tone of voice to be thankful." Anne glanced at her wristwatch. "I've still got twenty minutes," she said, before I could ask her what time it was. "So, do you think it's trivial that Ahlene wants to start using her maiden name?"

"*Maiden* name?" I shook the mushy apple at her.

"Excuse me." She rolled her eyes heavenward. "*Birth* name."

"Thank you. But it's not *her* birth name. 'Paloma,' is her mother's original, or pre-marital, birth name. Surname. Whatever."

"That's as back to the source as you can go," Anne said.

"I don't think it's trivial. It's obviously important to Ahlene, for some reason."

Anne raised her left eyebrow, perhaps involuntarily.

"Now, don't jump on that," I said. "I know that I probably can't fully understand why it's important…"

"Who said, 'can't'?"

"…*why* it's important to her, and neither does she, right now. It's not definite. She's just considering it."

"Anything else she's considering?" Anne cradled her arms in front of her chest. "Or should I say, *you're* considering?" She smirked, and rocked her arms from side to side.

"God, you're nosy."

"Hey, who phoned whom?" Anne jumped down from the desk and slapped at the back of her skirt. "Dusty old thing. Okay, Dear Abby, I'll MYOB on that subject. But you wouldn't be offended if she changed her name now, after four years. Wouldn't care what people would think?"

"No. I wouldn't enjoy all the paperwork."

Anne shook her head. "Laws vary. You might not have to do that, in California. You'd be supportive, then?"

"Of course. Look it up in the dictionary: 'supportive, adjective. Giving support and assistance, as in, "He is a supportive husband." See Figure One.'"

"And your picture is 'Figure One'?"

"In color."

"I should have guessed." Anne smiled, and patted my knee. "What's in a name, after all?"

Ahlene Nada, and Daniel Robert. When it comes to first and middle names, she's the exotic, quasi-ethnic, and I'm white bread, hold the mayo. But we're both, at present, Spanglers. Her marital surname betrays her ASP ("WASP is redundant," she says) association.

Ahlene vehemently decries the fact that, as she sees it, ninety percent of the males on this planet answer to variations of eight names: Dave, Bill, John, Mike, Bob, Carlos, Mohammed or Chang.

"My Star-Spangled Daniel," she calls me. She gives people nicknames; she gives *things* nicknames. She insists I skip my morning run before church—Sunday mornings are "Snuggle Sundays."

I can live with that.

I can, and will, live with a lot.

This Daniel entered the lioness's den of his own accord.

Stop.

Start. Testing, testing. It's later, nine-thirty-ish, still Thursday. Reminder: purchase more micro-cassettes, and check the voice activation switch on this thing.

I met my wife at Sacramento University, at an orientation to the teaching credential program. Ahlene and her best friend, LaDonna, arrived late, as did I—five minutes after the presentation had begun. There were no empty chairs left so we three stood in the back of the auditorium. The professor who gave the presentation had some sort of speech impediment. He flattened and drew out his vowels, especially his *O*s; he pronounced the word "good," which he used frequently, as "guuuuud." LaDonna, Ahlene and I exchanged glances whenever he said something odd.

"That was so guuuud," Ahlene drawled, during the polite applause that greeted the end of the presentation.

"I bet this program turns out the guuuudest teachers in the state," LaDonna added.

"I usually know a guuuud thing when I see it," I said, "but I'm not so sure about this."

LaDonna put her hands on her hips and turned to face me. "If you really know a guuuud thing when you see it, why don't you walk on over to the coffee shop with us? Forget their degree program; if it's a guuuud school it'll have a guuuud coffee shop."

"Not that we'd know a guuuud cup of coffee if we fell face first into a vat of French roast." Ahlene nodded her head toward LaDonna. "We attended a Lutheran college."

We exchanged introductions on the way to the campus coffee shop. "LaDonna is Spanish for 'The Donna,'" Ahlene told me, "but her guuuud friends call her 'L.D.'"

L.D., Ahlene and I went for coffee. L.D. got my phone number, under the pretense of sharing information about the credential program. L.D. joined the program; Ahlene and I did not. Ahlene and I went out for coffee, again, the next night. L.D. had given my phone number to Ahlene, and insisted she call me...

"...'or I'll do it myself, woman.'" Ahlene imitated LaDonna's voice, swinging her head from side to side, flicking imaginary beaded braids across her face.

"She does that when she's trying to emphasize a point." Ahlene looked at me over the rim of her cup as she sipped her decaf. "It's a form of punctuation. When she's really serious about something she almost gives herself a black eye."

"So then she'd have three black eyes?" I cringed immediately after saying that, thinking Ahlene would take my feeble joke as a racist remark.

I was relieved, or reprieved, by her gentle sneer. "That's *African-American* eyes to you."

"L.D. is quite intuitive about certain things," Ahlene said, two hours later, when glasses of red wine had replaced our coffee cups. "She could tell you were…how'd she put it? 'A feminist man who'd never call himself that, and without the dreaded double B: beard and Birkenstocks.' A red rose in a mud garden."

She told me this when I asked her, after my first glass of wine, why she had telephoned me. I then asked if she agreed with LaDonna's assessment.

"Not entirely," she said. "Not yet."

"Why didn't LaDon—L.D. call me? Why pass this mud rose to you? Does she think I'm more your type, or is it because I'm white?"

Ahlene shook her head. "I don't think that matters to her, as long as you're not Indian, as in India, not Native American. It's a long but interesting story," she said, in response to my raised eyebrows. "Details, someday. She recently returned from India…she'd been doing work similar to the Peace Corps, only church-sponsored. She helped organize small business co-ops and study groups for village women, and her experiences left her…under-enthused, shall we say, about men."

"Indian men?"

"Definitely. But I think she's burnt out on all Y-chromosome holders, for now." Ahlene leaned back in her chair and folded her arms across her chest. "It's the common, post-feminist intellectual crisis: a guuuud man is hard to find."

I could listen to that laugh for the rest of my life, I remember thinking. It must be the wine. I think I'll have another glass.

"And you?" I asked. "Any problems with Y-chromosomes?"

"Pass." She waved her hands in front of her face. "I don't know about all this honesty on a first date."

"I hate that word."

"Which one? Honesty or date?"

"First." I leaned across the table toward her, thinking, I am flirting outrageously—like a debutante, for God's sake. Why not flutter my damn eyelashes, dahling, and get it over with?

"Birkenstocks I can do without, but I've nothing against beards," she said. "On some men, I prefer them."

I could start growing one tomorrow, I thought.

She tapped her finger against the stem of her wineglass. "But don't stop shaving your face on my account."

We were married one year later, the week after LaDonna got her teaching credential.

"You aren't just gaining a wife," L.D. said, as she gave me a last minute beard trim before the ceremony, "*I'm* losing a room-mate. I'll be expecting some demonstrable appreciation for my sacrifice."

Stop.

No; start again. Libby, I can't remember: is this the tape I'm supposed to transcribe for myself or for you or for all of us?

I'm beginning to think this is not such a good idea. Maybe I'll just drop this tape off at the next session. Ahlene can still come to the individual sessions, if she likes. I'm sure she finds them entertaining if not useful.

My dropping out is not a criticism of you or of your sessions. On the contrary, it's an affirmation. I got it, already. And I'll prove it to you. Here's my summary, my guess as to what's probably on Ahlene's tapes. You owe me a bottle of your favorite wine if I'm right. Are we on?

One: As far as she's concerned, I can stay at the map desk as long as I like, as long as I am content. Two: She wants children, someday, if she—and I bet these are her exact words—"can guar-antee they won't be accessories."

She has a way of turning a phrase, as you've probably no-ticed.

Moving along. As for my great issues, Ahlene can call her-self Lucy Ricardo, or anything she likes, as long as it fits on our mailbox.

Stop.

Ahlene had flexible working hours during the first year of our marriage. She preferred to go to the office early and leave early to avoid the rush hour traffic.

I got home at about five-thirty on the first day we both went back to work after returning from our honeymoon. Ahlene, who'd been home for about two hours, was in the living room, slouched in front of the sofa, reading a book.

"What're we having for dinner?"

I actually said that. We kissed hello, I changed shoes in the bedroom, walked back into the living room and then I said that. Like the title of a bad horror movie, it came from within.

"How should I know?" she mumbled.

I waited for her to realize what I'd said. She obviously hadn't really *heard* me. She had a new book. Ahlene gets lost in books.

I hung my jacket in the hall closet and strode into the kitchen. I stood in front of the refrigerator.

"I think I'll make a curry," I said, loudly.

"Mmm hmmm?" I heard from the living room.

"Where did we put the large cast iron skillet?" I yelled again.

No reply. It was in the first place I looked: in the cabinet below the stove.

"Turmeric?" I queried the living room. "Do we have any turmeric, and cayenne?"

"What am I, the spice-monitor?"

Ahlene feigns irritation when I ask where something is. She says, "If you were the powdered ginger, where would you hide?" or "It's probably where you left it the last time," or, finally, "How should *I* know?", belying the fact that she does, of course, know.

She knows where everything is, at any time. Sometimes I can catch her off guard—in the early morning when she's not quite awake, or in the late evening when she's not quite asleep, or when she's into a new book—and she'll tell me.

It's in the top cupboard, left side. It's in the carport storage locker, by the rowing machine. It's in your pocket, dummy.

All other times it's "How should *I* know?"

She never asks *why* she should know.

I don't know why she should; I don't know why I don't. I only know that she does.

Stop.

Clinic

The patient grimaced when the lancet pierced her finger.

"It's okay," Elaine said. "Everybody hates this part." Deftly kneading the patient's finger as if milking a cow, Elaine filled a small, thin glass tube with blood. "You can finish reading your post-surgical instructions while I run the test. I'll be back in five minutes."

"Whoa, don't start the centrifuge yet! Incoming!" Another medical assistant scurried into the lab. "'Lainey, you're here? What gives?"

"Good morning yourself, Amy." Elaine removed her gloves and washed her hands. "It's you, me, Chris and Carmen today. Sue's on vacation. I'm filling in."

"A vacation, that's what *I'd* like," Amy said. "Especially after my first intake. Didn't ask a single question; chewed gum the whole time. Teenagers drive me nuts."

"I feel it in my bones." The receptionist waved the schedule sheet at Elaine. "It's gonna be one of those days when everyone waltzes in twenty minutes late. If you're looking for the tea bags, they're by the typewriter."

Elaine made herself a cup of tea and returned to the lab. Chris dropped her patient's chart into the "Intake Complete" file holder and loudly announced, "Dibs on the next one."

"Don't be such a chart hog, Chris!" Elaine tried to sound exasperated, but as she looked down the hall at Chris, who leaned against the wall across from the reception office, the mock accusation stumbled in her throat.

A young woman checked in at the reception desk and then sat on the couch in the waiting room. A man sat down beside her. Elaine hovered by the reception office door, and reached for the new chart the moment the receptionist placed it in the "Intake" file holder.

"You thief, that's *mine!*" Chris snatched the chart from Elaine. "Dr. Lee's here; you're up."

Elaine stood by the lab sink, humming softly to herself. She donned gloves and dumped the contents of a used surgical pack into a wash basin.

"Yo, Elaine." Chris entered the lab. "What happened in there? We almost sent in a search party."

"The patient had a…*complicated* medical history, shall we say." Elaine rolled her eyes. "Minor childhood operations were recounted in mind-numbing detail. Did I miss anything while reliving Great Moments in Surgical History?"

"The usual dog and pony show," Chris said. "Amy's first patient had her dates wrong and…"

"I'll make a deal with you." Elaine feigned nonchalance. "Let me go in with your second. The next two scheduled to arrive speak Spanish, so I'd have to wait for you or Carmen to do the intakes."

"Bueno by me. She's ready to go, room four."

"Anything I should know?"

"Nothing out of the ordinary. Her boyfriend came with her, but he's the squeamish type…"

"Retches if he cuts himself while shaving?"

"No doubt," Chris snickered. "I advised he wait out front. I promised to speak with him, afterward, so if you could…"

"No problem."

Elaine stood outside the exam room and scanned the chart.

Melanie Anderson. Twenty-two, 5'1", 100 pounds...great. Some jive, sitcom "Father Knows Best" munchkin. No previous pregnancies; previous contraception: condoms.

Elaine rapped on the door and entered the room. The patient sat at the edge of the exam table, tugging at the neck of her short, pale, salmon-colored exam gown. She squeezed her legs together, alternately extending and contracting her feet, as if performing some sort of yoga warm-up pose, Elaine thought.

"Hello, Melanie. My name is Elaine. I'll be with you during the procedure."

"Oh, okay." The patient nodded. "Um, Chris...?"

"Chris's bilingual skills were needed up front," Elaine explained. "I'll quickly review your medical history. Dr. Lee will join us in a minute."

"Is he the Japanese guy I saw in the hall?"

"Chinese-American; yes."

Chinese, Japanese—they all look alike, eh, round eyes?

"Did Chris explain the procedure?"

"Uh-huh." Melanie crossed her legs, grabbed the sides of the exam table and looked at the floor. "I'm a little nervous."

"Quite normal." Elaine opened Melanie's chart. "You chose the pre-op Valium; that'll help the nerves. Prior pelvic exams uneventful, no history of STDs; contraceptive plans undecided..."

Elaine paused, anticipating the sound of crinkling paper. Melanie squirmed on the table and attempted to pull the gown down to her knees. Elaine reached for the paper lap drape that remained folded at the top of the exam table. "No, thanks;" Melanie said, "this is long enough. Why can't they cover the table with something that doesn't stick to your butt?" she implored.

Elaine tapped her pen against the chart. "Perhaps Chris didn't have time to complete your medical history form. Was your previous pregnancy a normal, vaginal delivery?"

"What?" Melanie paled. "I—I never...this is the first, ever."

"I noticed the stretch marks on your hips and assumed..."

"Oh," Melanie blushed, *"those."* She reached for the lap drape. "I had a junior high growth spurt. Two inches in a year."

Right! From midget to munchkin.

Dr. Lee entered the room without knocking. He spoke briefly with Melanie while Elaine readied supplies.

"Ready?" Dr. Lee handed the chart to Elaine. "Put your feet in these holders, Melanie. Lie back and scoot your bottom toward me; that's fine."

Melanie folded her arms across her stomach and fluttered her fingers. "I'd, uh, like some distraction now."

Elaine raised her hand. "That's my job. I'll also describe what Dr. Lee…"

"Can we talk about something else?"

Dr. Lee, humming softly, disappeared behind the paper drape covering Melanie's legs.

"He'll do a regular pelvic exam now, then take a pap smear and a chlamydia culture. Did Chris explain 'chlamydia?'"

Melanie lifted her wavering arm to point at a travel poster that was affixed to the ceiling. "'Visit the majestic fjords of Norway.' That's so pretty."

"Chlamydia is a prevalent, sexually transmitted disease. You'll be notified if the results are positive. As for future contraception…"

"I'm thinking of becoming a nun. Are there convents in Norway?"

A convent. Twit! That's what they all say.

"The Sisters of Saint Ole Olafsen," Elaine smirked. "Cold, reeks of herring—not the most spiritually uplifting of places. As per your instruction packet, you must refrain from intercourse until after your two-week checkup, so you've time to consider your options. I'm sure you don't want to be back here again."

"You can say that again…oooh—*yeeouch!*"

"He's injecting the local anesthetic into the cervix. About birth control: Norplant, the 'Pill' or the Depo-Provera injections are the most effective methods, and convenient if you are frequently active, but they don't protect against STDs. You should insist your partners wear condoms."

"Partner," Melanie whispered. "Singular."

Elaine reached for a box of Kleenex. A tear rolled down Melanie's temple and into her ear. "These days it can be deadly to assume you're in a *mutually* monogamous relationship," Elaine said, dabbing a tissue against Melanie's cheek.

"It hurts," Melanie whimpered, touching her abdomen.

"Cervical dilations," Elaine said.

"Number eight, please," Dr. Lee requested. Elaine handed him a thin, plastic tube. "Melanie, you'll hear the machine; we'll be done in a minute, okay?" Dr. Lee tapped her toe with his gloved finger. "You may continue to feel some cramping."

"I'm fine," Melanie winced, her lower lip quivering.

"Finished." Dr. Lee removed his gloves and patted Melanie's knee. "Everything went well. I'll see you in recovery."

"Thank you," Melanie mumbled. Dr. Lee nodded and left the room.

"Any dizziness, nausea, cramps?" Elaine reached under Melanie's back. "Buns up!"

"Huh?"

"Lift your bottom please; I've got to hook your pad on in front. Remain prone while I take your pulse and blood pressure readings. Your uterus is contracting, returning to its normal, non-pregnant size. The cramps will subside shortly. You can sit up now."

"That was quick." Melanie slowly pushed herself up on her elbows. "No cramps, but I'm a little dizzy."

"When you're ready I'll walk you to recovery."

Melanie's chin trembled. Elaine reached for the tissue box, but Melanie shook her head. "I'm okay." She wiped her eyes with her hand. "Relieved, actually. But maybe I shouldn't be."

"Many women think they're supposed to feel bad and then they don't, so they feel guilty because they *don't* feel guilty." Elaine patted Melanie's hand. "But *I* know it's not your fault."

Fascinating, how color flees the face so suddenly...it's like watching a silent sink drain.

"I don't feel so good."

"Lie back and raise your knees." Elaine reached for an emesis basin.

"My kind of day: two reschedules and a no-show." Carmen walked with Elaine from the recovery room to the reception area. "I promised myself not to work clinics when I was made Manager." She ran her fingers through her salt-and-pepper hair, glanced at her wristwatch and made a sour face. "What'd you want to ask me?"

"I need more hours." Elaine placed her hand over her heart in mock obeisance. "Por favor, my Blessed Lady."

Carmen put her hands on her hips. "I've tried to get you to work more hours for over a year!"

"You know how it is." Elaine smiled. "Things change."

"Such as?"

"I'm devoting my life to public service."

Carmen furrowed her brow, and lasered her infamous, don't-mess-with-me-girl stare at Elaine.

Elaine avoided Carmen's gaze. "I'd rather not go into it; I don't know all the details myself, and you…"

"Got another damned meeting." Carmen tapped her watch and did an about-face. She marched down the hallway, Elaine at her heels, toward the clinic's rear exit door. "Monday, ten-thirty. We'll work out a schedule. Remember, you're no good to me if you burn out. I'll try to get you some Family Planning hours, too, if you need full-time."

"I appreciate it, ma'am." Elaine bowed deeply. She held the door open for Carmen, and called out after her as she strode through the parking lot. "Don't you worry about me burning out. There's a lot of good work to be done."

"You're with Ms. Anderson?"

Elaine stood beside the waiting area couch. Scott Stoller, her husband, looked up from the magazine he'd been reading.

"Oh, Jesus."

Elaine cleared her throat. "Although patients often consider me to be God-like, I prefer to be addressed as 'Ms. Stoller.' Ms. Anderson requested that you be notified…"

"'Laine, I, I had no idea…I thought you'd cut most of your hours, and you *never* work on Thursdays."

"She'll be in recovery…"

"'Lainey, I'm… I thought you weren't… What happened?"

"…for approximately twenty…"

"You're not supposed to *be* here!"

"She'll be tired today, but can resume most normal activities tomorrow. No intercourse until after her post-op checkup."

"This was Melanie's idea. She insisted; she'd heard good things about the clinic. You never work on Thursdays. 'Laine, if I'd had *any* idea I'd have suggested…"

"The important thing is to make sure this doesn't happen again."

"Shhh," Scott whispered. "*Please*. And please don't talk to me like, like I'm one of *them*." He gestured toward the other inhabiters of the waiting room's furniture.

"She remains undecided about future contraception. Whatever method she chooses, I advise using condoms as a backup. In order to be effective they must be used properly." Elaine tore off a piece of paper from the chart and held it out.

"Why are you here?" Scott took the paper, and softly closed his hand around her fingers. Elaine gently but firmly pulled her hand from his grasp. Hugging the chart to her chest, she stared past him, through him, at a faded movie poster that hung on the wall behind the couch.

"You're not supposed to be here." Scott shifted his weight from foot to foot, like a toddler with a full bladder. "We'll talk about it; Saturday, at the arbitrator's, before the meeting, okay?"

Elaine flicked her fingernails at the paper she had given Scott. "Here are the names of two companies that make prophylactics in assorted sizes." She raised her voice, turned on her heel and marched toward the reception desk. "Perhaps a smaller one would fit better. Or stick with your usual brand, Mr. Stoller. Wear two, in case one breaks or falls off."

Googie

"Don't even *think* about answering that."

Dorie flung a warning scowl at her husband and grabbed a box of cereal from the pantry. Tim sat at the kitchen table. He fidgeted in his chair and stared at the ringing telephone.

"I'm expecting a call from one of my subcontractors."

"It won't be him. It'll be reporters, or worse." Dorie slapped the kitchen counter. "Let the machine get it."

The telephone answering machine clicked on. Tim winced at the sound of Dorie's voice, stalwart and metallic, on the outgoing message.

"You've reached 681-8124. If you're the press or anyone wanting information about Ananda or The Chosen we have no comment, now or ever. Please respect our privacy in this matter. All others may leave a message after the tone."

The caller hung up. Dorie poured herself a bowl of cornflakes and muttered, "Surprise, surprise."

"Your decaf's waiting." Tim tapped the rim of the coffee cup he'd filled for her. "Maybe you should speak with one of 'em. That woman from the *Register-Guard* sounded aboveboard, to me."

"What woman?" Dorie opened the utensil drawer and reached for a paring knife.

"One of the first reporters to call, last week. Before you cut off my phone privileges." Tim took a ripe banana from the fruit basket and set it next to Dorie's coffee cup. "If you give an exclusive interview to one, maybe the others will go away."

"Or it might encourage them."

"Well, I refuse to feel like a prisoner in my own house and I'm going to answer the phone if I feel like it." Feigning nonchalance, Tim picked up a section of the morning newspaper and sipped his coffee. "Besides, what if it's Danielle? She probably only gets one call at a time."

Dorie sat down at the table, across from her husband. She leaned over her coffee cup and inhaled deeply, savoring the bitter aroma. "I haven't changed my mind."

"What if it's the school calling?"

"Nina's at the sitter's. I took her while you showered. She can skip the compassionate support of her peers for one day."

Tim sighed. "Were they teasing her again?"

"Teasing?" Dorie peeled the banana and set it next to her cereal bowl. "'Nina's aunt's a cult-killer, Nina's aunt's a cult-killer,'" she sang in a nasal whine. Wielding the paring knife like a cleaver, she rapidly and methodically sliced the banana into precise, half-inch rounds. One by one she plunked the slices on top of her cereal. "I think that goes beyond teasing, for an eight-year-old. Words like 'torture' spring to mind."

"Nina's aunt didn't kill anyone and those kids know it. Where are the teachers when these things happen?" Tim pushed his chair away from the table and stood up. "We'll call the parents and…"

"We'll do nothing of the kind! It could backfire." Dorie gestured with the knife, flinging bits of banana onto the sports section of the newspaper. "Besides, Nina wouldn't…we might embarrass her. We should lay low until this thing blows over."

"I suppose so." Tim slowly sat down. "I still can't believe it, sometimes. Danielle, our Dannie, is in jail."

"*Ananda*. That's what she wants to be, now."

"She called herself Danielle when she phoned the first time."

"The first time?" Dorie tapped her spoon against her bowl.

Tim reached across the table and placed his hand on top of Dorie's. They both have that look, he thought. Despite the shrill morning light; despite Dorie's new face—a steadfast mask of disdainful indifference.

Tim shook his head. "It's the first thing I think of, every morning when I wake up: Dannie is in jail."

"That's what happens to gun runners." Dorie jerked her hand out from under his. "Let one of her cult siblings post her bail."

"I don't think there's any of 'em left on the outside. It says most have been apprehended." Tim picked up a section of the newspaper. "Besides the guy who actually fired the shots they got the others for conspiracy, weapons violations, assaulting federal marshals, some resisting arrest charges tacked on... The bails are being set pretty high."

"I've stopped reading the newspaper."

Dorie's translucent skin often appeared pale blue and bloodless in contrast to her coal black eyes and hair. She looks leaden and sallow this morning, Tim thought. If I didn't know better I'd think it was a reflection of the bananas from her cereal. Most likely it's overcompensation; she put on more makeup than usual and she's not very good at it. She denies insomnia but I know she's up at night. I wonder why she lies to me about such a thing. I wonder what she does when she doesn't sleep. I wonder what she'll do when she finds out what I've done.

"I have to read the papers; I have to know *something*." Tim raised his eyebrows in appeal. "She's still our Dannie."

"No, she's not. That came straight from her, remember? *A-nan-da*." Dorie slowly, distastefully elongated each syllable, as if the name was a gelatinous obscenity stuck to her tongue. "That supposedly means 'Daughter of Truth' in Coptic Hebrew, an ancient tongue lost to modern linguists. But, hey, there is *one* person living today who just happens to be able to translate it. And that person is Jameha, what a coincidence!"

"How fortunate for us all," Tim chimed in.

"*Ananda*." Dorie mimed spitting into her coffee cup. "Coptic Hebrew, my ass! It's crypto-shit for 'Sell me the Brooklyn Bridge.'"

"They still haven't found him; that Jameha, what's-his-name."

"Yah-MAY-ha. The *J* is like a *Y*."

"Apparently he's out there, somewhere."

"Of course." Dorie sneered. "His lackeys took the fall for him. I'm sure they threw themselves at the marshals, offering themselves as a sacrifice while he ran out the back door like the gallant little guru he is. That probably fulfills one of his needle-dick prophecies: the Great Leader shall elude the Army of Devils, or some other post-apocalyptic horseshit. He'll change his name again, then emerge in a few years in some other flea bag town to lead astray a new bunch of brain-dead, religious fanatics."

"That's a bit harsh."

"Oh, excuse me. Did I say brain-dead, religious fanatics? I meant, 'the theologically challenged.'" Dorie rubbed her forehead and squinted. "Is there any aspirin down here?"

"Will generic ibuprofen do?" Tim stood up and took his coffee cup to the sink. "There's a bottle here, somewhere." He rummaged through the utility drawer. "I find it hard to be angry with Dannie—Ananda, whatever, and the rest of his followers. But that Jameha I'd like to see hung in a public square."

"That's the problem!" Dorie pounded her fist on the table; her coffee cup rattled in its saucer. "You blame *him*, don't you?"

"Don't *you*?" Tim dabbed at the spilt coffee with a dishrag.

"It's the followers, don't you see? It's not the leaders who are dangerous. Jameha, Jim Jones, Manson...what would have happened if no one listened to them? Or if they listened—to be polite, or out of respect, curiosity or whatever—considered the messenger as well as the message, then said 'No thanks' and walked away? It's the followers that make them dangerous. Without them, Jameha is just another loser passing out tracts at the airport."

"Maybe." Tim shrugged his shoulders and returned to the table. "Did you see the TV show about the former People's Alliance members? It was a how-could-this-happen-here kind of story, comparing The Chosen with The People's Alliance."

Dorie nodded. "I remember them. That cult from Idaho, almost, what, ten years ago?"

"The reporter found some of them living in this area who were willing to go on camera," Tim said. "Most of them understandably don't want to be associated with that whole mess. The ones who spoke were quite articulate about coming to terms with their pasts and getting on with their lives. They're happy, successful, involved with their families and communities and such and they seemed so…*normal.* It was scary to hear their stories, to think that if it could happen to them it could happen to anybody."

"No, no no no no!" Dorie frantically waved her hands in front of her face and made the sign of the cross at Tim. "Get thee behind me, you horribly misguided sympathizer! You are *so* wrong! It is *so* wrong to say that—to even *think* that, don't you see? It doesn't just 'happen to anyone!'"

"You think those people volunteered to be deceived? That they wanted to be…"

"It doesn't matter *what* they wanted!" Dorie paused, and Tim pretended to sip his coffee. Dorie lowered her voice. Although she spoke slowly and softly, her tone was firm, deliberate, authoritative. This is what Nina's classmates hear when Dorie volunteers for hall monitor duty, Tim thought.

"I realize that these guys, the leaders, play on people's weaknesses." Dorie drummed a ragged, bitten-down fingernail against her coffee cup. "They've some kind of radar for the emotionally fragile, the intellectually flimsy—I'll allow for all of that. There is no evil in what those followers sought: spiritual guidance or answers or maybe even 'God.' We all want that, right? But if it really could happen to anyone it *would* happen to everyone and it *doesn't.* It happens, in fact, to a very small group. Those poor, confused, misled people are the real demons. Without them, the leaders are powerless."

"Okay; I see your…you've given this some thought," Tim stammered. "I get your point. But those people have friends and families, like us, who are concerned about them. They're affected, too. I can't help it if I feel sorry for…"

"For the poor little lost lambs of The Chosen? The meek sheep that gunned down that deputy in cold blood when he tried to give Jameha, what was it, a *traffic* citation?"

Count to ten, Tim thought. Staring at the newspaper, he let his eyes drop out of focus, and the headlines melted into a comforting blur. He imagined cool ocean breezes, and frosty breath on a chilly winter morning. He concentrated on dousing the scarlet warmth that crept up his neck, into his cheeks.

"That deputy had a family." Dorie looked past her husband, out the kitchen window to the backyard, where Nina's bicycle leaned against a maple tree. "How they must hate us," she murmured.

Tim willed himself to count to ten, one more time. "It's awful, I know. Think of how confused—how truly *sick*—you'd have to be, to justify such an act."

"They are adult human beings who willingly set aside their common sense and their ability, however limited, to discern. *Willingly*." Dorie curled a strand of her hair around her finger. "'Of my own free will.' Remember when she said that? When she told Mom and Dad she was with her 'real' family now? Remember their faces? One of the intensive care nurses told me Dad kept repeating that phrase, over and over: 'My own free will.'"

"That's not fair."

Tim rapped his fingers against his chair, attempting to mask the sound he was certain Dorie could hear: sprockets spinning noisily, desperately, in his head. It's finally come to this, he thought. She's been a clam since Dannie's arrest. Push too hard and she'll snap down again, but I'm sorry, Dorie. I can't let that stand.

"Your mother tried to get him to take a treadmill test. He'd been having problems for years. The doctor said there was scar tissue; that wasn't his first heart attack."

"Well, Ananda made sure it was his last, didn't she? I *know* Dad felt betrayed by her. Even Mom thinks so."

"Your mother blames Dannie? She said that?"

"She can't even bring herself to say Danielle's name. But then," Dorie smirked, "that's what Ananda wanted."

Tim searched for a tone of voice he wasn't certain he possessed: a voice whose pitch or inflection would somehow convey all the love, hope and frustration of his plea. "Poor Mom. It's as though she's lost a child as well as a husband. So, if there's a chance to get Dannie back, think of what it would mean to her…and to Nina. And us. Don't you feel a part of you is missing?"

"A part of me? You mean my other half?" Dorie spat out the words, and Tim started counting again.

"That's why I stopped reading and watching the goddamn news. If I see one more story playing up the identical twin slant…don't those people have any originality? A doppelganger in the flesh! The evil twin! Journalistic cliché heaven and they've milked it for all it's worth. One respectable citizen; one wild-eyed, religious wacko. Can our studio audience tell them apart?"

Tim watched Dorie's body language belie her protestations. She moves like her, he thought, even when agitated. The way she yanks her hands up and about her head to punctuate a denial; that odd angle at the elbows, arms flailing in a spasmodic ballet…just as when Dannie couldn't contain herself, her whole body a-flutter when she announced she was joining The Chosen.

"…One goes astray while the other goes to the PTA! It's Nature versus Nurture, tonight on channel twelve."

Don't you, won't you, see? Tim thought at his wife with all his might. He thought to her, and through her. Can't you see? The pictures in the paper; the TV news footage: a black-haired woman, tall and frail, drowning in a voluminous orange prison jumpsuit. She looks down at the iron shackles around her ankles and wrists, shields her petrified, ashen face, then glares at the cameras, un-bearably brave and defiant. Can't you see *her*, Dorie? All I can see is you. And I can't save you.

"It is," Tim weighed his words carefully, "a…compelling story, you must admit. No matter how cliché. I've thought about it myself, how you two would end up with such different lives."

"We didn't 'end up.' We made different choices. She had choices; I had choices. We made them."

"That's what fascinates people. And there *is* something special about twins. I haven't seen all the twins in the world but I've seen you and Dannie. Years ago, God! You were so close, almost…"

"Identical?" Dorie grabbed a clump of her hair and pulled it straight up from her scalp. "In what way?" She let go of the hair and pinched the skin on her forearm. "You mean like this?"

Tim attempted to smooth her hair; she pushed his hand away and laughed caustically.

"Forget Jameha's dumb-ass dogma for a moment. You know what's one of the hardest things for me? That she could so easily chuck her pride and kowtow to that *man*. The way the women are treated; the way they allow themselves to be treated." Dorie clenched and unclenched her fist. "Can you believe she actually fell for the 'holy vessels' line? How could *my* sister swallow that?"

She continued to pull at her skin while she spoke. Tim willed himself not to reach out and caress the red welts on her forearm.

"Mom and Dad took us to church. We were in the same Sunday School class; we heard the same stories, memorized the same verses. It's been years...I'll admit I don't know what I believe now. But I know what I do *not* believe. I do not believe I was ever told about how Jesus exhorted his followers to 'Gather up ye the weaponry; blessed are the heavily-armed for they shall intimidate the earth.'

"Jameha," she snickered. "Know what his real name is? Terence Wiley Wood. Former record store assistant manager. Former and current miserable failure of a human being."

"Forget that scum. I try not to think about him, but Dannie is still my sister, my sister-in-law...no wait!" Tim raised his hands in front of Dorie's open, scowling mouth. "Don't cut me off. This is our *life*, here; how can anything be more important? No matter what, she's still your mother's daughter; she's still Nina's aunt. She's still your sister."

"Still," Dorie murmured.

"Don't you love her?"

"Ever heard of tough love?"

"She's reaching out. If you could have heard her voice when she called...you know what it must have cost her to ask for our help?"

"You mean our money."

Tim realized he was mildly hyperventilating. He modulated his breathing. *Slow, deep, one-two in, one-two out. I will not beat my head against this wall. I know how she is when she makes up her mind; she's the kind of person who pulls up her slouch socks. I will not raise my voice. I will speak in the tongues of angels; like Dorie does, when she reads a bedtime story to Nina.*

"What about forgiveness?"

"That's her religion, not mine. Though it seems Jameha's interpretations allow them to de-emphasize such pesky concepts." Dorie stirred her cereal, spooning milk and soggy cornflakes over the now-brown banana slices. She pushed the bowl aside, sipped her cold coffee and grimaced. "That Ananda-person wanted nothing to do with us. She's got her wish."

Keep on, Tim thought. Keep on, or she'll pause. She'll know.

"That was before," he said. "She was probably afraid."

"Afraid of what? Of us? *We* weren't the ones steering every conversation into a sermon on judgment and divine score settling."

"Maybe she thought you'd kidnap her, have her deprogrammed or something. She was really upset when you tried to discuss…"

"There were no discussions. Ananda did not discuss, exchange ideas or even converse. Ananda lectured. Ananda relayed the Word From On High." Dorie snorted. "As high as Jameha's rectal cavity."

"Oh, geesh." Tim managed a weak chuckle. "She was right about one thing: you *are* profane."

"That's pro*found*. She always had trouble with her vowels." Dorie checked her wristwatch. "I told Nina's sitter I'd call at ten." She yawned, and rubbed her eyes. "Tim, I'm not abandoning Danielle. I simply refuse to abet The Chosen. Danielle no longer exists. I've been told that more times than I care to remember."

She picked up her dishes, started for the sink, and then turned around. Tim averted his eyes and folded the newspaper.

"I know this is going to sound weird, but I don't want you to contact her." She took a sharp breath and her ribcage trembled.

"I forbid it."

It seemed a non sequitur, coming from her. *Forbid.* They did not speak to each other in such a manner. I am not abetting The Chosen, Tim reassured himself. I would not play Judas in that way.

"Let her rot in jail."

Tim had never seen Dorie strive so hard to appear blasé. He felt a growing tightness in his chest and willed himself to remain rooted in his chair. *If I get up I will have to touch her, hold her; there, there, make it better.*

"Dorie, she's not eating." He spoke barely above a whisper. "They're on a hunger strike."

"Then let her starve," Dorie hissed. "It's what she wants. She'll be a martyr. She'll leave the living hell of this world."

Tim flinched. Dorie's voice, gaunt and frigid, emerged from a subterranean ice cave. He could offer no response, and the ensuing silence both separated and enveloped them.

"What time does the mail get here?" Tim finally asked.

"I'm not sure. Early, I think. You expecting something?"

Tim cleared his throat. "Sort of."

"When I come home for lunch it's usually here. I'm not going to work today."

"I figured that."

She's the one who does the books, he thought. Combs the bank statements like a chimp grooming her baby. She'll see it.

Tim watched Dorie load the dishwasher. Danielle was not yet in the cult when he and Dorie married. From deep within his mind he unearthed a picture, a memory: a photograph from Dorie's family album, now put away in the attic. *She can hide the albums, she can burn the pictures; I see it as though it is in front of me.* Two ten year old, gangling, black-haired, ghost-skinned girls, their arms around each other's shoulders. Below the photo is an inscription Danielle wrote to Dorie, the day they graduated from college: "To Googa—FAMILY!—Googie." In their favorite childhood game Danielle and Dorie were secret agents working for Interpol. Their spy names were Googie and Googa, and they devised a code language used only by the two of them. FAMLY, Dorie had explained, was a scrambled acronym that stood for "Love you madly, always and forever." They signed notes and letters to each other that way well into adulthood, and loved it when people thought they had misspelled 'family.'

Tim surrendered to the growing ache in his chest. I abet no Ananda, he silently cried out. I rescue the Googie.

"Remember that language you two used to speak?"

Tim flinched at the sound of shattering stoneware. Dorie picked up pieces of her coffee cup from the sink and piled them on the counter. She gripped the sides of the counter with both hands, her knuckles shining white beneath taut, scarlet-mottled skin. She turned her head to look at him, her eyes puncturing his. The fury of recognition desiccated her sudden tears.

"How dare you," she whispered.